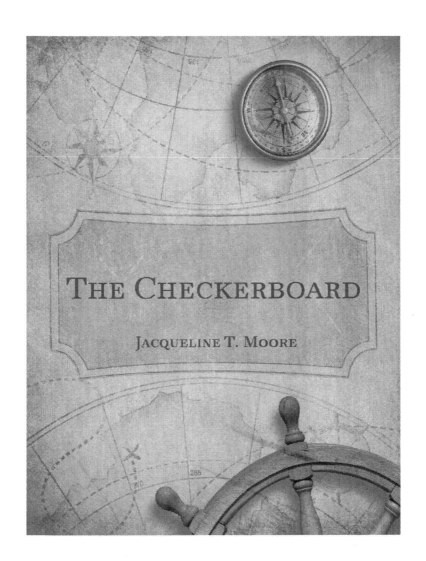

THE CHECKERBOARD

JACQUELINE T. MOORE

Cover Art:
Michelle Crocker

http://mlcdesigns4you.weebly.com/

Publisher's Note:

This is a work of fiction. All names, characters, places, and
events are the work of the author's imagination.

Any resemblance to real persons, places, or events is
coincidental.

Solstice Publishing - www.solsticepublishing.com

For Marjorie,

Enjoy!

The Checkerboard

By

Jacqueline T. Moore

Jacqueline T. Moore

2019

Dedication

For my colloquialism coach who is finer than frog's hair.
Thank you for all you have taught me.

Five Thousand Lives Blotted Out

The headlines said it all. Death, destruction, and desolation was everywhere on Galveston Island. The newspapers tell about the rescuers. Nothing is mentioned about the survivors.

The Checkerboard

Chapter One
September 8, 1900
Red Head in the Hotel

Bein' a red headed colored gal had its advantages, and disadvantages. The white folks liked you more and the colored didn't. Marguerite Black wasn't black. She wasn't yellow. Truth be told, she was red. Some say she looked exotic. She just called herself a red headed colored gal. She got the whole mess from her Cajun mama, Celestine, who she called Maman, and that discardin' runnin' red rat. She thanked the Virgin Mother every Sunday at Mass that she wasn't born a red headed colored fella. Their treatment was a whole different story.

She worked for the fish man, delivering baskets of oysters, drum, and snapper to the back doors of taverns. Marguerite sometimes helped her maman cook in the Tremont Hotel's kitchen when banquets were held. They were serving that fateful day when the hurricane hit, and were saved by the pure strength of the building. The flood washed through the lower floors, but the fourth one was spared. Only the beautiful windows were gone. After it was over, the word spread through the employees that a woman lay bloated under a mule carcass, blocking the front door. The guests were sent out on the back loading docks into the alley to find their own way through that hell that was Galveston Island. Now the staff waited. Marguerite and Celestine sat together on a cot in the far back corner.

The hotel manager, Mr. Eugene Brown, called all of the workers together in that banquet room, the grand hall turned survivor camp, with now empty cots lined in soldier rows. He climbed the steps to the speaker's platform. Except for his front desk staff and his chef, all the faces he saw were colored. It was then that he realized that the Tremont was not done saving lives.

"Oh, my wonderful, hardworking people, you have served and saved so many. I thank you." He spread his arms wide like a preacher with his flock, his voice rising toward the amen. "Our beautiful city has been destroyed. Most of the houses are timber." Weeping wails began amongst the maids and butlers at the realization of their own homes' destruction. *And their families, oh dear God, their families.* Mr. Brown continued. "Go out from here and find your people. Our hotel stands. Bring them here to be sheltered. Carry back what food you can. We will survive."

Most senior butler, Mister Charles, a stately man far past seventy, moved through the crowd to the dais. As he approached Mr. Brown, the sea of folks parted. Straight as a rod, he climbed the steps. His brown cheeks were smeared with toil and tears.

"Suh," he started. "Suh, I speak for us all when I say 'thank you.' May I say somethin' more?" The manager nodded, his own tears starting. Mister Charles turned square to his fellow workers, raising his not-so-white gloved hands palm up in supplication. "My family's been gone a long time now. I'm sure my house be flat. I will stay. Is there anyone else who won't be walkin' out the door?" Some in the crowd nodded. "If you others are comin' back, we will prepare a place for you and also for yo' kin." He turned to Mr. Brown. "Is that acceptable?"

Mr. Brown could only nod, eyes streaming.

Celestine murmured. Marguerite, squeezing her maman's hand, stood. No one waited for them in that two room shanty they called The Place. Neither ever felt it was home. The daughter spoke. "We stay, nothin's out there for us."

Stepping beside Mister Charles, an ashen-faced Mr. Brown spoke. "There is nothing out there for me, either. My friends, you have worked all these many hours. The cots are now empty. If you are staying, please find rest." Turning to his head man, he whispered, "I don't think I have the strength for this. Help me, please."

Mister Charles put his arm around his boss's waist and the two walked through the crowd as though two pals who were on a stroll. No one noticed the senior holding the junior. Once the door to the back office by the kitchen was closed, Eugene Brown crumpled into his seat. The butler stood, waiting. After a finger wave permission, Mister Charles sat in one of the brown leather club chairs facing the desk, leaned back, and immediately fell asleep with his gloves still on.

The two snored through the afternoon, each dreaming their own horrifying dream as they both saw the woman under the dead mule. Mr. Brown dreamed the carcass turned into Satan. The Evil One pulled out a covered table complete with silver and china, and invited Eugene to dine on the exposed thigh of the woman. He did, with a side of mint jelly. It was spicy. Mister Charles dreamed he climbed on the mule's rotting back. The duo rose into the sky, soaring over the island, taking in the sights of the destruction. They swooped low over the lost roof of the First Missionary Baptist Church on Avenue L. Just then the carcass split, dripping black rot and dropping Charles into the waiting arms of his long deceased Pastor-Preacher, Reverend Campbell. The holy man held him close as the lost lamb cried. Neither dreamer woke.

Marguerite and her maman took cots side by side. Disregarding the rows, they pushed their beds together for the closeness. Holding her daughter's hand, Celestine spoke, "*Mon petit*, sleep. I am so tired. My heart flutters." She took a breath. "I need rest. We will cook for them later."

Falling asleep was easy. The maids, kitchen girls, forty-eight hours sopping the rain that blew through all the great halls broken windows. With the help of the stranded guests, sheets, blankets, towels and such were brought from the rooms below to fight the filthy water. Soaking wet, they were returned to the third floor, wrung out, and spread in the rooms over water ruined beds in a futile attempt to dry them. Those saturated linens were very heavy and everyone was exhausted.

Waking several hours later, Marguerite rolled to her side, noticing the blanket had slipped from her mother. She stood yawning and stretched, moving her shoulders and neck to loosen the tightness. Others were stirring, too. They seemed to know what was coming.

"Maman, let me cover you." She pulled her mother's covers up to her neck and kissed her cheek. "I will go to the kitchen and start gettin' ready for Mister Chef. I will fetch you soon." Though she breathed, Celestine slept the sleep of a dead woman. Marguerite lightly stroked her mother's hair and headed to the back kitchen, crossing herself as she walked.

I be only a fish gal, but I got arms. Mother Mary, fill them with strength. Amen.

Other kitchen staff followed. Chef gathered everyone in the pantry. "Folks, I have not been down to the main kitchen. Do I have anyone willing to see what's in the mud and bring us what is useable?" Several serving girls nodded. "Good. We need whatever you can find." Turning to the others, he lowered his voice. "For some unknown reason, our plumbing still works, but I don't know for how long. I need strong help to fill every container we can spare for drinking, dishwashing, and toilets." Two waiters stepped forward. "Gentlemen, you are most important. I don't know if we will need the water, but I do know it will never go to waste. Thank you."

"Mister Chef?" Marguerite spoke up from the back of the group.

"Yes?"

"Will we have enough food to serve?"

10

Chef lowered his voice to almost a whisper. "I don't know, but this is what I plan. All meals will be plated just like a banquet. Everyone will be dining in style." He turned to the servers. "We will use the luncheon china. You will use the small spoons to fill those plates. We will eat, but we will eat less."

The crowd murmured their approval.

"Mister Chef?"

"Now what do you want?" A bit of impatience showed in his tone.

"Thank you."

"Oh, Miss Girl, thanks to all of you." He smiled. "Let us praise God for our safety and the bounty that will be found in the mud."

Marguerite crossed herself as she walked back into the hall to check her mother. Maman lay still with her mouth open. Marguerite screamed.

Celestine Black was buried the next day at St. Mary's Cathedral. Setting on high ground, it was one of the few remaining Roman Catholic cemeteries. Not one word was said about her being colored, as this was the home of the first Negro Catholic School in Texas. Everyone from the hotel who could be spared became part of the cortege. Mr. Brown and Mister Charles supported Miss Marguerite in the walk, holding her arms like family. Many caskets filled the sanctuary. After the funeral mass, Marguerite kissed her maman's casket. *Réquiem cetérnam dona ea.* Celestine was laid to rest in a row of fresh graves with only a wooden cross to mark each site. For the very first time in her life, Marguerite was alone.

"Come, child, let's go home." Mr. Brown took her arm and led her away.

Mister Charles walked behind as though on guard. Waiting for the mourners was coffee, sandwiches, and weak milk punch for toasting. Marguerite drank several cups, asking for extra brandy. She was soon asleep next to her mother's empty bed. When she woke, the cot was gone, moved to the space by the big smashed window. There it waited for someone in need.

Chapter Two
September 16, 1900
Jack Finds Marguerite

The ship *Sallie Lou* had her hatches full, heading home from Panama. All the dreaming men were on their way to the gold fields, having caught the train across to the Pacific. In Belize, Captain Calhoun got the word. Galveston was gone. The island was washed away by a hurricane two weeks back. The ship was loaded with mahogany and spices. The captain made the decision to bring her home anyway, hoping perchance that there might be a berth somewhere close that would take her. If so, he would give his sailors leave to seek out family and face whatever awaited them.

CB Ledbetter and Black Jack Smith had no home, having been on board the *Sallie* since they were nine years old. The only things Galveston offered were the friendships made in the taverns where the young men played their checker games. There were stories, music, and man movin' to be had. This all made for good times and almost a feeling of kin. CB did have his sister, but that was a secret he promised to keep. The sweet darling, Myra Gallaway, also lived there. He'd declared his love in a letter posted right before the storm. He needed to get on land, find her and her family. He had a wonderful thing to tell her, and then he would propose.

Jack didn't know if anyone waited for him. He had no ties, only dreams of the pretty girl he met on the docks. She spoke to him once, introducing herself. She spoke all Frenchy, sounding just like his mama. They never got a chance to talk.

Captain found a temporary new wharf built a bit south of their usual dock. A strange harbormaster allowed

13

them slip to unload and berth in exchange for his sailors on leave pitchin' in with the clearing of the timber left by the destruction.

Cargo unloaded, Captain Calhoun paid his men. "Gentlemen, find your people, attend to home. If you can, honor your *Miss Sallie* by helping in town. I'll stay aboard and call you back when we sail again." His voice broke. "This is hard times." He turned to Jack. "Be careful, son. There are some out there who…, well, you know."

"Yes sir, I do know." Jack's whippin' scars gave a mean itch. "I will."

He only hoped one of the taverns would take him. He was certainly willing to help with the cleanup, but he had little idea what awaited him. Walking down some unknown street, Jack quickly realized he had no place to go. The taverns were all along the shore and the floods took everything. He was lost. What he did recognize was the stench of carrion and smoke.

"Boy. You. Nigger, git over here."

Jack knew what that meant. Slumping his shoulders, he shuffled over to the caller, ready to lose his dignity.

"Yeah, suh, what cans I do ya for?" Jack hated talking common, but didn't want to add to his scars for not knowing his place. The man had dirty yellow hair and even a dirtier drooping moustache. He was wearing a badge and holding a gun.

"Nigger, you have just volunteered for the dead gang. See them bucks over there?" The man waved his gun toward a group of young blacks holding coal shovels, standing by four pushcarts, "You 'n' them have important work. Y'all gonna clean these here streets of them rottin' corpses."

"Suh?"

"Shaddup." He raised the pistol.

"Yes, suh, I's a movin'." Jack did his slave man's walk. The other men were lookin' more at ease than Jack felt. All the 'volunteers' shambled into a line. The badge man spoke.

"Thank you for volunteering. You're pay's a pint," he said, his rough face serious. "This town is full of the dead. There ain't no graveyards left. The high ones are full and the low ones washed away. You boys are gonna walk through the streets smellin' out the rot. Some bodies are still under the houses and these weeks of sun have... Well, you get the picture. Your job is to scoop 'em into them there carts and get 'em down to the corners. Sheriff's men left a can of kerosene for you to use. Dump, douse, and fire 'em up."

The man standing beside Jack gagged.

The badge man kept his word, handing out whiskey at the end of the day. Many of the dead gang planned to spend the night drunk, trying not to remember. Jack didn't drink.

"Sir?"

"Yes, boy?"

"Sir. You know where I can trade this for a bed?" Jack was too tired to keep up the common talk. "I think I'm not gonna make it back to my ship tonight. You know of any boardin' houses for colored?"

"Boy, they all blowed away. However, I do know that there's a standin' place in town that's puttin' up anybody. It's down on Mechanic Street. You know where that is?"

"Yes sir. That's up from the old docks."

"Go there. You might not even need to trade your bottle." The badge man turned to the group. "You boys show up here tomorrow at first light. That's an order."

The dead gang melted into the night. Not one came back.

Jack hid the pint in his shirt and started toward the water. The crews had cleared the center of the streets. The walk was easy, but he kept his eyes down, not wantin' to trip and break somethin'.

The man said the place still stands, should be easy to see. Mechanic Street's somewhere close.

Stopping, he raised his head. Down the way was a huge marble palace, a place like he knew King Arthur would stay. No other building stood.

"Jesus," muttered Jack. "I know they don't take colored there. Maybe they can tell me where to go."

He walked around to the back alley and climbed the steps of the loading dock. The door stood ajar. Pulling it open a bit, he hollered in.

"Anyone here who can help me? I need to eat. I need to sleep. I have money and trade." Jack looked into a dim, empty kitchen. "Walk with me, Jesus," he prayed aloud, and stepped into the room. "Hello. Hello. Anyone here?"

"*Oui.*" The reply came from the dining room, right out from the kitchen. Jack froze. *Frenchy.* "Miss Marguerite?" *It can't be.* "Miss Marguerite, the fish gal?" *Dear God, please be.*

"*Oui.*" Miss Marguerite Black, the girl of Jack's private dreams, walked into the kitchen. "Oh." She caught hold of the butcher table, her knees buckling. "You are alive."

Jack was quick by her side, taking her elbow. "Yes, and you are too."

She smiled her wonderful, sweet smile, and kissed him full on the mouth. "*Oui.*"

This time Jack needed the butcher table. It was his first real kiss.

"Oh, *Excusez-moi.*"

She stepped back, fingers over her mouth and nose. Jack had never seen colored turn red. She was beautiful. He felt warm too, in a good way.

"You are excused," smiled Jack. "Thank you for the kiss." She blushed deeper. "Where can we sit?" he asked.

Marguerite led him into the water-ruined dining room, seating them on molding chairs.

"This is the worst floor." She swept the hall with her eyes. "I help cook in the banquet kitchen on the fourth. That's where we all are, the ones with no homes." She looked at her hands, clasped in her lap. "Mr. Brown lets us stay in exchange for work. The second and third floors didn't flood, just got rain soaked from the broken glass." She stared hard at her fingers. "Crazy what rich people will do. Soon as those windows got fixed, people started checking in like they were on some kind of holiday." The corners of her mouth quirked. "We who have no place are living above those who come to see the sights. Humph, *insensé,* just plain crazy."

"Miss Marguerite, is there a place I can sleep?" Jack took a deep breath. "The dead gang man made me, uh, well, I am hungry and tired."

"*Oui*, and you smell." Marguerite knew what he'd been doing. The stench of death and fire had been in the city for a while. "Mr. Brown said all who need are welcome upstairs. Would you like to stay with us?" Wrinkling her nose, she said, "*Monsieur* Charles is tall like you. Perhaps he would spare some clothes. You can wash yours tomorrow."

"*Monsieur* Charles?" *Her husband? Naw, she wouldn't kiss like that if she had a man.* "Um, is her your...?"

"Head butler? *Oui.*" Marguerite's eyes flashed, showing her amusement. "*Monsieur* Charles is a wonderful man. He is like a *grand-pere* to all of us. The hotel manager, Mr. Brown, is very busy. He made *Monsieur* Charles our boss."

Jack smiled. "You think he will share his clothes? I've never worn a boss's pants before."

"You are silly," Marguerite giggled. "Let me show you where we all are." Holding tight to his hand, she led him back through the kitchen and up the dark serving steps. "Shhh, people stay on these floors," she whispered. "Even Miss Barton and her nurses are here." They climbed until there were no more stairs. "This is it," she said, dropping his hand. She knocked a rhythm on the swinging door they faced and pushed it open.

"Oh, Lord, look at this." Jack stared at the precise rows of cots, all made with starched sheets, pillows, and a folded blanket at the foot. Some were occupied. "Oh, Miss Marguerite, this is amazing. How many are here?"

"As many who need to be. Come, I will introduce you to *Monsieur* Charles."

All eyes followed as they walked around the edges to the front. On the dais were an upholstered chair and a real bed made up with a blue quilt. By the headboard was a small wooden table covered with a doily. On it, a coffee mug and the Holy Bible sat next to an oil lamp. Sleeping in the chair was a grey haired, long-legged Negro gentleman, white gloves resting in his lap. The steps to the platform creaked as the two climbed.

"Yes?" His eyes stayed closed.

"*Monsieur* Charles, it is I, Marguerite."

"I know. What is it, dear?" He slowly looked up. "Who have you brought me?" Stiffly he straightened in his chair. He looked at Jack, sniffing. "You get 'volunteered' today?"

The young man nodded, frowning.

"Son, are you alone?"

"Yes, sir, my mates are all with their families."

"Where're you from? You sound like you went to school."

"I went to sea, not school." Jack smiled. "My mama taught me how to read and my best mate taught me how to talk. I've been aboard the *Sallie Lou* since I was nine."

18

Mister Charles squinted through the lamp light. "You play harmonica?"

"Yes sir. How did you know that?"

"Maude's." Mister Charles chuckled. "They served anybody as long as we didn't sit in the front window. I heard what happened to you. Mighty sorry for that."

"Me too." Jack frowned, remembering his worst humiliation. "Maude? Clarisse?"

Mr. Charles shook his head. "Gone."

"Oh, Jesus." Jack sunk down on the steps. "Oh, Jesus." He looked up at Marguerite, who nodded. Maude owned the tavern where Jack and Marguerite first met.

"Son, do you need a bed, a meal?"

"Yes sir. I have money, and the dead gang boss man gave me whiskey. I can trade."

"Son, you need nothing to stay here. But if someone sees your liquor, they might help themselves. Give me the bottle for safe keeping." Mister Charles turned his attention to Marguerite. "Find him food and take him to the cot by the big broken window. You know the one."

She nodded.

"Sorry to have to put you there," apologized Mr. Charles. "It's windy, and the birds like to come in."

"Sir, that makes me no never mind. I'm used to it, living on a ship. Thank you for the spot."

Mister Charles gave Jack a questioning look. "Will you be going back to sea soon? You know this town could use some extra hands."

"My captain promised the harbormaster his men's work. I can't go back to the dead gang, though."

"Oh, holy Jesus, no. If you stay with us, I'll find you a crew away from the dead."

Jack shook his hand, trying not to look at Marguerite. "Thank you, sir. Thank you. I'll go to the *Sallie* tomorrow and tell my captain where I'll be. He said he would call us all in when we're ready to sail."

"You get stopped tomorrow, you tell the man you work for Mister Charles at the Tremont. You got that?"

"Yes sir." Jack looked at the beauty beside him. "Um, Miss Marguerite mentioned something about clothes. This dead smell is awful. Might I, uh, borrow something so I can wash out the stink on me?"

"I reckon. Go get a bite. I'll check what I got." The butler smiled at the two. "Miss Girl, feed him good and bring him back. I'll fix him up. By the way, son, what is your name? I only ever heard you called 'Mr. Music'."

"Sir, I am Jack Smith, son of Abraham Lincoln Smith."

"Welcome to the Tremont Hotel, Jack Smith. Now go find food."

"Yes sir."

When the young pair returned from the banquet kitchen, Mister Charles had a twinkle in his eye and a package of clothing. "Son, this should do ya 'til you get some washing done. Miss Marguerite, do you want to do his clothes?"

"Beg pardon, sir," Jack interrupted, "but no woman's done my wash in twenty years. I can take care of it."

"You sure about that?"

Jack nodded. "Yes sir. I'll do it tonight. Just as soon as I change, I'll get to work. They'll be dry in no time since my bunk is by the window. Where is the head? If you got water, I'll do it there."

"See ya directly." Gesturing with his chin, Mister Charles sent him on, watching to make sure Jack found his way.

"Miss Girl," he said to Marguerite. "Step up here. You tell me. What's he to you?"

"Oh, *Monsieur* Charles, he's just a man from the docks." Her flaming cheeks matched her hair. Head down, she whispered, "Perhaps a new friend."

"My child, I think you are fibbing to this old man. You know him." Mister Charles lifted her chin. "Tell me."

"*Oui*, I know him, know him in my dreams."

Mister Charles smiled. "Good night, my dear. Get some sleep."

Jack had long ago learned to hold his dignity in most situations. However, he never walked into a room with an armload of wet laundry wearing some else's long johns. How was he going to explain to CB that, on his first night under the same roof with the red headed fish gal, he was in underwear, and they were way too big?

Mister Charles sat on his stage, watching over his room. Pulling out Jack's pint, he poured a small tot in his porcelain cup. "Here's to you, mister saggy bottom. Take good care of our Miss Girl." He drank the whiskey straight down.

Chapter Three
September 16, 1900
Marguerite Finds Jack

Jack and Marguerite fell into the rhythm of becoming acquainted under the watchful eyes of a banquet room full of chaperones. The very second the two walked the edge of the cots to speak to Mister Charles, the buzz began. With their beloved Celestine fresh in her grave, many of the women living under the roof of Mr. Brown's hotel decided the girl needed special caring.

"Blessed Lord, we know she's not a tease," said Missylou, one of the kitchen girls. "We jist gotta keep her tail tied to an anchor. We gotta be her mama."

"Well, that sure is some sweet daddy."

All the dish-washin' gals laughed. They could count on Cocoa's lack of shyness, what with her always talkin' sassy about men. Marguerite heard the giggles but kept away from the chatter lest she show her feelings. When a short, yellowed haired white man took him to Texas City for the day, the gals teased about "your Mister Man ain't coming back to you." Marguerite knew why he was gone and felt no worry.

Mr. Jack Smith was tree tall skinny, and that was mighty fine with her. She liked the way he carried himself, all straight up and proud. He talked nice, too. Then one evening she heard him sing. Jack was sitting on the stage, spending his after work time visitin' with Mister Charles. Marguerite was finishing in the kitchen when she heard a sound that brought tears. Jack was playing his harmonica. Very softly the beauty of 'Amazing Grace' floated over the room.

"Oh, Maman," she whispered.

As though pulled by a single invisible spider web, Marguerite walked through the swinging doors, between the cots and climbed the steps of the platform. Her Cajun mother's words escaped her lips.

"La Grâce du Ciel est descendue

"Me sauver de l'enfer.

"J'étais perdue, je suis retrouvée

Jack lowered his instrument and joined her with his mother's words. Their harmony was flawless.

"Aveugle, et je vois clair."

Silent tears sparkled on her cheeks. "How do you know this?"

"My mother." Jack was too choked to say anything else. His daddy had told him all her stories. Maybe it was time to talk.

Mister Charles interrupted Jack's thoughts. "Miss Girl, that was beautiful. I remember your mother singing as she worked. She made these old ears smile. Thank you for your song." He looked at Jack. "You got the Cajun, too?" The young man nodded. "Well, that just beats all."

"Yes, sir, but I don't remember much. Been on ship since I was nine."

"Sounds like you have enough to make sweet music." Mister Charles winked at the two. "Now run on. Tomorrow comes fast enough."

Jack walked Marguerite back to her cot like he was escorting her home. Without thinking, they sat together on the bed. "May I tell you about my family?"

"Oui, I would like that."

Jack began.

***

Black Jack's granddaddy had been a slave on a tobacco farm close to Louisville, Kentucky. You can't say much for being a slave, but Granddaddy had opportunity. His master, Walter Johnson, was landowning freed nigger, and kept his own like family. One day Mr. Walter called his slave into the curing shed.

23

"Nathaniel, wha's this I hear 'bout you 'n' Ma'belle?" Mrs. Johnson had told her husband that he'd better speak to his man. She knew things were heatin' up 'tween those two. "Missus sez you is courtin'."

"Yeh suh." Nathaniel was true dark. "I's gots mah eye on Marybelle. She be mighty fine."

"You bed huh yet?"

"Oh no, suh, no suh." Nathaniel's cheeks were feeling hot and his flush spread to his forehead. Truth was, that was his plan for the very near future.

"That girl's fresh. You keep huh that way. You's better plan to jump, you hear me, boy?"

"Yes suh, do it soon."

Granddaddy was allowed to marry, with promise of continuation, and that promise was kept. Mr. Walter trained him to be a smithy and gave him a last name. When the war was over, Marybelle and Nathaniel Smith stayed on as hired folk, living in the cabin they'd always known. Nathaniel was considered a fine iron wrought and Marybelle birthed and nursed for miles around. All the white ladies wanted Missus Marybelle's midwifery, and it was realized that cream rises, no matter the color. The Smiths could go to town without worry.

Mrs. Johnson knew Marybelle was a valuable commodity, free or not, and took to giving her the writing and the reading.

"Goodness, Missus Marybelle, you is a quick study."

Emancipation and marriage gave Marybelle spoken respect. Today the women were working through the sounds and spellings of words that had to do with the household. Mrs. Johnson was the mistress of the farm, but also understood that Marybelle was a smart woman. They became what friends they could, considering recent history.

"Yes, ma'am, I like learnin'." Marybelle knew that not many served in a Negro household. It made all the difference in this world. "Let's do supper. You write food and I'll guess read."

Mrs. Johnson marked out PORK, CORN BREAD, and COLLARDS on butcher paper. Marybelle squinched her eyes, thinking.

"Poke, co'n bread, greens."

"Look at the last. It ain't got no letter G. You's jist rememberin' last night." The two looked at each other and smiled. "That's a C, but I didn't write 'coffee' neither." The lessons lasted all winter.

Together the women kept a book of sicknesses. Marybelle learned quick what worked and what didn't to ease, keeping journal of it all. She also made lists of the birthings and dyings. This book became the first writings of colored history in the area. Mrs. Johnson's lessons were quietly passed on to the children. Marybelle was proud to have some young'uns who could write their names, and prouder still of the ones who could read. Mr. Johnson never knew what those women were up to, and that was all right.

Marybelle had eleven children of her own. Six were born after the Emancipation Proclamation. When the war ended, Mr. Walter had several cabins empty and Nathaniel was allowed to sleep his first five in one and keep the others next door with their mama. Those older ones worked the tobacco for their keep. Marybelle held the little ones in tow while she did her healing. They would help in the white people's houses for pennies. After a while, Mr. Walter expected the little ones in the field, too. He seemed to forget Mr. Lincoln's work when it suited him.

The oldest free child was named Abraham Lincoln Smith, born in 1863. He was taught from an early age about his name, and how to write it. The hero's namesake was told what was before, and what was now. He was never told what would come next. He took charge of that himself. At age fifteen, he stood in front of all.

"Y'all know I's gotta be gone. I's loves you, Mama and Daddy." He nodded to the Johnsons. "I thanks you, Mister and Missus." He kissed his tearful mother and all the little ones, hugged his daddy, and shook Mr. Walter's hand. Mrs. Johnson handed him a wrapped bundle, telling him to save it back, keep it safe.

Mrs. Johnson looked at the package. "Jesus walks with you. Be wise. Don't bring shame."

"Yes ma'am. I won't shame y'all or the family. That's my promise."

He left word to the older ones that he would miss them and boarded a flat boat that would eventually lead him working the river trade to Evansville, Cairo, Memphis and on down the Mississippi. He carried with him the only learning book he had ever seen, Mrs. Johnson's gift, *The Sovereign: A Collection of Songs, Glees, Choruses, & c.* Neither his mama nor he knew what those five lines and dots meant, but the book did have the letters he'd learned. Marybelle knew that odd book would be right with her best boy, and also knew Mrs. Johnson must love him to give it away.

Jack's mama, Lizzy, had sung the sweetest songs to him. She said that her mama, Granny Betty, learned all the new tunes because she was employed as a housemaid for Countess Willie Piazza in New Orleans. Many a fine gentleman went to this house for entertainment. The fancy ladies would play the piano and sing beautiful songs to start the evening. Little Lizzy's mother would serve the refreshments and, after the evening's end, change the sheets and prepare the rooms for the next day. When Lizzy was ten, the Countess asked Betty to her office in the back, by the maid's steps.

"You have a beautiful daughter."

"Yes, ma'am, I does." Miss Betty did not like the chill climbin' her arms.

"I would like to hire her as kitchen help. I'm sure you could use her being paid for what she does already. You do need money, don't you?"

That chill was makin' goose flesh.

"Yes, ma'am, I do."

"There are great possibilities waiting, don't you agree?"

"Yes 'um."

Betty kept her daughter close in the house. Lizzie was never allowed into the parlor when there were gentlemen to be entertained, but she heard the singing just the same. By the time Abe came to the back door, delivering the Countess' brandy, Lizzy was aware of what went on in those rooms upstairs, and was anxious to be gone, lest one of the gentlemen, or the Countess would call her out for the breaking at highest bid.

She became Mrs. Abraham Lincoln Smith within the week, loving him until she died.

After Abe married Elizabeth, he stopped traveling. When he showed her *The Sovereign*, Lizzy knew exactly what it was, as she had seen it before. Her mama would show her those wondrous pages as she shut that book each morning during the tidying. Lizzy told him that the lines and dots made songs. He told her that the other marks made words. Together they practiced, putting the lines, dots, and letters into what they were, the music of the day.

City life was hard for a man with a strong back and a free will. They both realized that there was not enough space in that town for Abe, a man always looking for what came next. They soon headed west with their newborn, Jack, working their way to Houston. The handbill read 'Farm niggers needed.' Reconstruction laws hit Texas with a bitter thud. The Texans who did fight traveled east to do it, and the majority of whites didn't see the need for the results of that far-away war. What they did see was that the

Cotton Kingdom needed paid hands that had once been slave labored.

The Smiths settled into what Abraham knew, field work. All the while, Abe and Lizzy sang the songs and taught the letters to their children. Lizzy died and was buried with her fourth, a stillborn, cradled in her arms. Abe cried for his own mother, knowing Marybelle's midwife skills could have brought the child alive. The childbirth fever left Abe with three sons to work the fields. One day Jack was gone and so was the book. Abe never knew where, but he always hoped the nine-year-old was safe. He knew that Jack Smith was just like him, born looking for what comes next.

It was hard traveling, but Jack knew exactly what he wanted. His daddy'd told many a story about that big river and how it led to an ocean called the Gulf. Cotton can't grow on water, so that's where he was headed. What his daddy picked was baled, and put on mule trains. The drivers had told him that the bales ended on big ships that went all over the world. Jack packed his kit with corn dodgers, tack, and hope. He stood by the high road, waiting.

First wagons rolled by. The drivers stared straight ahead. The day wore on,

"You boy, what you doin'?" This driver was white, with red hair, a stranger who met his eye. His mustache was waxed up like long horns.

"I's runnin' to the water. You take me there?"

"Your pappy know?"

"Yes suh," he lied.

"You got food?"

"Yes suh."

"Get on the back."

The driver and his men didn't mind the hitch. Five miles from the wharf, they wished him well, and Jack ended up on the *Sallie Lou*.

Captain Calhoun knew that hiring colored was wrong. A mixed ship does not sail well, everybody knew that. Yet, by the end of day, Jack Smith was given a hammock, a plate, and cup, and was sent below to work bilge. Mr. Calhoun had noticed that the skinny boy had strong arms, and few men kept at the pumps very long, anyway. Jack stayed down low for a year, out of the way, working those strong arms. The *Sallie* was dry and Jack grew tall. Sometimes the men forgot he was there, except when he was heard singing. And Lord, how that boy could sing. There seemed to be a tune echoing through the ship most of the time. The men would catch a bit of gospel or minstrel. One day, the Captain heard some of 'Jeanie with the Light Brown Hair' floating through the wind and headed into the hold. Jack did not know he was there. Mr. Calhoun stood, listened, and knew one thing. He had to get that boy out from below and onto the planks. Then he could hear the songs whenever he wanted. All of a sudden, Jack was a deck boy. He never knew how that happened, but he did not stop singing.

***

After a bit, Marguerite spoke. "You are a fine man."
"You are a fine woman."
"I will miss you when you go."
"Captain will call soon."
"I think I miss you already."

Watching eyes be damned, Jack leaned over to the beauty beside him and kissed her full on the mouth.

"Oh, *mon amour*. Yes, I do miss you already." Marguerite's eyes glistened as Jack walked back to Mister Charles' chair.

Jack knew he must tell his secret. He also wanted to ask Mr. Charles a question. Mr. Charles said "Not yet."

Within the week, Captain Calhoun called all of his sailors back on ship. He sent Jack up to LaPorte to fetch his best mate, CB. Every time the *Sallie Lou* came to port, Jack would stay at the hotel, courting Marguerite. After two rounds to Panama and back, Jack asked Mister Charles again for his 'Miss Girl's' hand. This time the answer was "Yes."

Marguerite and Jack were married at St. Mary's Cathedral in the side chapel. Jack had asked Mister Charles for Marguerite's hand the night he kissed her. Mister Charles loved that red headed child just as his own and was proud to be with her like a daddy. Eugene Brown stood as Jack's best man, 'cause CB was heading down from LaPorte, and they didn't know where he was on the road. When Father Gallagher asked for a ring to bless, Mr. Brown handed his late mother's opal to the bishop. As soon as the vows were made, Marguerite removed and returned the ring. Mr. Brown did not know that opals brought bad luck if worn after a death.

"This is your maman's. Please cherish it," was all she said.

Jack had to leave immediately. The entire wedding party walked him to the docks. The newlyweds kissed good-bye with the promise of hello. Jack climbed the plank walking backward, waving to his bride. He kept the wedding secret for the longest time.

Chapter Four
September 8, 1900
Miss Annie's Prayer

The Galveston Island Methodist Women's Guild met the second Saturday of each month to darn stockings and outdo each other with their best recipes. Miss Annie Hoffen learned long ago that dosing her mother with a special naptime tonic would ensure the chance for her to join the ladies for a rare afternoon out. While her sisters found husbands many years ago and lived proper married lady lives, Miss Annie dedicated her life to the care of their very contentious, bed-bound mother. That was what everyone expected her to do.

On the morning of the unexpected storm, the dinner repast was spread on the side table and the ladies were singing the Doxology when the warning bells began. The chimes were completely ignored as plates were filled and compliments given. All that changed when Reverend Nicholson rushed into the room.

"My God, Linda Sue," he shouted to his wife. "Don't you hear the bells? We are in a hurricane. Look at the floor."

"Dear God in Heaven, Mother, oh, Mother." Annie froze mid-step and started to scream, realizing their house was far downhill from the church. The speed of the water rising in the sanctuary spelled no hope for the invalid, alone in their home. The sisters joined Annie in her panic. "Mother, Mother, Mother. Oh my Jesus, Mother."

"Move ladies, now." All were in shock.

"The choir room is high enough," Linda Sue continued. "Fill your baskets and let's go. Jesus loves us, but we must help ourselves."

The women scrambled to collect the dinner and

their belongings. Quickly, they trailed the Reverend through the water to the loft door. Several were starting to push. All were weeping. Linda Sue Nicholson gathered up Annie and dragged her toward the steps.

"Come. Now. All of you." The command in her voice worked. Annie stumbled with Reverend Nicholson, her two sisters, Mrs. Emily Wallace and Mrs. Arabel Gaithers, plus almost all the other ladies, toward the safety of the church tower choir room. As she climbed, Annie fumbled with her cross chain, unlatching the clasp. She slid off her deepest secret and put it where it belonged, on her left hand. Miss Annie Hoffen was not about to die an old maid.

Once settled in and among the choir robes, the ladies of the Guild comforted themselves with what they did best, gossiping.

"I'm so glad Harry came for Ada."

"Wonder how he knew?"

"Poor Julia, I hope she finds her family."

"Whatever possessed her to go out in the storm?"

"I don't know. Maybe...oh never mind."

"What, what, what?"

"Well, she sure acted happier these last few weeks. Maybe she 'n' Ike were..."

"Ladies," Reverend Nicholson's tone said it all. "You need to stop this conversation now. We will pray for her safety, no matter what her reason is for leaving."

Chastised heads bowed and heart-felt prayers were shared, round-robin. The ladies prayed for their children, their husbands, and their city. They all prayed for Ada, Julia Jameson, and the mother of the Hoffen sisters. Reverend Nicholson offered the 'Amen'.

He headed toward the hampers of food. "Excuse me, everyone, but I never ate my dinner." He turned to his wife. "Linda Sue, please join me. I don't believe you got dessert. Miss Annie, did you bring your wonderful pound cake?"

Annie smiled through her grief. "Yes, sir, I did. Let me cut it."

Justine, the newest guild member, was the first to notice the emerald and diamonds on Annie's left hand.

"Why, Miss Annie, what a lovely ring. Is it from your mother?" Justine realized what she said, and clapped her hand over her mouth. "Oh, Miss Annie, I'm sorry," she murmured through her fingers.

"No. It is my engagement ring."

The entire choir loft fell silent.

"Your, your what?" Justine stammered.

Miss Annie raised her voice. "My engagement ring. I am betrothed to Mr. Carlton Wilson."

"Father's friend?" her sisters shrieked in unison. The ladies of the guild stared.

"Yes, Father's friend." Annie's pinched lips spoke volumes. "We have been engaged for several years. We were waiting for the right time."

"Why didn't you tell us?" Emily stood by the stacks of practice hymnals, arms crossed. "Don't you think your sister and I have a right to know?"

"Not really."

"But, but, uh, if you get married, who would take care of---oh, God." Emily stared blankly at Arabel. "Oh dear Jesus, Mother is dead, Annie's engaged. I can't take this. Where are our husbands?" She sank in a heap. "You got engaged. You did that on purpose just to ruin my life." Emily started sobbing.

Arabel stepped away from the pile on the floor and put her hands on Annie's shoulders, standing arms-length away. "I am shocked at your news, especially at your age." She looked her elder sister up and down. "Well, I, um, wish you two the best." Arabel shook her head in disbelief and walked to the other side of the choir loft.

"Um, thank you, sister." Annie turned back to the cake.

Miss Annie did not die an engaged woman. Miss Annie, her two married sisters, and almost the entire Women's Guild survived the hurricane. Sunday morning dawned with nary a cloud to be seen. As soon as possible, the ladies left the church to find their homes and husbands. Annie's beloved, Carl, lived upstate, and she could only hope he was untouched by the storm. She parked herself on a ruined pew in the narthex and waited.

"Be safe sisters, be safe," Annie called as Emily and Arabel made their way down from the loft and out the front doors.

"Humph," the both responded. The two walked out into the timber pile that used to be Galveston.

"I'll wait here," Annie called to their disappearing backs. "I'll wait here for my Carl."

The clergy and his wife brought her some of the food left in the choir room. Twenty-four hours of refuge made little dent in the monthly Saturday Stocking Mending Day feast.

On Tuesday, Carlton found Annie. After a chaste kiss on the cheek, knowing they were in a house of God, he sat beside her on her pew. He took both her hands in his.

"My dear, I am so very happy to find you." Carlton lifted her hands and kissed each one. "I thought you were dead." He gave an extra kiss to her left ring finger.

"My darling," Annie smiled. "I knew you would come."

"I have terrible news." Carl leaned closer. "I saw your house. It still stands, but …"

"Mother? Was she washed away? We knew she must have drowned." Annie started to weep silent tears.

"She's still in her bed. We can bury her." Carlton sighed. "I found nothing recognizable at your sisters' houses. I think the husbands are gone. I am so sorry."

"To everything there is a season, and a time to every purpose under heaven." Annie wiped her tears. "They will need us."

"Yes."

In utter desolation, Emily and Arabel made their way back to the church. Miss Annie was still sitting on that pew, but now she was holding the hand of her fiancé. The couple stood.

"We can't find our husbands," Arable wailed. "We couldn't even find our houses."

"I know." Annie nodded toward her sisters. "Carl told me. We will attend to Mother."

"Oh, what will we do?" moaned Emily.

"Sisters," Annie answered, "My Carl is here. We are not alone, are we, dear?" Annie squeezed his hand. She had never felt so empowered in her life.

Miss Annie became Mrs. Carlton Wilson that day, September 12, 1900. On a whim, she unpinned her hair, smoothing it out like her long hoped for veil. Reverend Nicholson blessed the couple with the Methodist wedding ceremony.

Carlton arranged for Mother Hoffen's burial and procured a room at the Tremont Hotel for the sisters.

"My dear sisters-in-law," he said, "You will stay at the hotel. I know you need things and there will be an account with the manager. Annie and I will go to my house in LaPorte for a few days. I am fortunate to have plenty of space, but there needs to be a woman's touch." Carlton shook his head. "I have been a bachelor too long." He smiled at his new wife. "We will make rooms ready for the both of you. I hope you two will find the stay in the Tremont to be satisfactory." Nodding to Annie, he took each sister by the arm. "We will be back in a week. Let me escort our sisters to the hotel."

Carlton marched the protesting women out into the horror and on to the hotel. Once in the lobby, they were directed to the make shift desk on the mezzanine where he registered them and reminded them of the money on account. "We will be back in a week to bring you to my, uh, our house. See you then." He turned, briskly walked straight out to the front steps, and was gone.

"Well, I never," grumped Emily. "Some nerve telling us what to do. He's practically a stranger."

"Oh be quiet," snapped Arabel. "We will pray for our husbands. In the meantime, let's find our room and dinner. Then we'll ask for all new clothes. My hems are filthy."

Carlton's upstate house was practically a mansion. He gave his wife the grand tour, ending in the master room. Laid out on the bed was a full bridal night ensemble. The dressing gown, negligee, peignoir, and bed jacket all matched, with blue bonnets embroidered around the necks of each piece. The tiny flowers were repeated at the edges of the sleeves and along the hems.

"Carl, but how…" Annie was speechless.

"My dear, all those years ago when you accepted my proposal, I went shopping for you." He smiled a shy smile. "Of course I had no idea when we could wed, so I put them away. Little did I know that it would be under these dire circumstances." He looked straight into her eyes. "My darling wife, will you accept this wedding gift?"

"Oh, Carl, my love, yes." Annie touched the silky garments, fingering the white gown. "I, uhm, I never have worn things like this before. Do you understand what I am saying?" She softly giggled.

"Yes, my beloved."

"Tonight will be my first time to wear this kind of clothing." She blushed. "Do you know how to take care of, uhm, sometime so precious?"

"Yes, my beloved. However, at my age, I will need to pray for strength. I have not needed strength for many years. Do you understand what I am saying?"

Annie smiled.
That night, all prayers were answered.

Chapter Five
September 18, 1900
Two Roosters, One Hen House

Junior Gallaway's daddy died when he was about seven. His mama did the best she could, selling sweets while Junior watched the four others, him growing up way too fast. Then the hurricane came and blew his life away. His mama got married to a stranger.

CB Ledbetter was no stranger to Myra Gallaway. The problem was that they courted by letters, and he never got a chance to come calling. The whole family, including Aunt Ada and Uncle Harry, was shocked to see Myra hand over a beautiful yellow diamond to the man she'd just finished kissing on the floor of the center aisle of St. Mary's Catholic Church. That man then asked Myra to get married. In less than a week, all of them were living in CB's house in LaPorte, and CB had to go back to sea. Him gone made everything feel the same, even if it was in a different house. Then, the week before Christmas, that man was back.

Junior did not like it. Not one bit.

It all started at the dinner table. Junior always led grace. Mama nodded the signal to begin. "Father, thank…" said Junior.

CB interrupted with, "Bless us oh Lord for these thy gifts which we are about to receive from thy bounty; fill our sails with fair wind, and bring us home to safe and loving harbors. Through Christ, our Lord, Amen."

Junior stared. Table grace was his job. "Father, thank you for this food. Amen." *So there.*

Myra smiled at her family. "Thank you, both. Let's eat." She turned to Theo. "Son, please pass your daddy the biscuits."

Junior cleared his throat, but kept his mouth shut. *Daddy, humph, my daddy's dead.*

Staring at his plate, he did not pass the rice, butter beans, or anything else. As soon as he could, Junior left the table without the usual honey biscuit he was accustomed to eating outside.

Aunt Ada excused herself and followed the boy. He was sitting on the ground, out by the back alley, drawing scribbles in the dust with a stick.

"Child."

He did not look up.

"Ma'am?"

"Darlin', I saw you forgot your honey sweet. I brought you mine."

"Don't want it."

"Child, I am too old to get down in this dirt with you. Please come sit with me." Not waiting for an answer, Ada walked back to the painted wrought iron bench in the middle of the yard, next to the gazebo. There she waited. After several minutes, Junior stood and followed. Sitting board straight, he reached for the dessert.

"Have you forgotten *all* your manners?" Ada reminded.

"Thank you, ma'am," the boy mumbled, licking the honey that was on his hand. He ate silently. "Aunt Ada?"

"Yes, my darling."

"Why did Mama do that?"

"Do what, my child? Catch that drip."

Junior licked the sweetness from the side of his thumb. "Why did she let him pray? That's my job."

Ada sat silent for a bit, and then spoke. "Darlin', I don't know that she thought about it. You started, he started. You both finished."

"Not his job," Junior said with a tremble. "Mine. And his prayer was all about ships. We live in a house." He took another bite. "Aunt Ada, that man is not our daddy. Mama made me real mad."

His tears started streaming. "My daddy's dead. CB is just some sailor, not our daddy." He sobbed. "Why did she call him our daddy?"

Ada gathered the boy into her arms. Rocking and cooing, she allowed the child his long hidden grief. Later they both stood. Aunt Ada dusted the remnants of the crumbled biscuit off her apron, and walked back to the house. Junior went straight in and up the stairs to the room he shared with his brothers. Ada took up a tea towel and silently dried the supper dishes as Myra washed.

That evening, after prayers and kisses, the grown-ups sat in the parlor playing Shut the Box. CB brought his set from the *Sallie*, and it never left the parlor. Betting was involved, but the family used buttons, not pennies. Uncle Harry had enough winnings in front of him to sew up a shirt. Everyone was chatting, laughing, and enjoying the game. Winners were slamming the lid, indicating that they had 'shut the box.' No one noticed Junior standing at the foot of the steps, watching.

"I wonder if Missus Annie and Carlton would like to play this game." Ada was so glad her dear church friend was resettled in LaPorte. "We had coffee the other day and she mentioned how happy she was to have a husband." Ada arranged her buttons in front of her according to size.

"I'll bet she is." Harry did not have the same talents as his wife, and his tumbled button pile sat undisturbed. "You think she'd play a wagering game?"

Ada smiled, and picked up her largest coat button. "She took a bet on marriage. I don't think settin' down buttons would distress her." *Tink*. "I ante the purple square one."

CB claimed a kiss from his bride every time he won. "I like this game," he said with an eyebrow wiggle.

"What do I get if I ever win?" asked Myra with a return wiggle.

"Sweetheart, anything you want." CB's eye dance was workin' its way to his shoulders.

"Hush." Myra's sparkling eyes were doin' their own talkin'.

"All right, you two," interrupted Uncle Harry. "If y'all don't mind, it's my roll. My buttons are lookin' for new friends."

Ada patted his arm. "Just make sure all those new friends spend the night in the sewing box."

Harry rolled a seven and a one. Before he could flip the tiles, the box and buttons went flying. Ada and Myra both screamed. A furious Junior had kicked the tipped game table across the room. It stopped just short of their decorated tree. He walked straight to where CB sat, his boy-sized hands in a ball.

"You quit kissing my mama. She don't need you or nobody else to kiss her." He raised his right fist.

CB stood, gesturing to Uncle Harry to stay back. "Son, you..."

"I am not your son," Junior yelled.

"Son, you need to apologize to the adults for your behavior." CB unconsciously realized the boy was his same height.

"You need to apologize for, for, for..." Junior stammered.

"Apologize now."

"Hell, no." Junior turned and bolted for the porch. Throwing open the screen, he yelled, "You apologize for living. My daddy's dead."

The slam shook the doorframe. The boy was gone.

No one followed him.

Silently the women righted the table, collected the buttons, and put away the game. Harry and CB retreated to the kitchen. When the women arrived, Uncle Harry's fresh pot of coffee was almost ready. CB, chin quivering, talked to his new uncle.

"My daddy was the meanest skunk. I was nine years old and couldn't wait to get aboard the *Sallie Lou* after Captain Calhoun paid my bond. I grew up on that ship with the Captain as sort of a good step-daddy." CB gulped air. "That's all I want to be, a good step-daddy."

"Your father sold you?" asked Ada as she set out the mugs.

"Yes, ma'am, it was the second best thing he ever did for me." CB looked at his wife. "The best thing was to die."

Myra gasped. "No."

"Yes. Someday I'll tell you. Not now." CB stood. "Can I pour everyone a cup? Myra, is there something in the pie safe?"

"Yes, dear, do you want jumbles or plunkets?"

"Both. Any Christmas jam thumb prints?"

Harry looked hopeful. "I like jam thumb prints."

"Darlin', enough is enough." As usual, Ada was supervising her husband's waist line. "Niece, I'll take a half cup. Don't need to stay up all night."

A plate of cookies and a plan later, the adults said good night and climbed the stairs to their rooms. Ada stopped Myra at her door. Kissing her cheek, she whispered, "All we can do is try."

"Yes, ma'am. Thank you."

The day after Christmas, the Dickensons and Junior stood with CB at the LaPorte train station. "Son?" CB's tone had the slightest hint of questioning.

"What?" Junior's curt reply answered CB. Nothing had changed.

"Son, I hope you are a good help for your Uncle Harry and Aunt Ada. They need help with the new store and he really appreciates your work."

"Yeah." *If you like having a slave.*

The two waited in silence. Off in the distance was a low rumble and then a whistle.

"Here it comes," said CB, a bit too loudly. "Your mama's gonna miss you."

"I'll miss *her*." Junior's inference was evident.

"I will miss you, too." CB put his hand on the boy's shoulder. Junior shrugged it off, standing stock stiff.

"I doubt it," he snarled under his breath.

"Son, try to understand…"

"I don't have to. I know that you showed up and I was sent away. You win, the end."

"It's not like…'

"You win, the end." Junior did not say another word to his stepfather. The boy adjusted his new cap, his only Christmas gift. He climbed aboard the car behind his aunt and uncle, offering a very loud "Thank you, sir," to the porter as his valise was handed to him.

"Good bye, my son," whispered CB. "May God, or Uncle Harry, show you the way."

Chapter Six
March 30, 1901
CB At Home

The little bungalow that Myra had lived in was swept away with the wind. They called that house The Shoe, because of all the children. CB called the house in LaPorte 'The Boot' because it was bigger.

"There was an old lady who lived in a boot," chanted Nora Lee as she marched up to CB. "She had so many children before she ever knew it."

"Now watch yourself, child." CB gave his new daughter a developing 'Mama look.'

His mother had used her eyes to say so much. The rhyme stuck in his head. 'There was a sweet lady who lived in a boot. Her husband was handy at getting the loot.'

Shush brain.

CB knew that he and Jack needed to get back into the man smuggling business. Rumors said that the beaches of Nome, up in Alaska, held gold just for the sand sifting. Now that the docks were rebuilt, and they were back at sea, maybe their business would keep the children fed.

Oh, dear God, please.

CB's new family lived in a very fine house, which had been payment to CB and Jack for the stowaway passage to the land of dreams.

Sweet Jesus, please.

Unfortunately, this house required what seemed a king's ransom in taxes, something CB did not have.

I can't tell Myra. She doesn't need to know. At least not right now.

"Daddy CB." Nora Lee's voice brought him back to the here and now. "Daddy CB, would you push me on the swing? Mama said to get my bottom out from under foot."

"I don't doubt that," CB smiled. "What does that have to do with me?"

"Since you are Sure Foot you could swing me high and then I'll be over foot."

"Come on, silly bump, meet you by the tree." CB's sailor name was Sure Foot, his bowed legs allowing good stead when the ship rocked. Nora Lee settled herself on the plank and grabbed the ropes. "How high?" he asked.

"High as the sky, high as the stars, high as the waves of the sea." Giggling, Nora Lee knew what came next.

"One." Covering her hands with his, he pulled her back a bit.

"Two." He softly pushed her forward.

"Three." Letting go of the rope, he let her drift slowly forward.

"No, no, no, I gotta go."

"Where?"

"Sailing."

That was their signal. CB pulled her middle back, bringing the swing high.

"Hold tight. WHEE."

"Sailing, sailing, over the bounding main." The two sang at the top of their lungs for the many verses of the song, daddy pushing daughter, daughter loving daddy. Only a holler for dinner brought the two back to shore.

"Time for mess."

"Aye aye, sir." Hand in hand, the two walked toward the kitchen, making sure to stomp the dust off their shoes before climbing the stoop steps. CB found Franky, Benjy, and Theo sitting at the table, Myra cutting bread at the sideboard.

"Child, go wash." Myra flicked her eyes at CB, inviting him to join her. He nuzzled her neck. She let him. She buttered a thick cut heel and popped it in his mouth. "Husband, go wash."

"Yes, missus." He rubbed her round belly, savoring the crust on his way on his way to the basin.

I do like this married life. He smiled, licking the last delicious crumb from the corner of his mouth.

CB's shore leave was almost over, and summer was headin' to fall. School was starting. Soon Aunt Ada would be coming back to help Myra through her last month.

This dinner meal seemed bigger than usual. There were three meats and five vegetables, jarred chow-chow, plus the usual biscuits and jam. When CB returned, he noticed an extra place set.

"Who?"

"Look beside the plate."

"What?" The children were giggling.

"Look beside the plate."

"Yes, man, look beside the plate. Don't you see a harmonica?" CB knew that voice well.

Stepping around the corner from the parlor was his best mate, Jack Smith, smiling broadly. That mouth organ had earned the two sailors passage into many of the taverns along the Galveston wharves. They would sing and play their checker games, signaling the traveling dreamers that it was time to get in a specially marked stowaway barrel to be on their way to the Klondike gold fields.

CB returned the smile, with a lift of his eyebrow. Jack turned to the table. "Missus Myra, this spread looks might fine. You didn't need to put out for me."

"Don't be silly. We all could use a feast now and then." She touched her stomach. "Especially me. Seems the two of us are always hungry."

Jack flushed. He was not used to household familiarities, and this was a white household, t'boot. He picked up his harmonica. "Might I play the blessing for you?"

Myra nodded and they all bowed their heads. The clear sweet notes of *The Golden Gate* filled the room. CB's eyes sprung open, staring at Jack. That song was their signal to get the gold seekers on board. Jack nodded. No one else knew what had just happened.

"Amen."

Praise God. We can start movin' again.

All were seated and CB handed Jack the meat platters first. Jack did not defer, taking a nice slice each of ham and beef, leaving the cold slices of souse for the others. Myra thought her husband was welcoming their guest. Jack knew CB was honoring the news he brought.

Nora Lee asked for the chow-chow.

"Yes'm." Jack passed the jar to the wiggly child beside him. "Missus Myra, where's the rest of your folk?" He made an exaggerated circle with his eyes. "This here table seems to be missin' a boy. Did he get lost somewhere in this fine house?"

"Off to the Island with Uncle Harry and the buildin'. Seems we could all use some help."

Myra patted her bulge. "With you two men headin' back to sea, Aunt Ada will soon be here, bless her. It's going to be very busy with the baby comin'." Just then, her dress shifted in front of her. "Goodness child," she said, looking down. "Settle darlin'. Dinner's on its way."

"Mama's baby needs a piece of bread." Theo handed her the basket.

"Yes, darling, we do, and pass some of that good jam, too. The figs are from our tree."

The meal was well appreciated by all. CB had two slices of the souse, loving the vinegar tang. He scraped the last bits onto the other heel and called it dessert. Jack just shook his head.

Crazy white folk, too close to slave slop for me. Jam was his dessert. Then Missus Myra stood.

"Mister Jack, I know you didn't make your way all these miles just to eat dinner. Is there another reason?"

"Yes, ma'am. Cap'n sent me."

Myra nodded. She'd figured it was time. Jack looked at CB and then around the table at the children.

"If I may be excused from this fine table, there's business needin' to be talked about."

CB tilted his head toward the door.

"Excuse us, family." He loved saying 'family.'

Myra nodded, wondering and realizing all at the same time. Something was up, something more than call to duty.

Hmmm.

The men walked out and stood on the stoop. Colored could not be seen on a front porch, that's just the way it was. A bit later, they returned with giant smiles on both faces to find jumbles and coffee on the table.

"Fresh? Hot?" Myra tilted her head, eyebrows up.

"Fresh, hot, and straight from Panama." CB's words said it all. The three clinked their mugs together in an unspoken toast.

Chapter Seven
April 28, 1901
CB and Jack at Sea *or*
What Do You Do With A Drunken Sailor?

Captain Calhoun was dead drunk. Must have been since one bell. CB knew because he served the brandy. Captain always had drink on his dinner tray.

"Sir?" CB shook the captain's shoulder. "Sir, time for charts, we gotta get to work." Captain Calhoun snorted, but did not lift his head. "Come on, sir, we need to work."

The captain opened one eye, the one buried in his arm.

"Hush boy. Can't you see it's night?"

CB gave him another shake. "Open your other eye, sir. It's day."

"Damn." Captain was not one to swear sober. "Damn."

"I'll get coffee from Cookie. We gotta do charts, or tiller man will drive us who-knows-where."

"No coffee, brandy," argued Captain, closing his free eye.

"Yes coffee, no brandy. I'll be back lickity-split. Don't make me get Jack to give you a walk about. You know he will."

"Damn it." Slowly Captain raised his head from the desk. "You keep Jack away from me. His walk abouts are more like run abouts. Damn, his legs are long."

"Yes, sir, you need to sit up and quit cussin'. The men know you're drunk when you cuss."

"Shit."

"Stop it. I'll get coffee and Jack. I can tell the brew isn't gonna do it by itself."

CB found Jack topside.

"Again?" Jack put down his swab mop.

"Yes, come on. I'll get the coffee pot. You meet me at quarters. He's 'specially ornery this time."

Jack sighed. "Is it going to take singin' or walkin'? Singin' him straight is so much easier on my back."

"Both." CB headed to the galley and Jack went below, where he waited outside the captain's door.

Snores roared inside. Noise was so loud, it practically rattled the heavy chain and open padlock Cap had hung on a hook on the door frame. Cap said he put it there as a reminder. He never said of what.

CB was soon beside his friend. "Cookie was one step ahead of us. He had a fresh pot waiting."

Nodding toward the door, both men knew what to do. Jack pulled out his harmonica and opened the door. CB clanked the coffee pot on the desk. Jack leaned directly by his captain's head and blew.

"Honk. Tweet. Squawk."

More snores.

"Squeech. Squeal."

Captain jerked. "Shush, damn it. Can't you see I'm sleepin'?"

Jack squatted by the captain's ear and began to play "Camptown Races." He 'n' CB'd made up a special song to the tune. CB let it rip.

"Cap'n Calhoun, he got drunk, do dah, do dah.
"Cap'n Calhoun, he got drunk, all the live long day.
"He's been drinkin' all day,
"He's been drinkin' all night.
"He better get a'walkin' while we got daylight."

Pocketing his instrument, Jack went behind, put his hands under the captain's armpits, and yanked. "Get up, man. We gotta move."

50

Half pushing, half dragging, the two seamen circled Captain Calhoun around and around the cabin until he could walk on his own. He found his desk chair and sat. CB poured him a mug of some of the blackest jamoke on ship. As soon as it was half gone, Jack topped it off with more.

CB waited. He needed some semblance of sobriety sittin' in that chair before he said what he had to say.

Finally he spoke. "Sir."

"Yes?'

"This is a bad one, a really bad one."

"I know."

"You're not gonna stop."

"I know. Oh, Jesus, I know."

"You want to keep sailin'?" Jack asked.

"You boys know I have nothing else. The *Sallie Lou* is the only home I got. I can't leave her." Captain William J. Calhoun started to sob. "She's my girl. She's my life. You know I've owned her 'bout as long as I've known you." His head sunk into his hands. "Oh, Jesus, what am I going to do?"

That was the cue CB had been waiting for. "You're going to stay with her, but you cannot captain her."

The captain started to hiccup. "I, uh, know, uh, I know. Oh, God, uh, what's gonna, uh, happen to me?"

Jack spoke. "You are going to give command of the *Sallie* to us. You will promote Sure Foot to Chief Mate and me to Second Mate. We been doing that work, anyway, and you can stay drunk in your quarters all day long."

"And you will back pay us for everything we've done," CB added.

Captain stared at the both of them. Opening his mouth, he started to speak, but all that came out was a hiccup. He nodded.

"Boys, get me to the head."

"Yes, sir," the newly promoted sailors said in unison.

CB and Jack knew that nothing had changed except their pay. It was Cookie who figured things out. CB was in mess, pickin' up the Captain's tray. Everything was set just a usual, with good strong Chinese tea that always went with dinner.

"Hey, Sure Foot, what'd ya do to the Cap? Hide the brandy?"

CB straightened the butter knife and looked up at Cookie. "Huh?"

"You two haven't come after coffee mid-afternoon in a long time. Y'all dryin' him out?" Cookie added a small plate of marzipan to the tray.

"You gonna give some of that to us? Jack and I got a sweet tooth." CB knew he was on cracked ice. "You remember my Myra's jumbles? They're all full of nuts, too,"

"That don't answer my question. I ain't seen the Captain in days. You two got him locked up, or somethin'?" Cookie's usual squint got tighter.

"Um, no, you got some time? Best you come to quarters with me." CB knew he'd better get this handled quick. "Carry something so the men don't notice."

"Shit, man, did you two kill him or something?"

"Come on. Bring a kettle of hot water. We many need it." CB picked up the tray and began whistling 'Camptown.' Less than ten seconds later, Jack was by his side.

"You bringin' Cookie?" Jack hissed between smiling teeth.

"Do dah, do dah."

"Why?" another hiss.

"All the live long day." CB kept on singin' and walkin', Cookie following.

The cabin smelled like piss and dead fish. Captain Calhoun was in his bunk, mouth open, arms crossed on his chest like he was laid out. There was puke in his whiskers.

Cookie gagged. "Oh, God in heaven, ya kilt him."

CB set down the tray. Jack took the kettle and poured water in his basin.

"No siree, he's killin' himself. We're just doin' the best we can." Jack's disgusted tone said it all. "Now you can help, too."

CB spoke up. "Cookie, we got big troubles down here. He won't quit. All we can do is keep his glass full to keep him quiet so's the men won't hear him holler when he sees the rats and spiders."

"Rats I understand. Spiders? Where they comin' from?" Cookie looked around. "Show me his kit. This man's a mess."

"No rats, no spiders, DTs. Jack and me been keepin' him drunk so he don't scream." CB pointed to the leather shaving box under a pile of charts. "He gets so far gone, we can't sit him up to shave him. We're lucky to get him to the branch hopper. Smell like he didn't make it this time."

Jack looked in the chamber pot sittin' by the bunk. "It's dry," he said. Pulling back the blanket, Jack took one look and stepped away. "He's not."

Cookie stared at his captain. "Damn, boys," he said. "We can't let this get out. Shit, we'd have a mutiny, for sure."

"Gosh darn it, Cookie, we been tryin'." CB's face said it all.

His dead daddy had been a mean drunk. His captain was a nice drunk, but all that drunk tending was wearing him down.

"We been tryin' real hard," he repeated.

Jack chimed in, "Yeah, real hard. Damn it, Cookie, it's been like keepin' a really big baby. And that's not countin' the ship runnin' time. We need help."

"I see that." Cookie was setting out Captain Calhoun's grooming gear. "Let's get him sitting. I'll wash and shave him. Sure Foot, you figure out what we're gonna

53

do with his bunk. Jack, look in his drawers' drawer for something to put on him." Cookie turned to CB and Jack. "Come on, boys, let's get him up."

The three men raised the dead. The corpse was not happy.

An hour later a clean but shaky captain, one sweating cook, and two exhausted mates stepped out on the deck, with CB carrying a quarter's chair. The sailors who saw them didn't say a word, keeping about their work. Captain Calhoun was seeing the light of day for the first time in weeks.

From then on until they got back to Texas, CB and Jack put the captain on display. Sitting in his deck chair every afternoon drinkin' Cookie's good, black coffee with a double shot of brandy, Captain William J. Calhoun took in the sun. Every evening he fell asleep plastered but not piss drunk. Breakfast tea had the hair of the dog. CB and Jack kept Cookie out of it, only asking for the coffee. It was just better that way.

Chapter Eight
June 14, 1901
Childbirth

Rain on the garden was one thing. Plants danced. Rain on a house full of children was another, and this day was a real toad strangler. Myra's house and belly were both filled with young'uns. Everyone wanted to go out to play, including little unborn CB or Flossie Mae, depending on its nature. This one was taking its own sweet time. It was not like Myra'd been sitting around, not with four, sometimes five children in the house. No, Mrs. Myra Gallaway Ledbetter was not a lazy bones. However, today she barely moved off the settee, keeping her ballooning feet high up on a pile of pillows balanced on the hassock.

"A watched pot never boils," said Aunt Ada, patting her niece's huge stomach. Aunt Ada Dickenson was in from Galveston for Myra's confinement. She was settled in the second floor screened sleeping porch. It had six cots made up, and many a night the family would join her to escape the heat.

"Hah. This pot had better start boilin' pretty darn soon. My lid looks like it has a handle on it." Myra pulled her dress tight across herself and pointed to her protruding belly button. "I'm 'bout to pop."

"Goodness, child, you sure are."

All of Myra's other birthings were done before she was widowed at twenty. Now she was twenty-five and adding to the family with her new husband.

"You sure you have a baby in there and not a watermelon? That thing looks like the stem." Both women smiled.

"Maybe it's a boy, and he's just too crowded." Myra chuckled.

"Shush, darlin', the children might hear you. They'll want to see his little wing-ding a pokin' out your middle." Ada smiled. "Next thing you know, Nora Lee'll be pitchin' one of her cat fits. She wants a sister more 'en anything in the whole wide world."

"That little missy can pitch all she wants," said Myra. "She gonna have to take what she gets. I just want it over with. Look at my ankles. They're almost as swollen as the rest of me."

She was spending most of her days corset-less in her bare feet. Not even her garden shoes could be laced. Thank heavens Aunt Ada was there, since CB was out to sea until next month. Lord knows you couldn't time a baby.

"Darlin', baby comes when baby's ready and not a minute before. You know that. Just how soon are you?"

"If I worked the calendar right, it'll be a couple of weeks, around the first of July. Heaven's sake, I'm big. Mrs. Turnborg didn't seem concerned. Said I had plenty of time, but I just don't know. Thank goodness we have the layette ready." Myra shifted her bulk and gave up trying to stand. Her midwife, Sue Anne Turnborg, seemed almost nonchalant.

Humph, let's give her four youngun's runnin' and one sittin' on her lap not going anywhere.

"She did say she'd come by tomorrow. Auntie, could I be carrying twins again? Good Lord, let's hope not."

"Stay on the settee, darling." Aunt Ada stood. "What do you want? I'll get it. How 'bout some fresh coffee? Sounds good to me."

Myra snuggled back into the cushions. "Oh, please, and a crybaby too, if there are any left. Maybe the cookie's name will work its magic." She smiled. The memory of walking the wharves, selling jumbles, plunkets, and crybabies seemed so far away. "I love crybabies."

Myra was starting to doze, dreaming about Galveston and her life before marrying CB. Aunt Ada found her in tears.

"Oh, my precious, what's wrong?" She put down their coffee mugs and cookies on the side table. Sitting as close as her niece's bulk would allow, Ada pulled Myra to her bosom and rocked her like the baby she was carrying. "Tell me. Is it the waiting? Are you getting your pains? Let me ease you, my love."

"Oh Auntie," Myra sobbed. "I miss Julia so much. I miss the wharves, I even miss the Guild. I am so homesick for what will never be again."

The hurricane of 1900 destroyed their houses, the wharves, and killed over five thousand souls. Her dear friend, Julia, her future sister-in-law, was killed that day, crushed by a mule carcass. Had Julia stayed in the church with the other ladies, she would be alive. Then, maybe, there would still be the adventures. Myra kept the secret about how she and Julia, whose real name was Flossie Mae, were moving smugglers' jewelry, the payments given to CB and Jack. Besides, who would believe that a poor widow and a snooty church lady would even speak to each other, let alone be partners in crime?

Ada continued the rocking. After a bit, Myra pulled her handkerchief from her sleeve, sniffled and dabbed. She sat up and reached for her coffee. The mug was cool.

"I have got to get a'movin'." She struggled to stand. "I need to go to the bathroom. I'll warm our cups when I get back. Can't lay about all day long."

"Let me help." Ada stood in front of her, offering her hands.

Myra grabbed hold and ever so slowly got to her bare feet. She could hear the children upstairs, thumping and shuffling around. As long as she didn't hear hollerin' and cryin', she didn't care if they were taking the paint off the walls. Nora Lee would come tattling if anything horrible was happening. Ada took Myra's arm to steady her. The women did that time honored dance of assistance as they shuffled their way across the room.

"I'm fine now," Myra said, and fainted straight down. Ada stifled her scream.

Checking to make sure Myra was breathing, Aunt Ada yelled for the children, grabbed their slickers, and got them all out on the side porch. Ada had not been blessed with a child and was never privy to a birthing. Not one of the children knew where the midwife lived. Ada thought quick.

"Darlin's, do you know where Miss Annie, uh er, Mrs. Wilson's new house is?" That they did know, having visited several times. "Run to her. Tell her Mama needs help and ask her to find Mrs. Turnborg. And, for God's sake, be polite." Everyone knew that Annie appreciated manners at all times. "Hurry darlin's, hurry."

They ran, buckling their coats on the way.

Myra yawned.

That was a good sleep. Wonder why the house is so quiet?

She tried to roll out of bed, bringing her arm around her belly, pushing palm down on the mattress. The sheet felt rough, odd. She opened her eyes. She saw eagle claws holding clear soap bubbles. Raising up on the other elbow, she looked straight down at the Persian carpet that came with the house.

Why did I take a nap here?

"Auntie? Where are the children?" Myra noticed her voice didn't sound.

Hmmm that's not right. Try louder.

"Auntie? Where are the children?"

Her movements and whispers seemed burdened. *Gotta stand, gotta find the necessary. Oh no, too late.*

She was alone in the room. Drawing her legs closer, she, forced herself to hands and knees. She saw the settee across the room and started to crawl. Her belly and wet skirts were in the way. She was not moving.

"Nuuuuuh, nuuuuh."

In the time it took to wink a blink, Ada was back in the house, screen slamming behind her. Her niece was on the floor, poised like cat in heat, knees wide. Ada slowly lowered herself beside Myra, who stared straight ahead, seeing nothing.

Myra suddenly realized who was making that sound, the primal grunt that indicated birth.

"Nuuuuuh, nuuuuh, ahhhhh."

"Oh dear Jesus, CB, Auntie, anybody, Help me."

The last words came out in a scream. She closed her eyes, arched her back, and pushed.

"Nuuuuuh, nuuuuh."

"I'm here, child I'm here. Look at me. Tell me what to do."

"Hunh, hunh, hunh," panted Myra. "String, scissors, bath towels, Lister towels...in box in pantry...hunh, hunh, hunh. NOW," she howled as she pushed.

Ada rushed for the supplies. Myra was humming.

"MMMMMM, MMMMMM, MMMMM. NOW, Oh God, NOW."

Myra fell deadly silent. There was a slippery being held tight against her, caught in her clothing. It wasn't moving.

"Auntie, baby, my drawers. Help me, oh Jesus, help me."

Ada threw Myra's skirt up over her back and clawed at her niece's underwear. They were soaked with urine, blood, and fluid. Grabbing the scissors, she cut up the side where the buttons were, and pulled them off her hips, down to her knees and away. The baby slid to the floor with a solid 'plop'. The umbilical cord was stretched taut. Myra instinctively curved her back, lowering her hips.

"Tie two tight knots, one against the baby, another one a bit higher. Cut between. Hurry, we gotta get it crying."

Myra stayed statue still, knees apart, instructing her aunt. Ada had tied many a shopping bundle at the mercantile, and was quickly done with the knots.

"Cut, Auntie. Hurry, I feel the afterbirth moving."

It wasn't a snip as Ada had always imagined. It was like cutting thicknesses of wool.

"Done." Ada pulled the baby free just as Myra collapsed, landing flat on her belly. The child opened its eyes. Ada knew what to do with newborn kittens, so she instinctively did the same, gathering the child in a towel. She patted the silent child, rubbing and jiggling. Nothing. She blew on its face. It blinked, opened its mouth, and hollered. Myra started crying. Ada slid the baby under the settee.

"Auntie, get another towel. We need to look at the afterbirth, gotta make sure it's whole. Oh, nuug, nuug. Gotta roll over. Help me over, Auntie, help me. It's coming."

Ada spread another towel and rolled her niece. Now on her back, Myra planted her feet firmly on the carpet, pushed one more time, and expelled the placenta. She seemed to sleep while her aunt gathered it, saw it wasn't torn, and put it aside, secured the Lister towel.

Myra mumbled, "Bring me the baby. Nursin' will slow the bleedin'. What is it? Boy? Girl?"

Ada scuttled on all fours to the settee, finding it easier than standing 'cause of the rheumatism in her back.

"I don't know, didn't look." The child was chewing its fist. "Hungry, though."

Scooping the bundle and putting it on the settee, she used the leverage of the cushions to pull herself upright. A quick peek inside the towel answered the question. Babe in arms, Ada walked to her niece, who was trying to sit up.

Myra adjusted her stained skirt to maintain modesty. Still on the floor, she scooted her bottom until she was backed against the wing chair and unbuttoned her bodice.

"My darling," announced Ada, "I present Miss Flossie Mae Ledbetter, in all her hungry glory."

Myra reached up, took her daughter, and put her straight to breast. The pre-milk was dripping from her nipples. Little Miss Flossie latched on as though she had done it all of her life. Each suckle brought cramps of tightening.

"Thank you, my beloved child. Thank you for being here. Mama loves you." Myra's murmurings soothed the baby and Flossie Mae was soon asleep, her mouth slack. "Aunt Ada, please take her. I have got to get off this floor. The layette is ready in the humpback chest by the cradle in our bedroom. All the diapers and gowns are there. I bought more Lister towels for me. The extras are there with the baby blankets." Myra took a breath. "Just don't wash her yet."

"Why?" Ada took the baby and sniffed. "She stinks."

"No, no," Myra protested. "The white stuff's good for her. We can bathe it off soon enough." Just like her aunt, Myra used the chair to bring herself upright.

That's when she saw the carpet.

"Oh dear God, look what I've done," she moaned, waves of memories washing over her like that killer hurricane flood.

Oh Julia.

Their whole adventure with the jewelry started with a carpet stain, a pot of coffee intentionally spilled.

Ada glanced at the rug. "Darlin', darlin', we can clean this. Don't fret. We'll find somebody to do it. Right now, I need to get both of you to bed. Are you strong enough to climb the steps?"

Within the hour, Myra and Flossie were sound asleep, clean and in the matching nightgowns Ada embroidered. However, no Missus Annie and no passel of youngun's came banging through the door.

Ada said a quick prayer. "Lord, can't leave here to find them. Keep them safe and get them home. And please forgive me if I use the switch. Amen."

Tap

As though an answer to her prayers, she heard a soft rap on the back door.

Thank you, Lord.

Then she realized that no one she knew would be coming to the back door, and definitely not knocking. Her skin went to chill bumps. She did not know the people of LaPorte. Galveston, yes. They would come to the store all the time looking for meals Harry would hand out. Ada grabbed the broom handle. She could always give the stranger a whack if need be.

Chapter Nine
June 14, 1901
Hens and Chicks

Standing on the stoop was a girl, almost a woman. She had a black straw mourner's hat, long plaited red hair, and brown skin. She held two suitcases in clean-gloved hands. Ada looked through the screen. "I think I know you."

"*Oui*. Fish gal."

"Pardon?"

"I brought fish to your store. You are Missus Ada."

"Oh yes. My goodness, what are you doing here?" Ada smiled and set aside the broom. "Come on in." Pulling the door wide, she said, "Let me help you with your grip," and took one of the cases before there could be any protest. "Do you want coffee? I promised myself a hot cuppa hours ago." Ada gestured to the kitchen table. "Sit, child, sit."

"Ma'am?" The girl did not move. "Ma'am, I'm colored."

"Goodness, I can see that. Now sit." Ada put two mugs on the table. "What is your name? Harry always called you 'fish gal'." She didn't add that Harry always called her 'Injun fish gal' in honor of her braided hair.

"Yes ma'am, thank you, ma'am. My name is Marguerite." She sat. "It has been a long train ride." She looked at the coffee. "Um, uh, ma'am?"

Ada was rummaging in the sideboard. She never got those promised cookies, either.

"Yes?" She turned to the table with the plate of crybabies and two saucers.

"Please, ma'am, might I have some milk for the coffee, if it isn't too much trouble."

"Oh, of course. I have fresh skimmed cream, if you would like that."

"Milk's fine. Thank you."

Ada sat. After a decent sized bite of cookie and sip to wash it, Ada put her mug by the saucer. She waited, listening for the front door and for sounds from upstairs.

Where were those children?

She nodded to Marguerite. "Now tell me, dear, what brings you here to this house?"

"Jack Smith."

"Oh?"

"*Oui*, I love him." Marguerite felt that answered all questions.

"CB and Jack are at sea. Surely you know that."

"*Oui*." Marguerite started to cry. "I love him. I can't live without him. I am here."

"And…?"

"Please let me stay. I cannot go back to the hotel."

Crash. Holler. "Finally. Excuse me, the children are back."

Marguerite nodded.

Ada hurried into the parlor. "Where's Missus Annie? Did she go for the Mrs. Turnborg? You children knew I needed help."

"Nope, couldn't find her." Nora Lee shook her curls. "We got a baby?"

"Yes, now hush your voices. You all had me scared to pieces. Where in God's name have you been?"

Benjy, Franky, Theo, and Nora Lee grabbed hands and circled their aunt Ada.

"Hooray. Hooray. We have a baby."

They were dancin' ring a rosy when Nora Lee stopped still. The boys crashed into her. Hands on hips and bottom lip pouted, she said, "What is it? Better not be a boy."

64

Ada smiled her most loving smile. "The baby's name is Flossie Mae. Don't you dare wake her, or I'll get the switch. Do you understand me, little missy?"

The children began pantomiming their celebration.

"Ma'am?" Marguerite was standing in the kitchen door.

The children froze, staring at the stranger in their house.

"Ma'am, did you say there was a new babe? *Monsieur* Jack said his friend was soon to be a papa. "

"Yes dear, today. My great niece was born about an hour and a half ago. "

"You did it yourself?" Marguerite looked amazed.

"Yes." A huge wave of exhaustion hit Ada. "Oh my, suddenly I am so tired myself." She sank into the depths of the settee. "I feel a bit faint. Benjy, would you get me your mother's church fan? It's in the seat of the hall tree bench. Thank you, sweetheart. By the way, this is Miss Marguerite. She's looking for Mister Jack."

"Here, Auntie." Benjy handed the pasteboard fan to Ada, and dropped the hinged seat with a crash.

"Waaaaa." The new one made her presence known from upstairs.

"Sorry, Auntie, sorry," Benjy mouthed.

"Ma'am, let me attend the baby. I want to help." Marguerite headed to the steps, bold as brass. On the first step, she stopped and turned. "May I take the young *mademoiselle* to meet her sister?"

Ada waved weakly from the couch. "Please, and Marguerite, thank you."

"Come, *mademoiselle*, show me where your maman is." The two new friends climbed the steps hand in hand.

Ada turned her eyes to the boys. "Now, where have you been?"

With the baby awake, the boys found their voices. "We were watchin' the sign man."

Ada pulled the boys close and snuggled them on the settee. "What sign man?"

Only Franky stayed in the hug. The other two jumped up and started jabbering what sounded like nonsense.

"Whoa, boys, hold your horses, one at a time. Put your bottoms on the floor." Then she remembered the stain. "Uh, wait a minute. Let's go in the kitchen. I have a cup of coffee and cookies there." Ada held her hands out. "Help your old Auntie. My rheumatism's acting up"

The boys pulled her to her feet and all found spots at the table, cold coffee and cookies waiting.

After hearing the story of the sign man, Ada said, "Guess we'd better get Junior in on this. What do you think?" More cheering. "I'll ask Uncle Harry to send him when I telegraph about the baby."

"How many cookies are we allowed?" Franky's one-track mind always led to cookies. His crybaby was half gone in two bites. "Can we take some to Mama and see, ugh, the guurl?"

As much as Nora Lee wanted a girl, Franky wanted a boy. He just knew that another girl would be like his tattletale sister.

"Darling, just remember that babies are God's blessing."

"Yeah, but a guurl?"

"Yes, even a baby girl," Ada winked. "Now I'm going up to see if your mama would be willin' to let you visit, even though she just had a baby 'guurl.' Y'all wait 'til I call you." She turned to Franky, "You bring the cookies, and be nice. I don't want to start calling you Cranky Franky."

The boy giggled, and stuffed another crybaby in his mouth.

Ada found Nora Lee in bed with her mother and the swaddled newborn in Marguerite's arms. Myra was holding her big baby girl close. "Auntie, look who's come."

"Yes, dear."

"Marguerite and I are friends from the docks."

"Really? You never told me about her." Ada was feeling the need to sit again and lowered into the nursing chair. "How long have you two known each other?"

"Since Everett died." Myra smiled up for her new daughter. "I'm ready. Scoot over, Missy, your sister needs feedin'." Babe to breast and covers pulled, she whispered to Nora Lee. The child popped out of bed and ran down the steps. "Get ready, everyone, I've sent for the troops. Told her they had to count to one hundred first." The baby was sucking hard. "Oooh, the tightening's working. Auntie, I need to tell you something before, oooh, the boys are here. I've asked Marguerite to stay with us. Is that all right with you?"

"Darling, it's your house, not mine. Why do you ask?"

"With Marguerite's help, you can go home to Uncle Harry."

"I see." Ada's smile was straight.

"Auntie, are you mad at me?" Myra's tone showed uncertainty.

"Oh, no, darling, it's just, well, I'd hoped to be here to see CB hold his daughter for the first time." Ada lifted an eyebrow. "Now I have to go wrangle your uncle and you know that's a whole lot more work than a house full of children." Ada stood. "Do you need the chair?"

"Not until tomorrow. Today I am a lady at rest, and a hungry one at that. Auntie, will you show Marguerite around the kitchen? She used to help her mama cook at the Tremont. How is she, by the way?" Myra had not noticed Marguerite's hat.

"Maman went to the Blessed Mary two days after the hurricane."

"Oh. I am so sorry."

Marguerite nodded. "*Oui*. It was her heart, I think. I will tell you the story later. Uh, Missus Myra...?"

"Call me Myra. We are friends."

"But I'm colored."

"Hush, my friend. Does Jack call CB 'Mister CB'?"

"*Non*." Marguerite smiled. "Uh, Myra, I have to tell you something."

Myra frowned. "What is it? Are you sick? In man trouble?"

"Oh no, it's just the opposite." Marguerite blushed. "It's just that, um,"

"What?"

"It's just that," Marguerite rushed on, "I am Mrs. Jack Smith"

"You're what?" Myra was astonished. "Does CB know?"

"I don't know who Jack has told. You see, we, um, have never, um...uh." Marguerite was beet red.

"Oh." Myra smiled. "You and Jack have never been private."

The bride nodded. "*Oui,* never. We are not really married yet."

"My dear, that will never do." Myra shifted her sleepy bundle to the other breast. "We've got to take care of that little problem as soon as possible." Flossie latched on and farted at the same time. All the women smiled.

"Where do I put my suitcases?" Marguerite asked Ada.

"Follow me, child. We live in the sleeping porch, the best place to be in the summer. It's just down the hall." Aunt Ada led Marguerite out of the bedroom. "Good bye, darlings. Holler if things get to be too much."

The roommates left the family to get acquainted.

68

Marguerite had never seen a sleeping porch. With screening stretched on the three open sides, what breezes blowing could cool all and there would be no bites. Maman and she used to sit on the back stoop, dozing in kitchen chairs, waving their fans trying to cool off before going to bed. Sometimes they would fall asleep in those chairs, but usually the mosquitoes would run them back into the heat of the house.

"This is wonderful, ma'am. Where do you want me to put my things?" Myra had offered familiarities, but Marguerite knew the manners of house-help. "Ma'am? I saw the carpet. I know how to take care of that kind of mess. We do it in the banquet hall when there is a spill. I will clean it tonight so the stains do not set."

Ada smiled. "Thank you, so much." She gestured to the beds. "I sleep by the door. Take your pick of the others."

Marguerite pulled a faded quilt from her valise. "This was my maman's. Now it is mine." She smoothed it on the cot closest to the screens where she could feel the breeze.

Chapter Ten
January, 1901
Junior and the Store

The only good thing about living with the Dickensons was the prospect of not going to school. Junior was sorting the apple barrel, basketing the bad ones for the rot dump. When he heard the argument, he squatted down behind it to eavesdrop.

"Work will teach him life," stated Uncle Harry.

Aunt Ada and Harry were arguing the benefits of 'The Boy's Grand Plan,' as Harry was fond of calling it.

"School will teach him how to live life." Ada pushed back her white curls and reset her comb. That was the signal she was diggin' in for a fight. This was the third time for this 'discussion' in a week. "He must be able to do more than—"

"What? Work hard to earn a good living?" Harry grumped. "Look at me. I stopped—"

"Yes, I know, after fourth grade. And, yes, you work hard and earn a good living. But, my dear, that was many years ago. Don't tell me about back when you did… whatever. These modern times require more than the basic three R's. Look at me, I graduated from eighth."

"Well, that settles it. You can schoolmarm him at home." Harry knew he had won. "Yessiree, you are the smartest woman I know."

"But—"

"No buts. Junior is not going to a schoolhouse with one teacher. He is going to attend the Harry and Ada School. End of discussion."

"This is not over, husband."

"Yes it is. I'm starting my lessons right now." Harry walked to back door, picking up his .22 on the way.

"Junior," he hollered. "Let's you 'n' me teach those rot dump rats how to add 2+2."

Junior skittered around the barrel with the peck of bad apples and joined his uncle. "Yes sir, I like shootin'."

Ada walked to the school, now meeting in a church until the new one was finished, to withdraw her nephew from enrollment.

I'll stir this pot later.

Principal Dirkman lost his wife and his mind in the hurricane and had to go live with his sister in Kansas. The school's new headmaster, a mere child sent in desperation straight from Southwest State Normal School with 1 ½ years college, did not know Junior from Adam.

"Ma'am?" The young man barely looked up from his cluttered desk in what once was the pastor's study. "What do you want?"

"Your secretary said you need to sign this." Ada handed him the form." I am taking my nephew, Everett Gallaway Junior, out of school. He is having difficulties and we are going to teach him at home."

"Good." The man did not care if another unruly boy was gone. He scribbled on the line and handed back the paper.

As Ada left, she thought she heard, "God help you. I can't."

Uncle Harry sure did appreciate having Junior staying on the island with him while Ada was helping Myra wait for that baby. The new store was a showplace. The shelves were stacked like pyramids with cans of anything you could want. Right below the displays were the bins of dried fruits, flour, sugar, crackers, and coffee beans. Frank B. Hale High Grade Tea—oolong, y hyson, orange pekoe—sat right there for all to see through the glass tops. Oranges and apples were piled in the windows beside the small burlap bags of pecans. It was Junior's job to build the pyramids.

71

The iceman returned to his route after the streets were cleared and the houses put up. Harry proudly sold fresh meat from the new walk-in cooler. The folks of Galveston Island had been mostly surviving on rice, beans, and tack. Now there was meat to buy and store in their kitchen iceboxes. It was Junior's job to tend that ice.

Harry was especially proud of his candy case. It was glass all around with oak for the side supports. These days candy was about as important as fresh meat. Mothers brought children on shopping day. One look at that big glass box was all it took. Nonpareils were the most favored, but plain lemon drops came in a close second. It was Junior's job to clean and fill the candy case.

Once a month on Saturday night, after the OPEN sign was flipped to CLOSED, Harry would sweep the store extra good. Then he would pour coal oil on the wood floor and rub it in with his wire brush push broom. He said it kept the dust down and the critters out. It was Junior's job to help with the scrubbing and clean the wire brush when done.

Yessireebob, Harry sure was happy. Junior wasn't. Just because he was away from CB and all that kissin', did not mean he was anybody's slave boy. No man would tell him what to do. That was his mama's job, and she was up in LaPorte, about to have another baby. Uncle Harry seemed to think that the answer to all Junior's problems was more work.

"Do this, do that," Junior muttered low as he stood outside, washing the front window glass with vinegar water, old newspapers, and rags. "Who do you think you are? You're not my boss."

"What say?" Uncle Harry came around the side of the building, taking his cigar from his mouth. "Who are you talking to? All I see is a reflection of a hard workin' helper." Harry smiled at his nephew.

"Nothin'. Nobody." Junior scowled. He kept polishing.

"Windows looks good. When you're done, I could use some help in the back with the dry goods." Harry stashed his half-chewed cigar in its hiding place and walked through the door. The bell hanging above tinkled his arrival.

"Shaddup bell." Junior gave the window a rough swipe, picked up his bucket of vinegar water, and followed, not caring if he slopped as he walked. Leaving splashes with every step, he went out back and threw the water on the new, but still nasty, rot dump. "Take that, you rats," he grunted. There was a scurry heard. "Yeah, you go home to the garbage, Uncle Harry'll git you soon enough."

Thinking of taking target practice on the critters with Harry's .22 seemed to raise Junior's mood. He set down the bucket, laying out the rags on the rim to dry.

His uncle wasn't in the storeroom. Junior found him standing at the counter, talking to his Masonic Brother, Eugene Earnest. Brother Earnest was the telegraph man for the neighborhood. Uncle Harry was smiling.

"Thank you, Brother, thank you. Always happy to see you bring good news," said Harry with a big grin. He turned to Junior. "Son, you have a baby sister." He handed over the telegram.

HARRY DICKENSON
BABY GIRL FLOSSIE MAE LEDBETTER
BORN JUNE 15, 1901
ALL IS WELL SEND JUNIOR
WILL BE HOME SOON
LOVE ADA

Junior stared at the paper. His face couldn't be mad anymore. He was going home, home to his mama. "Yes sir, I've got a baby sister. When do I leave?"

Harry scratched his head. "Tomorrow, I'm guessin', gotta buy a train ticket." He noticed Eugene still standing there, waiting. "Son, would you get a quarter from the cash box for this fine man? Thank you."

"No, no, Harry. No tip needed. You're a Brother."

"Don't argue a proper day's wage."

Junior handed him the coin.

"Thank ye kindly," said Mr. Earnest. "Son, you know the telegraph is in the train station. Make sure you let me know when you leave and I'll wire your family that you're on your way."

"Thank you, Mr. Earnest, I'll do just that."

The next morning Junior boarded the train for LaPorte. He shook his uncle's hand like a man. He did not notice the ticket said 'Round Trip.'

Three days later, the family kissed, hugged, and bid farewell to their beloved Aunt Ada. The twins escorted her to the station, leaving Junior and Theo with their mother. Ada waved her handkerchief out the window at the boys, they sending kisses back. Ada settled into the velvet coach seat, and prayed.

Thank you, Heavenly Father, for not giving children to old women. Amen.

Chapter Eleven
1895-1901
Lulah Marie Dubonet

"You have the eye," her grandmother told her.

Sitting between Nana Moo's knees getting her hair twisted, Lulah Marie Dubonet had no idea what she was talking about. Lulah had two eyes, everybody knew that.

"I got two, and a nose. Ow."

Nana was makin' the knots real tight.

"Your mama's got the eye. I got the eye. All us women got the eye, even your Russian great granny. Girl, you got the eye. Now hush." Nana Moo added bits of thread to her twists. "You'll know soon. Baby, you'll know soon."

"What? Ow." Another wicked twist.

Lulah Marie learned not to ask. The girl grew up with threads in her hair and the belief that she had the eye, whatever that was. When she was twelve, her flowers blossomed, and she became a woman. Her mama and her grandmother were thrilled. On the third day, Lulah Marie went to Nana Moo's house, where she was led out back to the garden shed. There was a table, three chairs, a basin of water. Beside the water was a bundle of sticks wrapped tight with string and a burning candle.

"Sit, my princess. Your mother will be here soon." Nana Moo talked in a soft voice, stroking Lulah Marie's bright auburn hair. The twists had never been cut or tied and they hung past her shoulders. "Today is your washing day." Lulah Marie sat, utterly confused. At least Nana wasn't tightening her twists. The grandmother picked up the sticks. Lulah Marie watched as she put the bundle to the candle. The sticks flamed.

"Blow out the fire, my princess. You must make smoke. Burning sage shoos evil." Lulah Marie blew. Nana Moo waved the smoking sticks around the shed, humming. Then she circled her granddaughter's head with the bundle three times. The smoke settled on the girl. Lulah Marie blinked, her eyes irritated.

The shed door opened, and there was her mother.

"Hello, my princess. Today is your washing day." Mama carried some sort of cloth, piled up high.

The two women stood in front of the girl, each holding one of her hands. Lulah Marie started to feel uneasy. Her elder women always said odd things to her as though she knew; things like 'the eye' and 'auras' and other mumbo-jumbo that made no sense. This was different. Maybe it was because she got her flowers and was considered a woman. Maybe now they would tell her.

"Stand, my princess." Nana Moo and Mama pulled her hands, speaking in unison. "Today is your washing day."

Lulah Marie stood. She liked being called 'princess.'

Do you become a princess when you get your flowers?

She knew better than to ask.

Nana Moo spoke. "Princess Lulah Marie Dubonet, today is your washing day. Today you will begin your lessons. We honor you."

The women lifted the girl's hands to their lips and kissed each knuckle. Nana looked at Mama. Lulah Marie's mother nodded and picked up the basin. Without warning, they poured the water on the girl's head. Lulah Marie squealed in shock, but did not move.

"Sit, my princess," the women intoned.

Her hair was dripping, her dress bodice soaked. Now she was really scared. She sat. Nana Moo started humming while her mother took the end of the cloth and twisted it into a coil. Her mother joined in the unknown tune, turning the cloth like her nana twisted her hair, tighter and tighter.

The women stood still with the cloth rope draped between them. "Kneel, my princess."

Lulah Marie knelt, trembling. Her grandmother gathered her damp twists across her arm, kissed the cloth, and wound the rope twice under and around her hair. Her mother fed out the length as Nana Moo wrapped her head around like a turban, leaving the top with the beginnings of her copper twists exposed. Both women were *humh, humh, humhing* deep from their chests. It sounded like coughing, or maybe, growling. Lulah Marie was too scared to tell.

"Stand, my princess." Each elder woman then kissed her on the mouth, not like a lover, but as a blessing.

"Daughter," said her mother, "Now it is lesson time. From this day on, when the town ladies come for their sittings, you will watch us. You will serve the tea and learn to read the leaves. You will see what it means to do the work of our ancestors."

"Yes, my darling," added her grandmother. "You will learn and reap the benefits of your labors. You will live as the princess you are with the silver you earn."

For five years, the women gave the lessons to Lulah Marie, teaching her the words to use. They taught her about sight, powers, spells. She brewed and served the tea. Nana Moo and her mother told fortunes from the leaves. Lulah Marie loved to drink what was left in the pot, ignoring the debris in the bottom.

They never said her name, just calling her 'princess.' She learned to twist and wrap her hair, but she learned very little else. Lulah Marie always said the right words, and she was very good at nodding. The elder women never knew, and rewarded her with flavored sugar cubes when the daily lessons were done. When she was old enough, she was sent by train from Louisiana to be met in

Austin for more training. She figured she could see out her eyes, say munbo-jumbo, and keep her long hair wrapped as good as the next princess.

When the man called out "Houston," she stepped off the train.

I am a princess. I don't need any more lessons.

Her appearance was startling, with her crown of cloth wrapped around her head and under her hair with colorful yarns, bits of rags, and a few feathers woven in her twists. Her skirts swung wide as she walked away from the station. The ladies gasped, putting their gloved hands over their mouth. The men stared at that colorful brown bird walking up the street, swinging the woven carpetbag with her bare hand. They watched as she stepped into the first tearoom she could find.

Princesses drink tea.

Two steps in and she was stopped by a frilly-aproned white woman, holding a painted china pot. "Girl." The painted pot holder barely spoke through her tight lips. "You are in a ladies tea room." She sniffed.

"I know."

"This is no place for colored."

"Madam, I am Princess Lulah Marie Dubonet, and today is my birthday." She walked past the woman into a room of staring tea drinkers. She sat at a small table near the sideboard, and smoothed an invisible crumb off the doily. "You may serve me now. Do not forget your best cream."

This time painted china pot holding lady opened her mouth. "Girl, I don't care if you are the queen of Araby, you are not welcome here. Leave now."

"And two vanilla sugar lumps. Don't make me wait." Lulah Marie was very used to getting exactly what she wanted. She had no patience for truck like this.

"Get out or I will use the telephone and call the sheriff."

"If you feel the need, go ahead. I had not planned on chatting with a gentleman on my eighteenth birthday, but if you think he will enjoy my company, please be my guest. Remind him to bring a gift." Lulah Marie unwrapped her head. "I need to adjust my crown. Please hurry with my cup."

The service did not arrive. She said some mumbo jumbo to the tea lady, putting a curse on her painted china pot.

Lulah Marie spent the night in the colored jail. Sheriff woke her early the next morning.

"You, Miss Princess, gather your things. I'm throwing your wild self out of here." He was someone Lulah Marie'd never seen before. "Get you and your hair out of town. Do you understand me?"

Lulah Marie waved her arms and cast another gibberish curse.

I don't need any more lessons. I do this good.

As she walked toward the door, she heard the deputy tell the sheriff, "That one's plain tetched."

Lulah Marie Dubonet completed her curse by spitting straight down. It hit her skirts instead of the doorway.

Damn.

Using part of her ticket, she boarded the first train she saw. It was headed southeast.

Chapter Twelve
June 17, 1901
Circus

It was the children's opinion that grown-ups should've closed school for summer break early, that way no one wouldn't get in trouble. Good grief, almighty, the circus was in town. The Great Abel Hindone Show & Traveling Zoo was set up for today and today only, no holdovers. The Gallaway children went missing from class. Their mama knew all about it because she paid them to play hooky.

"My darlings, I see you are ill." A chorus of sniffs, coughs, and giggles confirmed Myra's diagnosis. "I couldn't possibly let you go to school and make your friends sick. I see you have circusitis."

"Mama, I'm not sick," Theo protested.
He'd been working toward the yearly perfect attendance medal.

"Yes you are, now hush," admonished Junior. This was his last full day visiting and he knew what was going on. No one was going to spoil it. "We're all staying home, aren't we, Mama."

"Of course, sweetheart, circusitis comes just once a year and y'all are quite fevered." Myra pulled back her hair, slipping in a side comb. Little Miss Flossie Mae was crying her hungry cry. Marguerite was out shopping, getting dry goods for baby gown sewing. "I'm putting five dimes on the table so that each of you can go to the circusitis doctor right after dinner." She headed toward the steps, her milk already starting. "Junior, make sure Theo understands about this disease. I would hate for him to ruin a perfectly wonderful Monday by going to school."

Theo still didn't get the joke. His mother leaned over and whispered in his ear. His face went from grumpy to smiles in the speed of that kiss.

"Hey everybody, we're going to the circus!"

Marguerite left behind their filled dinner buckets. Nora Lee took the pails and set up the kitchen table as a schoolroom with each meal properly in place. Noon took forever to happen. "We gotta sing grace." She stood at her mama's place and dramatically raised her fork like a baton.

"Father for this noon day meal,
"We would speak the praise we feel.
"Health and strength we have from thee
"Help us, Lord, to faithful be."

"Let's eat." Benjy opened his bucket.

"You forgot the 'Amen'." Nora pointed her 'baton' at him.

"Aaaaamen," they sang in unison, digging into their dinners.

Fifteen minutes later, dimes in hand, they were out the door, Junior leading the way. He knew where the circus was, set in an open field right by the tracks, close to the stockyards. Mama gave him the directions, but every child around could have found their way with their eyes closed. The children had spent Flossie Mae's birthing day watching the sign man nail his posters when they should have been hunting Missus Annie.

They saw the big tent. Sure enough, it was up wind from the yards, thank goodness.

"Peeuuie." Nora Lee said it first.

"Poopuuie," replied Benjy.

They ran past the pens, holding their noses. Only Franky needed to breathe, what with his cough and all. The poor child got the full effect, one lungful at a time.

"Gack, glick, bluck."

Then they saw it. Way in front of the big top there was a lemonade stand. It was a little, three-sided tent with faded yellow striping, dirty blue pennants hanging limp from the spire in the center of the stripes. The children only saw the sign. ICE COLD LEMONADE-2¢ They could do that. They each had a dime.

With a paper cone of sweet coolness and coins jingling in their pockets, they entered the midway.

"Lookie, lookie, there's the zoo! Can we go?" Theo long forgot his desire to get the attendance award. This was a lot more fun than school. He started to run. Three steps forward and his lemonade was 'bout gone, splashed in the dust. "Dang it." When he realized he almost cussed, he stopped, threw back the rest of his drink like he'd heard cowboys in saloons do, and wiped his mouth with an exaggerated swipe of his forearm. He grinned. "Yep, this is a whole lot more fun than any ol' school prize."

The zoo was another two cents. Nora Lee thought the Shetland pony was so-o-o-o cute. Junior and Theo wanted to ride the elephant home, and the twins just knew they could take care of the zebra if only they had a barn and corral in their back yard.

"TA TA TA TAAA" Someone was blowing a trumpet. The zoo man was at his ticket stand. "Ladies and gentlemen, boys and girls, now is the time to head out to the big top. Get your tickets, get your seats, show starts in fifteen minutes."

Nora Lee blew a kiss to the pony and joined her brothers. They followed the crowd as all the people headed to the main arena. Junior covered Nora Lee's eyes as they passed the tent with the half-naked dancing girls standing out front, wiggling, wearing pink tights, and shaking their shoulders and their bottoms all at the same time. He had to look twice, never seeing anything like that in his life.

The children were standing in the ticket line when Junior, the tallest of them all, saw the sign. ADMISSION-

10¢ They didn't have ten cents. Junior pulled them all aside.

"Gee Manetti Petes, we don't have the money. We spent it." Junior dug in his pocket and held out his change, a nickel and a penny.

Everybody else did the same. They had five silver and five copper coins. That made thirty cents and they needed fifty. Suddenly the lemonade wasn't so sweet after all. Franky coughed to hide his crying feelings. Nora knew one of her fits wouldn't do any good, so she didn't pitch one. She just stood there, pokin' out her lower lip.

Junior jingled his coins in his hand. He was thinkin' they should just go home and give Mama back the money. It was Benjy who came up with a plan.

"We don't need money, least not all of us. There's enough for three to get in. I'm willin' to sneak in the back under the tent wall. Who wants to go with me?" He looked at his brothers. They all knew a girl wouldn't do it. Cowboy Theo spoke up.

"Count me in. I didn't spoil my school record not to see the circus. Dang it, I'm ready!" He handed his money to Junior. "You two take the little lady and get seats, us men will find you later."

"Then it's a deal." Benjy handed over his coins, grabbed his brother, and took off before Junior could say a thing.

"Those two are just plain nuts." Franky knew anything his twin did would somehow end up square in the end. It was the between time that was questionable. "Let's get back in line." Each child handed over their fare and received a blue ticket. The man said they were to find the blue seats. Holding hands with Nora Lee in the middle, they went through the arch into the biggest space they'd ever seen. When the three found the right color bleachers, they were almost to the top. Being that high up was almost as exciting and scary as all get out. Junior and Franky kept

Nora Lee squeezed between them as they sat down. They stared at the center of the ring. A man in a fancy suit and top hat stepped up on a big platform and was blowing his whistle. The show was about to begin.

Benjy pulled Theo to the edge of the big tent and out of sight of the others. He stopped and turned in front of his brother. "You sure you want to do this? We can just stay outside and wait if you want."

"Dang it, we're gonna see the circus." Theo was likin' his cowboy cussin'. "Let's go 'round back. When we were gettin' in line. I saw a place that looks like where the animals go. We can sneak in there." His brother smiled. Theo, always the quiet one, was getting brave. If this worked, Benjy just might let him into some of his other schemes.

Theo took the lead. "I'm littler than you. I'll go in first."

The boys were almost there. The back side was full of wagons, tools, and cages. They knew this was no place for them and that made it even more fun. Benjy saw a little lift of the canvas close up ahead. Maybe that's where they could skinny in. They got down on their hands and knees and crawled the next few yards. The lift was about six inches high. Theo bellied up to the opening.

"What 'cha see?" Benjy was hangin' back, giving Theo plenty of scootin' space.

"Too dark. I'm gonna stick my hand and feel around." His exploration revealed nothing solid. "I'm goin' in."

Theo flattened himself like a mouse going where it shouldn't. He elbow dragged through the hole, keeping his eyes closed because of the dust. Once he felt his bottom pass the canvas, he got his legs under himself and stood. Then he opened his eyes. He was in front of a cage, face to face with Hercules, King of the Jungle.

ROAR.

The bars were as far apart as Theo's head was big.
ROAR.
Hercules' mouth was bigger than Theo's head.
ROAR.
Theo peed his pants right there. "Oh Jeez, oh Jeez, oh Jeez, I'm dead."

He dropped to the ground and arm raced back out the tent hole, right past his brother. He stood up and started to run, tripped over a coil of rope and landed belly down in what had to be an elephant patty, all fresh and steamy.

Slowly he opened his eyes. Giant purple shoes were as close as his nose. Theo raised his head, cricking his neck upward. Standing over him was a not-so-happy clown, holding a crowbar. His red painted frown and his white star eyes were almost as scary as the lion.

"Well look at you, you little puke," he said. Beside him was a really fat lady with a beard.

The lady sported a big blue bow in her hair and was wearing a dirty blue and white polka-dot ruffled dress that was shorter than her knees. "You're up to your keester in shit." She sounded all teeny-squeaky like the voice Nora Lee would make when she played baby dolls.

Neither boy'd heard words like that from any woman except their mother, and only when she thought they weren't around.

"Ain't that just too bad," continued Bearded Lady, swishing her ruffles. "Well, ass wipe, I sure am glad I ain't yer mama. Whacha gonna tell her about this mess?"

The clown hooked the curved end of the bar in the back straps of boy's coveralls and lifted him off the ground.

"Damn, you stink." Unhooking the bar, he let him fall. "Go home and take your friend with you," the clown snarled. Bearded Lady started laughing. Mr. Not-So-Happy pointed his hook at Benjy. "You want to join him?"

"Uh, no sir, no sir," Benjy said, walking backward away from the crowbar. "We'll be going. Sorry, sir, sorry, ma'am."

The couple walked away arm in arm laughing and muttering about "goddam little weasels." Benjy ran to his brother and started to offer him a hand, but changed his mind. Theo was covered with wet, green goo mixed with hay. It was all over his clothes, and he smelled worse than a privy. Theo stood himself up.

"Wow! Did you hear her? She sure don't sound like what she looks like." Theo gawked at himself. "What are we going to do now? Mama'll kill me. I can't go home like this."

"What happened in there? How come you ran out like that?"

"Dang it, I 'bout got eaten by a lion. I'll tell you later. What am I gonna do about my clothes?"

It was one thing to be a cowboy, and another to be covered in elephant poop. And...he'd destroyed his perfect attendance. He felt his tears stingin'.

"We better get out of here before those two come back. Good Lord, you stink. Mama's gonna kill you for sure. We better get you rinsed off." Benjy looked up. There were a whole lot a circus people standing around, and it seemed all were giving them the eye. "We gotta git. I see that clown. He's still got the crowbar."

"I'm scareder of the lady," said Theo. "Have you ever seen anything like that before? Eeegads."

The boys started running lickity-split. They were around the front and heading back toward home before the count of three. They didn't stop until they got to the fences of the stockyards.

"Dang it, the yards smell better than me." Theo was catching his breath, sucking in air.

"You're right about that one," Benjy agreed. "Hey, look at that." Benjy noticed a cattle trough right by the fence. It was almost full. Giving his brother the eye, he said, "Wanna go swimmin'?"

"What?" Theo was in no mood for play. Then he saw what his brother was talking about. "You want me to go inside that cattle pen and clean off in that water? Good grief, a cow might get me."

"Didn't you just say something about a lion eating you? And now you are scared of an old cow? I'd be scared of mama's whippin' if I was you, not some old cow." Benjy started pushing Theo to the fence. "Ya just gotta climb over and jump in. I'll stand guard for ya."

Theo did just that. He dunked, splashed, and scrubbed at himself. The young cowboy hoisted himself out of the water and climbed over the fence, back to his brother. He was stained, yes, but the stink was gone. The two walked around in the sun until the crowds started pouring from the big top. Franky, Nora Lee, and Junior were close to last coming out.

"Did you see it? I thought the doggy would catch on fire when she jumped through the hoop." Nora Lee was jumping through her own imaginary fire ring, acting out what they saw.

"And who thought an elephant could stand on such a little table. It was wonderful." Franky was talking so fast that he forgot to breathe and started to cough.

Junior pounded his brother's back. He looked at Theo's overalls. "What happened to you?"

"Aw, nothin' much." His voice was gettin' the cowboy back. "We couldn't get in, dang it, but I did see Hercules, King of the Jungle." Theo noticed that the others were staring at him, in awe of his every word. "I snuck into the lion tent and faced the brute." He did not notice who was behind them.

"Uh, Theo, Benjy, uh, we better get home." Junior grabbed Nora Lee and Franky, pulling them away from the group. Standing behind Theo and Benjy were three clowns and a very strange looking woman. She spoke.

"I told you little shits to git. You got a problem with that?"

Bearded Lady held Not-So-Happy's crow bar and she was smackin' her hand with it. "What's the matter, turd pile?" she squeaked. "You need to be taught a lesson about trespassin'?"

She took the bar in both hands and jabbed the hook end between Theo's shoulders. The force sent him stumbling' forward.

Junior hollered, "RUN!"

A woman sat at the end of the circus' entry lane. She wasn't there when the boys ran to the trough. They would have notice her, that's for sure, what with her brown skin, her hair all twisted, and her skirts so many colors. They stopped, staring warily.

"*Monsieurs, mademoiselle,* would you like your fortunes told? I am Princess Lulah Marie Dubonet. I can see your future. Come here. Come here."

"You say *mademoiselle* like my friend." Nora Lee was three steps ahead, out of grabbin' reach of Junior.

"Nora Lee, get back. Mama said never talk to strangers." Junior's voice was loud. "We gotta go home."

"*Mademoiselle.* If you come over here, I will tell you your name and where you will go."

Nora Lee sat straight in front of the Princess, crossed her legs, and plunked her chin on her knitted fingers. The boys gathered behind her. Junior did not cross the lane, standing, hands on hips, scowling.

Princess Lulah Marie smiled. "I will tell *petit mademoiselle's* fortune. First tell me about your friend. You say she speaks like me?"

"Yes. Her name is Marguerite."

"Oh? Does this Marguerite have a last name?"

Nora Lee giggled. "It's Brown, but she's red."

"Oh, I see." *Could it be?* "Is she old and ugly?"

More giggles. "No. She's pretty and red. She's from Galveston. She lives with us. She sleeps down the hall from our bedrooms in the screen porch over the dining room."

Aha. It is her.

"Well, *mon chere*, give me your left hand. It is time." Lulah Marie studied the small open palm with utmost care. "I will now foresee your future." She closed her eyes and hummed that tuneless sound. "Om be ju ba, om be ju ha."

She opened her eyes and released Nora Lee's hand. It went right back to supporting the girl's chin.

Lulah Marie made her voice soft and deep, "You are named Nora Lee." The seer waited for the expected gasp. "You are going to a rich man's house, one with many rooms." Pause. "You don't like anyone telling you what to do, especially a tall male in your family."

Nora Lee jumped up and gave the princess a hug and kiss on the cheek. "Oh, you know everything. You are wonderful." The girl noticed a tarnished copper pot on the ground beside the Lulah Marie. There were a few coins in the bottom. "Oh, princess, we have no money."

"No, *mon chere*, you are wonderful. You have given me more than coins. You have given me your kiss." *And everything I need.* "Run to your mama. You do not want to be thrown to the lions."

That always gets the kids to leave.

They did not stop until they were home. Myra found them faces washed, nightshirts on, and eating Marguerite's supper when she came down from nursing.

"Goodness, what are you doing? It's not bed time yet," their mama said. "You all look nice and clean. Was it dusty?"

"Uhuh," Theo murmured.

"We had so much fun at the circus. We're tired. " Junior hoped his voice didn't betray them.

Myra kissed each of them on top the head. "If that's what you want, well then, my babies, good night."

All five skittered off to their bedrooms. As Myra sat to her own supper, she could hear the upstairs chatter. She called up the steps.

"I'm so glad y'all had such a good time. I hope you will always remember this day."

"Oh yes, Mama, we certainly will."

The children fell asleep hugging pillows. The scary dreams lasted years. Blue polka-dots, whiskers, and crow bars...all those images floated through the night. Sometimes someone would wake up crying but never told Mama why. The children did not ask to go to the circus again. It was a very long time before Nora Lee used a baby voice when she played dollies, and when she did, it was only to make the baby 'waa-waa' sound, never to talk.

Chapter Thirteen
June 20, 1901
Lulah Marie Shows Up

She pulled the front bell fob as though she had the right.

"I'll get it, Mama." Nora Lee scampered to the screen and reached to flip the hook.

"*Mademoiselle* Nora Lee, 'tis I, the princess."

Nora Lee squealed, spun on her heels and ran into the kitchen. She hit Marguerite smack dab in the middle of her apron. Luckily, there was no cooking water in the pot she was carrying. Myra was standing at the sink, rinsing okra. Marguerite loved to make gumbo. Said it reminded her of her maman, and if you didn't cut the pods, the slime would stay where it belonged.

"Mama, Miss 'Gurite, there's a princess on the porch. Come see, come see." Nora Lee was back in the parlor, swinging open the door before the women could blink, which they both did at the sight of what awaited them in the parlor.

Lulah Marie Dubonet stood there, her dirty shawl and fading skirts looking nothing like a princess. Marguerite's lips clamped tight. Myra stared at the wild haired thing that was in her house.

"Mama, Mama, this is a real princess. I know her from the circus." Nora Lee was a'wiggle with excitement. "Mama, she tells fortunes. Just ask her. She knows my name. She knows everything."

The child was practically a dervish.

"Now Missy, settle down and hush." Tiny bits of prickles were making their way from Myra's neck to her scalp. This apparition of head rags and hair snakes was downright scary to look at. "What can I do for you?"

"She cain't do nothin' for you." Marguerite pushed past Myra. "Who do you think you are, coming in front door? Get out of this house, now."

Lulah Marie held out her arms. "Darling."

"Go back to hell, witch. I am not your darling."

Myra stood in shocked silence.

"Miss 'Guerite, she's not a witch." Nora Lee skittered herself between the two. "She's a princess. I like her." The girl pooched out her lower lip. Cocking her head, she asked, "Are you a witch?" Turning to Lulah Marie, she stood, fists on hips, waiting for the answer.

Myra put a strong hand on the girl, pulling her from between the two. She shoved her toward the kitchen, muttering about cuttin' a switch. Nora Lee got the hint and scooted in behind the swinging door. There she could listen, see, and not get swatted.

Turning to the women, Myra spoke. "Miss Marguerite, is there a concern with this stranger?" Marguerite's face was flaming. "How do you know her? Is she—?"

"I am her—" Lulah Marie interrupted.

"You are not. You are nothing," Marguerite seethed. She made two steps toward Lulah Marie, swinging back a flat hand. "Get out of this house. Get off of this porch, get out of this town."

Lulah Marie ducked just as Marguerite struck. The slap hit the crown of twisted rags, knocking the rat's nest a kilter on her head.

A shriek came through the screen. Everyone froze. Myra walked around the combatants and opened the door.

"Oh my goodness, I forgot. Missus Annie, please come in." Myra carefully led her friend around the edges, into the next room. She gestured to a dining table chair, shrugged, and left Annie to her own devices.

"Marguerite, please make some coffee. We have guests."

"Only one, that other thing is leaving," Marguerite mumbled as she stalked into the kitchen.

She clanged around the enamel coffee pot and didn't care if it chipped. Nora Lee stayed behind the door, now having two vantage points.

Lulah Marie sat on the parlor settee and began adjusting her crown. She seemed unaware of Missus Annie's stares from the dining room. Myra stepped in front of that very odd stranger. She was losing her patience, and her voice showed it.

"What is your name, and why are you in my house?" Lulah Marie continued to work her wrappings, leaning over to retrieve a stray feather. "Please leave if you cannot answer me." Myra walked to the screen and waited. Finally the wild thing stood up. She ignored Myra and turned, directing her words to Missus Annie.

"I am Princess Lulah Marie Dubonet. I am from a lineage of great women."

"No she's not." Marguerite did not hide her feelings.

"I know Miss Nora Lee and come to reunite with my—"

Clang went the pot. "Go to hell, witch."

"I thank you for your hospitality." With that, Lulah Marie sat down at the dining table across from Missus Annie, glancing at her hands. She then looked straight ahead and started to sway.

"I see a recent wedding, a wedding of an older woman. " Lulah Marie began to hum. "I see the bride crying with joy." The sway and the hum got more intense. "You are that woman, are you not?"

"Oh my goodness, yes," Annie put her left hand out to the seer. "How did you know?"

"I am a princess. It is my duty."

Slam went the back door. Myra followed the sound. Marguerite stood shaking on the back stoop.

"Get her out of here."

"Marguerite, is she your—?"

"She's the devil's spawn. Get rid of her." Marguerite began to cry. "Please make her go away. Please."

Myra went back through the kitchen just in time to see Missus Annie and Lulah Marie step out on the front porch. She rushed to the door.

Annie turned, beaming. "My dear, thank you so much for finding this charming woman for me. I told you I could use a girl." She returned her attention to Lulah Marie. "I know you will enjoy my home. Now, tell me more about yourself."

With that, the two walked down the street, Missus Annie gazing in rapt attention.

Chapter Fourteen
June, 1901
Gypsy Rapture

Missus Annie escorted Lulah Marie into the parlor where the princess enthroned herself in Carlton's new Eastlake side chair and waited. Annie loudly announced their presence. The spectacle of her royal highness finally got the sisters Emily and Arabel out of their rooms. The women sat three across on the settee.

"Sisters, oh sisters," began Annie. "I want you to meet Princess Lulah Marie, uh, uh…"

"Dubonet," Lulah Marie prompted.

"Dubonet." Annie smiled. "This wonder before us is royalty from an ancient line of women." She stood and walked across the parlor to Lulah Marie. "Sisters, this dear lady tells fortunes and unravels mysteries. She knows all about my recent joyful nuptials. I can't wait to tell Carl tonight when he gets back from Houston."

Both sisters unconsciously pinched their lips. Annie continued her introduction.

"I have invited her to stay here as my guest. She agreed on one condition." Annie nodded to Lulah Marie.

"My lovely ladies, I am pleased to be a guest, but I will only stay if I may be of help in this house. Ack" Lulah Marie's face went slack, eyes closed. The humming and swaying began.

"Oh my," Arabel exclaimed. "She's having a fit."

"No, no, no." Spirits want to talk through her." Annie smiled. "She told me all about it on our way home." She returned to the settee. "Just watch."

"Ooh ba, noo ba, jeebie jaw." Lulah Marie sat straight in the chair. "Ooh ba, noo ba, jawbie gee. What say, spirits, talk to me." He eyes flew wide. "Yes. Yes. I will."

With that she slumped into the chair and sighed.

"Princess, princess, are you all right?" Arabel approached the chair, but not too close. "Are you going to have another fit?"

Lulah Marie looked straight at Arabel. "I have a message from beyond."

Arabel took a step backward and practically fell in her seat. "Who is it for?"

"You have had death in your family. Is that true?"

"Our husbands and mother died in the storm," Arabel offered. "Who is the message for?"

"The spirit said 'I know all about what you did.' Does that mean anything to either of you?"

"Absolutely not. Perhaps the message was for either of them." Emily made a wide gesture, indicating her sisters. "I have no secrets." With that, she walked out of the room, and the ladies heard a door slam.

Annie spoke. "Please excuse my sister, Emily's, rudeness. I have no idea what brought that on."

"*Mon cher*, do not give it another thought." Lulah Marie smiled. "I will take my things to my room, now. I get so very tired after a spirit visit, and must rest."

"Of course, of course," twittered Annie. "Let me show you the way. Arabel, please excuse us."

Arabel stood. "Of course." She looked hard at the seer. "Um, Miss Dubonet—?"

"Call me Princess Lulah Marie."

"Um, Miss Princess Lulah Marie, you are welcome to visit my room sometime. I would like to continue this conversation."

"Yes." Lulah Marie returned the stare. "Yes, we will."

Annie showed her to the guest room and bid Lulah Marie 'rest well.' The sisters soon heard deep snores. At supper, Annie returned, tapped quietly, softly opening the door.

Princess Lulah Marie Dubonet slept fully clothed on top of the coverlet. Her crown of head rags shared the pillow like a pet cat.

"Princess." The snores continued. Annie gently shook her shoulder. "It's time for supper, please wake now."

Several minutes passed before her guest was fully awake and down the stairs.

Carlton was surprised, but not shocked, at the sight of the woman at the dinner table. He'd seen the like of her kind before. Annie explained how they met and why she was in the house.

"So, Miss Dubonet, you tell fortunes and unravel mysteries. And, according to my dear wife, you are here to help." Carlton was on his second serving of roast chicken. "Do you cook?"

"My family never taught me. My training is otherwise."

"Hmm, I see. Do you clean?"

"No."

Carlton cleared his throat. "So what is this help that you do? I thought my wife brought home a girl to cook and clean. Why are you here?"

"Husband, do not be harsh with our guest." The sharpness in Annie's voice could not be denied.

"Wife, I am not being harsh. However, it is a little bit curious, don't you think, that we have this hired woman sitting in our dining room eating instead of serving."

Lulah Marie stood. "Please excuse me. I did not know I would be unwelcomed here. I will go." She turned to leave the table.

"Wait. Don't." The sisters spoke in unison.

Carlton wisely kept his mouth shut, being outnumbered three to one.

Annie held out her hand. "Come, my dear, sit back down. We want you to stay." She turned to the head of the table. "Carlton, dear, Princess Dubonet is our guest. Please ask her to return."

"Humph. Sit down, girl, and eat. We will talk about how you can help my wife after pie." He looked around the table. He had no idea which woman had baked today. "There is pie, isn't there?"

Arabel nodded, smiling. "Yes Carl, it's pecan, your favorite."

"Pecan must have been your husband's favorite. It's not mine."

"Oh." Arabel started to cry. "Oh."

"Stop that." Emily's tone was cutting. "You don't need to bawl over something as simple as pecan pie."

Arabel cried harder. "You are just jealous because…"

"Sisters, we have a guest. Hush." Annie's admonition brought silence to the room. "I will get the pie. I am sure it will be wonderful."

Annie returned with dessert plates, forks, the pie, and a piece of pound cake for her husband. They all ate their slices without a word. When dessert was over, all except Lulah Marie cleared their own places. The Princess settled herself in the parlor, leaving behind her dishes and an unmentioned caramel stain on the tablecloth where the pie filling did not find her mouth. She soon dozed.

"Miss Dubonet." Carlton was standing in front of her. "Miss Dubonet, you are in my chair."

"Yes?" Lulah Marie opened her eyes.

"Please move to the settee. You are in my chair."

Lulah Marie smiled up at Carlton. "Oh, thank you for the offer, but I was sitting here earlier, and I find it so very comfortable."

"Madam," Carlton's voice was edgy. "Madam, you misunderstand. You are in my chair, and you are to move out of it."

He waited until she finally gathered herself together enough to stand.

"Madam," Carlton lowered himself into the Eastlake. "It would benefit you immensely if you would go into the dining room, clear your plates to the kitchen, and assist in the washing."

Lulah Marie stared at him. *Princesses do not wash dishes.* She sat on the settee, ignoring his request. *I'll show him what princesses do.* With calm and deliberate motions, she took off her head wrap and began to retwist the cloth. She started to hum and sway as she worked.

"Ohh ma ha, ooh. Ohh ma ha, ooh." The sway went wider, the chant louder. "Hoahh, uh." She jumped up, spilling her crown, and pointed at Carlton. "You, sir, have sorrow and happiness around you. You are challenged in your life." She waited, but Carlton didn't say a word. "You are loved and resented. You know your own mind, but sometimes change it to get along." Another pause. Nothing. *Money always works.* "I see fortune in your future. I see travels." She began her sway again and collapsed on the settee, barely missing stepping on her crown.

"Woman," Carlton's words were low and distinct. "You may stay at the pleasure of my wife and her sisters, but you may never put on your ridiculous show for me again." He wagged his finger. "You are nothing but a mongrel my wife brought home to pet. Do you understand me? Do not harm me, them, or this household."

"I bring no harm. I am of royal training, raised only to do good." Lulah Marie's wide-eyed response was just as low.

"Do something with that pile of rags and get yourself in the kitchen. Now."

Lulah Marie gathered her crown and quickly wrapped her head. As she passed through the dining room, she picked up her plates and silver. She was tempted to pocket the spoon out of spite, but didn't.

Chapter Fifteen
June, 1901
Tea Punch and Tumbleweeds

"Yoohoo, where's my Myra?"

"Yoohoo. where's my Marguerite?"

The men were home from sea, calling from the back stoop. The women ran to their husbands' arms, sharing more kisses than could be counted.

Myra stepped back. "Darling, come upstairs and meet your daughter." She took him by the arm. "Leave your kits on the porch. Some child will get them." Turning to Marguerite, she winked. "You two bring your kissin' in. Don't want to set the porch on fire."

"Yes, ma'am," the newlyweds responded in unison, following hand in hand. Marguerite led Jack through the kitchen to the settee where the kissing continued.

Jack finally broke the embrace and opened his eyes. Nora Lee was standing directly in front of the love birds, staring in rapt attention.

"Hello Mister Jack." Nora Lee was squinting. "Why are you kissing my Miss Marguerite?"

"Because."

"Mama says 'because' is not an answer." Nora Lee cocked her head toward Marguerite. "Is he allowed to do that?"

"Oh, *oui, mon cher*, he is allowed." Marguerite smiled. "Mister Jack is my husband."

Nora Lee wiggled herself in between the two and climbed on Marguerite's lap. "Sat so? Where's your ring?"

"In my pocket, little miss." Jack patted his right leg. "I will give it to her soon."

"Are you going to give her a baby? That's what Daddy CB gave Mama when they got married."

Marguerite smiled. "I hope so, but not yet. Right now we have plenty of children under roof."

Nora Lee turned her attention to Jack. "Are you going to live here, too?"

Jack's face went blank. "I don't know. Never thought about it, I live on the *Sallie Lou*."

Marguerite stood, dumping Nora Lee. "You. Never. Thought. About. It?" she echoed her husband. "You'd better put mind to it. I am your wife, not your occasional stop over." The back screen rattled as it slammed behind her.

Nora Lee looked up from the floor. "Mister Jack, you're in trouble now."

"Hush."

Jack headed toward the stoop. He could see his wife in the yard, back turned, standing on the gazebo path. The sun made her hair flame. Five long strides and he was beside her. They talked for the longest time.

Nora Lee ran upstairs to her mama and Daddy CB. "Mister Jack's in trouble."

"What?"

"Mister Jack got my Miss Marguerite real mad."

"Damn," CB swore under his breath. "I'll go. Child, where is he?" He handed his newly acquainted daughter to her mother.

"Backyard. You want me to come?"

Myra grabbed Nora Lee with her free hand. "Absolutely not." She pushed the child into the nursing chair. "You are going to sit and mind. Do you understand?"

"Yes, Mama."

"Here, hold your sister. I'm going to see if Marguerite needs help." Myra headed toward the steps. "Check her diaper, please."

"Yes 'um."

The adults stayed outside for almost an hour, having found shade and seats. Nora Lee put her clean, sleeping sister to bed and stood watching from the bedroom window. When she saw the men shaking hands and the women hugging, she tiptoes down the stairs and parked herself on the settee. There she could spill the beans about everything when the boys got home from fishin'.

They must've been tellin' jokes, 'cause Mister Jack was grinnin' big and Daddy CB kept laughin' and wackin' Mister Jack on the back.

The grown-ups walked into the kitchen, smiling. The women went straight upstairs. Nora Lee heard some furniture scraping, some giggling, and lots of whispers about clean sheets and 'maman's quilt.' Daddy CB and Mister Jack were sitting at the kitchen table, drinking coffee.

That night all of the Ledbetters, even baby Flossie, stayed in the sleeping porch. Mr. and Mrs. Jack Smith slept in the master room. The next morning a tray of steaming coffee, biscuits, and sweet honey in a pot was placed outside the closed door. The children were threatened within an inch of their lives to not make a sound as they walked through the hall and down the steps to their breakfast. It was half pass noon before the door opened again.

The honeymooners had only one thing in mind, the necessary. Neither lover wanted to leave that wonderful room, but the coffee won.

"Ladies first, but, darlin', hurry up, I don't want to find a bush."

Waiting for a turn to use the bathroom was another new experience. The ship's head had ample space. Too bad this house didn't.

Marguerite was quick about it, and soon Jack joined her in the kitchen. The children were off somewhere, and Myra and CB were setting out dinner fixin's.

"Well?" CB's raised eyebrow said it all. "Are you two officially married?"

Marguerite lowered her eyes and stepped closer to her husband. *"Oui,* we are husband and wife." She extended her left hand, proudly showing her wedding band.

"Good." The men broke out in a hearty laugh.

Marguerite scowled at CB. "Why do you say 'good' and then laugh like it is a joke? This is not a joke."

Jack turned his bride and kissed her softly. "CB and I laugh with joy. We spent our entire boyhood talking about women and wondering. He loves Missus Myra. I love you."

CB spoke up, looking at his own wife. "We are so very happy we had to wait." The couples kissed that deep kiss of promise.

Marguerite pulled away from Jack. "You mean to tell me that you were a—"

"Yes, ma'am, just like you." His kiss this time was hard and intense.

"Oh," came the breathless reply. "I'm glad."

"So am I."

The Ledbetters stayed in the sleeping porch that night, too.

The household rearranged itself to include the Smith family. The agreement made at the gazebo included a permanent address for Mr. and Mrs. Jack Smith in exchange for Marguerite helping with the children and the house, plus a few dollars rent to make it official. Theo's bed, which held Junior's empty trundle, was moved into the twins' room, giving Marguerite and Jack a place of their own, Maman's quilt proudly folded across the foot of their new bought bed.

Myra wanted to celebrate the newlyweds, but hardly knew anybody in LaPorte, and especially did not know if people would come to a white reception for colored folk. Missus Annie and her husband Carlton, maybe; her widowed sisters, Emily Wallace and Arabel Gaithers, well...they barely left their rooms. When the hurricane hit Galveston, they found their eldest sister had a secret beau, and a rich one at that. Now they were living under his roof, tables turned, mourning the loss of their mother, husbands, homes, and social status. Myra doubted Emily and Arabel would make their debut at *this* party, but sent invitations, nonetheless.

Missus Annie quickly replied that she, Carlton, and their new houseguest, Lulah Marie, would be proud to wish the newlyweds well.

Marguerite hit the roof. "*Aucun moyen en enfer.*"

Myra didn't know French, but had ample knowledge of Marguerite's opinion of Lulah Marie. However, she also knew that she had bigger fish to fry than to get between a squabble that made no sense to her.

Two days later, with the tea punch in a faux gilted china serving bowl and cake slices on matching plates, the Ledbetters were ready for their first social. Myra was proud to show off the linens, dishes, and crystal that came with their house. The children thought it was silly to float orange slices in sweet tea, but knew that Mama's cakes were delicious. They were sent out back after promising to stay clean. Myra and CB were in the kitchen, waiting for the coffee to boil. The honorees were planted in the parlor to wait.

"White folks are crazy," Jack whispered.

"*Oui,*" his bride agreed.

"Let's sneak upstairs and hide under the quilt." Jack's left arm snaked around Marguerite's back, his hand heading north.

"Shush. Stop that." She scooted sideways. "Missus Myra means well."

Jack started inching himself toward her. "Mmm, so do I."

The front bell rang. Marguerite stood to answer it. Myra rushed past her.

"Sit down. I'll get it. You are the honoree. Let them come to you."

"White folks really are crazy," Jack repeated under his breath.

Myra opened the door to Missus Annie and Mr. Carlton. "Come in, come in. Welcome." Myra looked past them as they entered. They were alone, no sisters or princesses in tow.

Annie walked straight to Marguerite and took her hand. "Congratulations, my dear. Isn't married life wonderful?"

"Yes, ma'am." Marguerite had no idea what else to say.

Annie turned to her own new husband. "Isn't married life wonderful?"

"A-hem," Carlton cleared his throat. "Yes, dear. And, you, sir," he directed his attention to Jack. "Have we met? I am Carlton Wilson."

Jack stood. "I am Jack Smith, and——"

"The groom," Annie interrupted, beaming.

"I am Jack Smith. CB Ledbetter and I have been mates on the *Sallie Lou* since we were boys. This is my wife, Marguerite Smith. Pleased to meet you." The men shook hands.

Gesturing to the side chairs, Myra excused herself. "Coffee's almost ready. Make yourselves at home." She disappeared through the kitchen door, leaving the couples in awkward silence. They sat.

"Mr. Smith," Carlton spoke, "Congratulations on your nuptials."

"Thank you. Call me Jack, that's my name."

"Of course, Jack. Tell me about your ship. Was it damaged in the storm?" Carlton's business sense was alerted. "I'm very curious about boats. I buy and sell flour, carried on trains. Do you know if there is opportunity with sea export?"

"Carlton, darling, no trade talk now." Annie's soft comment and sharp eyes hushed her husband.

"The *Sallie Lou* fared well. We were many points south." Jack smiled and took his bride's hand. "We all lived to see another day."

"We sure did." CB swung the door into the dining room, with matching coffee pot, cups and saucers on a tray.

"You look like you're ready to serve the captain." Jack smiled at his friend.

"Yep, but Myra said 'no brandy' on this tray." CB set the china service by the punch and turned to Annie and Carlton. "Our captain knows his drink, taught me about fine liquor." Nodding to his guests, he turned to leave.

"Mama, Daddy CB, everybody come out back." Nora Lee was hollering, the boys were whooping. "The Princess is here. She's gonna do magic."

Marguerite gripped Jack's hand. "*Merde. Salope.*"

"Shhh." Jack hoped no one knew French curses. "Let's go out. The children won't hush until we do."

"*Je crois que non.* You go watch that witch. I'll stay in the kitchen, thank you." Marguerite's flashing eyes sparked flames.

"Mama, Mama, look at her. She's wonderful. Princess Lulah Marie is going to make all the bad spirits go away."

Nora Lee was jumping up and down, pointing at what appeared to be a big tumbleweed wearing a wild colored skirt. All circled around the apparition. All, that is, except Marguerite, who stood by the door, crossing herself and murmuring what may have been a prayer.

"Oh my friends, oh my people, I come to bless and protect this house." Lulah Marie raised the dead bush above, revealing her face. She had red rouge on her cheeks and mouth. "I am here to give the ultimate wedding gift to my beloved."

"*Merde,*" came from the kitchen.

"I bring the wisdom of our mothers. I bring the strength of our generations." Lulah Marie swayed, waving the bush around her head.

"Oh, Carl, isn't she amazing. We are so lucky to know her." Annie said. Carl snorted.

Lulah Marie continued, adding a guttural hum to her voice. "My mother, *hahum*, my grandmother, *hahum*, trained me to drive away, *hahum*, the evil spirits." She circled the bush above her head. "My grandmother taught me the cleansing power of sage. Evil will go."

"Uh, Miss Lulah Marie, I'd know if there is any evil in our house." Myra's voice showed the offense she felt. "You are our guest. Please come to the party."

"Evil is as evil does," came from the house.

"I, *hahum*, bring a gift for the bride." Lulah Marie threw her words toward the porch. "I will use my heritage and training as a princess to assure that all will be safe."

Lulah Marie remembered that burning a sage bundle made a smoke that drove out evil. She couldn't remember where her Granny Moo got the sticks, so she figured a sage bush would do.

Same stuff, different shape, that's all.

"I shall begin."

Holding the bush in front of her like handing over a stinking baby, the Princess made slow deliberate steps toward the back porch. Her chant was of her own making. Family and guests stared at the spectacle. The children started marching behind her, step for step, making up their own chant. Marguerite continued to swear in French.

Lulah Marie stopped at the foot of the stoop. Holding the bush with one hand like Atlas, she produced a match from somewhere in her skirts. "May this sacred smoke remove the evil that lingers in this house. May this sacred smoke keep out any work of the devil. I bless this house and the ones who live here." Lulah Marie struck the match.

Sagebrush was not sacred sage. *WHOOSH*. Lulah Marie screeched and took off toward the alley hollering, throwing the fireball backward as far as she could. It landed on the porch, catching the sisal rug.

Everyone started screaming. Marguerite ran to the dining room. The men rushed up to put out the flames. They were met with flying fruit in their faces as Marguerite threw the tea punch onto the fire. *PSSSS.* The men stomped the smoldering rug and dragged it to the yard. The bush was completely gone, burned to ash in seconds.

Jack, CB, and Carlton stood around the steaming ruin. Jack, taller than the other two, started to laugh.

"What's so funny?" CB said. "That crack-pot just 'bout burnt my house down."

"You." Forgetting that he'd just met Carlton, he nudged him and pointed.

Carlton broke out in a grin. "You got a new hat on."

Sitting square a'top CB's blond head was an orange slice. Jack snatched it off and gave it to his pal. "Here you are, sir, fits you just right."

Marguerite bumped open the screen with her bottom, still holding the punch bowl. "That witch gone? You want I make more sweet tea? Ain't got no more fruit. Coffee's ready."

The party reorganized themselves around the dining table. Theo led the children with their cake and drinks to the kitchen. Carlton offered to help CB and Jack repaint the porch where it was blistered. Flossie Mae summoned her mama upstairs. After a short nursing and a change, mother and child rejoined the party.

"May I hold her?" Carlton extended his arms. Myra's eyes questioned her guest. "I never had a baby. My first wife died in childbirth."

"I'm sorry, Of course. Here." Myra handed over child and burp rag. "I'm getting me some cake and coffee. Who wants another piece?"

"We do," was the unison reply from the kitchen.

"Y'all, I was talking to the grown-ups, but get in here before I say 'no'." She smiled to the adults. "My guess they've been listening to every word we've said. Anybody do any cussin' while I was upstairs with Flossie?"

Jack spoke up. "No, ma'am, you want us to start?" He got a wifely elbow in the side for that comment.

Carlton jiggled Flossie on his leg, humming. "I remember your Auntie Annie playing on her daddy's knee," he told the baby. "Her daddy was my friend."

"Husband," cautioned Annie. "I don't think we need to talk about that. Someone might think you robbed the cradle."

"My dear," he replied. "Look at us. I do not believe anyone has ever thought that." Carl reached over and fluffed his bride's silvering curls. Annie giggled and held out her arms for her turn with the baby.

Chapter Sixteen
July 1, 1901
Serving Soup

Missus Annie located Lulah Marie holding court in Arabel's room. The seer was deep in her spell. Mrs. Gaithers was enjoying her daily Tarot card readings, and Lulah Marie was glad to oblige in exchange for the silver dollar left on the corner of the crocheted dresser runner. Arabel Gaithers loved to spend money and bought several of the jewelry pieces Julia sold at the Methodist Ladies Guild. She never knew the pieces were payment for stowaway passage on the *Sallie Lou*. It was just Arabel's very good luck that she was wearing her finery the day of the hurricane. All possessions were lost. Emily was penniless. Annie was rescued by Carlton, and Arabel wore her jewels to every meal. No one mentioned the missing brooch she pawned to provide the fortune telling dollars.

"Excuse me," said Annie. "I must speak with the princess." The burning bush incident could not be ignored. "Unfortunately, this woman has caused a problem that needs an explanation." Annie usually did not have a cross voice. This was an exception. "Lulah Marie, please meet me in Carl's study. Now."

"Wonder what she's upset about?" Arabel didn't like her special time interrupted.

"I don't know. Maybe it has something to do with the party at the Ledbetters. You know they have a girl there who hates me. I had to leave before refreshments." Lulah fidgeted with her turban. "Don't touch the cards. That will break the spell. I'll continue soon."

Crown reset, Lulah Marie entered Carlton study. There was no throne waiting.

"You idiot. What in the devil were you thinking?" Carlton's clothes were disheveled and his face red. "You caught their back porch on fire. Have you no brains?"

Lulah Marie stared. "It was a wedding gift. I needed to remove the evil spirits." Her eyes swept the room. Finding a side chair, she sat, uninvited.

"Stand up, woman. You are not a guest in my study, even though you think you have the run of my house." Carlton's voice was getting louder by the word. "You are a blasted imbecile."

Lulah Marie once again began to sway and mumble.

"Stop it. Your tricks mean nothing to me." Carlton reached for Lulah Marie's arm and pulled her out of the chair. "These women may think you are some kind of gypsy princess, but I do not. You are a charlatan and a cheat." He let go of her and she started backing toward the door. "You are not going anywhere until you answer my question. Why did you throw a burning bush at my friends' house?"

"I was taught burning sage removes evil. I didn't have any sacred sage bundles, so I thought the bush would work. It's not my fault it flamed like that." Lulah Marie shrugged. "I was only doing my best."

"That proves it. You are an idiot. Now get out of my study and ask my wife to step in."

Carlton opened the center drawer of his desk and pulled out a ledger. He sat, busying himself until Annie kissed him on the forehead.

"Husband, you are smoky. Let me get you fresh clothes." Annie pulled the chair close to his desk. "Did you get everything settled with her? I hope you didn't send her away."

Carlton's lips were set. "She's a hugger-mugger. I just hope you haven't fallen for her mumbo-jumbo like your sister has. Did you know that woman and Arabel meet every afternoon for fortune telling?"

"Yes, Arabel's really lonely. What would you like me to do? She seems to enjoy Lulah Marie's company. You know, Emily won't speak to anybody and still won't leave her room except to cook."

"Speaking of cooking, isn't that head wrapped excuse for a colored girl supposed to be helping in the kitchen? We're lucky to get the table set without her chipping a plate or forgetting a fork." Carlton's color was rising again.

"Husband, I am trying." Annie stood and patted his hand. "I don't see that she's ever had any training. You know, I think her mother really thought she was a princess. She certainly didn't teach her daughter how to keep house." She chuckled. "Perhaps she will kiss a frog and get a prince, because she sure doesn't know how to care for a regular husband." Annie raised her eyebrow. "How am I doing in that department?"

Carlton pulled her onto his lap, and kissed her hard. "You are a fine little wifey, Missus Annie Wilson. Who would have thought we'd be doin' this smoochin' at our age? Not me."

"I love you, husband." She kissed him back. "I am so very glad you visited us that day so many years ago."

"And I love you." Carlton shifted under his load. "Sorry to ask, but, sweetie, could you stand? Seems my old legs have fallen asleep."

"Of course, my dear."

Annie was almost to the door when Carlton spoke. "I'd like to get to know those two sailors. I think there's business to be had. Could you invite them all to come by for supper?"

"Them *all*?" Annie emphasized 'all'. "Do you understand that *all* means the children, too?"

"Of course, I would love to see them again. We can seat the adults in the dining room, and put the children around the kitchen table if we open one drop leaf. That should be plenty big enough."

Annie nodded. "That's true, but it can't be supper. A proper supper starts at nine in the evening. Would you like me to make the invitation for nice dinner?"

"That sounds fine, but please makes it soon. I don't know when the men sail. And," Carlton continued, "I want that sorry excuse for a princess to earn her keep. She will serve us. Do you understand?"

"Yes, dear, but don't expect her to cook. I think that's a lost cause." Annie smiled and blew her darling a kiss. "Is tomorrow soon enough? I'll start the girl's table training right away."

Lulah Marie took to her house keeping lessons with the same indifference as she did her childhood princess lessons.

"Missus Annie, you know I wasn't meant to do this. I am royalty," she whined.

"Of course you are, my dear, but you still need to remember where to place the silver."

Lulah Marie perked up at the word 'silver.' "I like my tea poured from a sterling pot. Do you have one?"

Annie ignored the question. "You are going to serve my party, not sit at it. I told you that. Now, for the third time, the butter knife is placed across the bread plate, not beside the dessert knife."

Lulah Marie returned to her glazed expression. "I don't understand why you're making me do this. It's just not right." She took off her head wrap and started to tighten the coils.

"That's another thing. You will not wear your crown tomorrow." Annie pointed at the goose down Lulah Marie was reinserting. "I do not want any of your feathers or charms falling in the soup."

Lulah Marie looked up from her rag twisting. "Missus Annie, I am a princess. You will not make me take off the symbol of my birthright."

"We'll talk about it tomorrow." Annie walked toward the kitchen. "Carlton expects you to serve our guests. Please continue practicing. I'll check on you later."

As soon as the door swung shut, Lulah Marie moved to the end of the table and continued her wrap repair. "I like Missus Annie, but this is too much," she muttered. "I might need to move on soon." A hand clamped on her arm.

"Once again I see you are sitting in my place." Carlton jerked Lulah Marie up. The rags fell to the floor. He stepped on them and dragged the pile back. "I believe my wife asked you to learn to serve. My wife also asked you to dress properly for our guests. I will insure my wife's pleasure by removing this mess under my foot."

"Give me back my crown, give me back my crown." The princess stamped her foot in a tantrum. "You have no right to take it. It's mine."

Carlton placed his other foot squarely on the mounded turban, crushing three feathers. "Madam, you may have that filthy thing back after properly serving tomorrow's meal. Until then, it is mine." Carlton leaned on his chair and, using a linen napkin, gingerly picked up the yards of fabric. "Do you understand?"

"Yes. Sir," Lulah Marie grouched. "I understand that I have never been treated this way before in my life. I am a princess."

"Well, girl, understand this. You will dress properly, cover your hair, and serve my guests. You will not do any of your unholy hocus pocus and you, as you just said, will move on the next day." Carlton and the bundle of rags left the room. "I counted the silver the day you arrived," he called from the hall.

The next day it was Annie who answered the door chime. The four children stood on the porch in their best clothes.

"Well, look at y'all. Your mama did a fine job of polishing you up." Carlton stood.

"Yes, Missus Annie," said Nora Lee, with a twirl of her dress. "Mama said she'd kill us half way to next Sunday if we got dirty on the way over."

"There'll be no need for that. Come on in." Annie looked over their heads.

"Where's all your grownups?" asked Carlton.

"Flossie Mae decided to explode," said Benjy. "They all are a comin' after they finish cleanin' her up."

"Yeah," added Theo. "She's covered. Momma started crying about the mess. Next thing ya know, the baby, diaper, and dress are all in the bath tub. Peeuuie."

"Marguerite told us to go ahead." Franky smiled his shy smile. "I hope you don't mind. Mama was pretty mad."

"Of course, sweetheart." Annie smoothed his hair. "Why don't y'all go in the kitchen and see if the lemonade is ready. Miss Lulah Marie will fix it for you."

Nora Lee shrieked. "The princess is here? Hooray. Hooray." She crashed through the door and spun back into the dining room on the return swing. "Where is she? Some colored lady's in there. She's got a fish net on her head."

"Nora Lee." Carlton grabbed at the dervish. "Stop." He was eyeing the crystal stemware. "That is Miss Dubonet, our helper for today."

Nora Lee froze. "Yes sir. Uh, where's the princess? Missus Annie said she was in the kitchen."

"She did her magic and turned into Miss Dubonet, and that is what we will call her." Carlton took Nora Lee's hand. "Let me introduce all of you to her."

"But we know her. She's Princess Lulah Marie."

"Child, you will call her Miss Dubonet." Carlton's firmness worked. She nodded and scampered away.

"Miss Dubonet, Miss Dubonet." Nora Lee put on her pretend voice. "It is I, your friend, Miss Gallaway. We are here. Might we have refreshments?"

"Yes," Lulah Marie grumbled the kitchen. "Make sure *he* will let you."

"Miss Dubonet, I heard that. Remember our agreement." Carlton nodded. "Go get your lemonade, children. We bought ice."

By the time the lemonade was gone, all the adults and one very sweet baby girl were gathered in the parlor. Flossie Mae's wicker buggy was parked by the front door. Annie was offering the very weak excuse that her sisters would not be joining them. "They often take trays to their rooms. Poor things are still mourning."

"Maamaa," Nora Lee called out. "We stayed clean. Can we go outside and play Annie Over in the alley?" She giggled. "Hey, we're over at Missus Annie's playin' Annie Over. That's perfect."

"Yes, darling, *after* you eat. Just try not to do too much damage to your dress." Myra handed the baby to Carlton's out stretched arms. "Go to your Uncle Carl. He likes holding you 'bout as much as your Uncle Jack."

"After today's excitement, probably more," said Marguerite. "Mister Carlton, Missus Annie, thank you for inviting Jack and me to your house. We are honored."

Carlton nodded. "Thank you for coming. We all need to get to know each other better, don't you think?"

Jack looked at Marguerite and raised one eyebrow. His wife stiffened.

Whites don't want to git to know colored 'less they want something, he thought, and she understood.

CB caught the exchange. "What do you want to know, if I may be so bold?" He took his daughter back. "We are just hardworking sailors with hardworking wives."

"Of course, of course, it's just that my Annie is a friend of your wives, and, well, you told me something that has really piqued my curiosity."

Annie stood. She smiled at Myra and Marguerite. "My Carl is anxious to talk to your men. He has some business news to share. I apologize for his lack of manners. Now I must supervise the kitchen. I'll feed the children in there." Annie disappeared. The sing-song of grace floated through the air.

CB placed his sleepy bundle in her carriage. "Let the women visit," he said to Carlton. "What is this business you have to talk about? Is there someplace we can go?"

"Absolutely. Gentlemen, come to my study. I have a proposition for the two of you." Carlton led the way. "I want to talk about your shipping routes. Do you go to Havana?

Myra stood to check her baby. Bubbles of drool were shining in the corner of Flossie Mae's mouth. Gently her mama wiped her cheek and quietly bent to kiss her. "I love you, my angel," she whispered.

"Ahh," sighed Myra, settling back in the settee. "The thought of an adults only table, except for little miss darlin' child over there, sounds heavenly, doesn't it?"

"*Oui*," Marguerite agreed. "My Jack and I have never sat all the way through a meal together since we got married." She giggled. "He calls me Missus Frog because I keep hopping up to help the children. I should call him *Monsieur* Lily Pad because he stays put."

Ting, ting. Annie was standing at the dining room archway ringing a small silver bell. "Come my friends, dinner is served."

Annie and Carlton sat at the head and foot. The Smiths were seated, backs to the sideboard with the Ledbetters across. Marguerite had served so many banquets working at the hotel that she knew the ins-and-outs of place settings. Jack was not so lucky. Leaning to his wife, he whispered, "I've never seen so many to-dos at one plate."

"Just start on the outside. Watch me." Jack smiled his thanks.

After grace, Annie reached for the bell. "We have extra help for this afternoon. First course will be julienne soup with toast points." Ting, ting. No response from the kitchen. She rang again.

"I'm comin', I'm comin', hold your horses. Give me a minute." The children's voices hushed.

Marguerite's eyes went wide, and she grabbed her husband's hand under the table. "Oh, no, oh no, not here," she mouthed to Jack. She looked at Myra and repeated the silent words. Myra shrugged.

Lulah Marie swung through the kitchen door, a blue willow tureen on her hands. She wore an apron that covered her bright skirts, and her hair twists were pulled up into a black mesh snood.

"Place the soup on the credenza and serve the toast. Thank you." Annie gestured toward the sideboard.

Lulah Marie did as she was told and stepped away from the soup. Marguerite felt a slight tug. One of her pins fell to the floor, releasing a long red braid, leaving the other wrapped around her head.

"Toast?" Lulah Marie asked innocently, offering the plate to Jack. "Missus?"

Marguerite shook her head 'no'. The braid swayed. Tug. Ping. Another pin hit the floor, and both plaits were down.

"Miss Dubonet, serve the soup." Annie watched her lift the steaming pot. Marguerite jerked her head straight back, and the julienne sloshed as Lulah Marie flinched away from the movement. Tomato broth spotted her apron and the weight of her twists caused the snood to slide back, exposing most of her hair.

"For heaven's sake, girl, watch yourself," warned Carlton. "You need to be much more careful with the food. You know our agreement. Serve the soup and fix your appearance."

The soup was ladled into each bowl and the tureen carried into the kitchen.

"*Je suis desole*," Marguerite apologized to the table. "My hairpins have fallen. Please excuse me."

"Oh, no, my dear," soothed Annie. "No need to be concerned. You have such beautiful auburn hair. It is to be admired."

Marguerite blushed.

The next course was one of Annie's favorite recipes, poached fish swimming in dill sauce. Lulah Marie had changed aprons, but the snood was forgotten. It was barely clinging to the end of her twists. Once again she walked behind Marguerite. Jack crooked back his elbow, blocking access to his wife. The fish plate and server were detoured. Lulah Marie sidestepped backward away from Jack and walked around the table to serve Carlton. As she leaned to offer him some extra sauce, the hairpiece fell in the dish. She squawked and dropped the plate, which broke neatly in half. Sauce seeped into the white damask. Lulah Marie Dubonet stared at the mess. The snapper looked fresh netted.

Annie screamed. That brought the children from the kitchen and woke the baby. Chaos reigned. The meal was forgotten as the diners all jumped to save the linen. Only Carlton noticed the culprit was missing.

"Miss Dubonet," he boomed. "Come here right now. I will drag you into to this room if I have to."

Lulah Marie cracked the swinging door, peeking into the dining room.

"Now." Carlton's voice was menacingly low.

Princess Lulah Marie Dubonet slouched against the wall and stood in silence.

"Mama." Franky was tugging his mother sleeve. "Mama."

"Ask Missus Annie where it is," Myra whispered.

"No Mama, not that." Franky pointed. "Mama, look. Missus Marguerite and the princess favor. They have the same hair. Look." All turned and stared.

Princess Lulah Marie Dubonet and Marguerite Black Smith could easily be related; the twists and braids looked identical.

"Are you two sisters?" Nora Lee broke the spell. "You look just like each other."

"Go out and play, all of you. Take the baby buggy with you." Myra's voice was no nonsense. "Now."

The children knew to skedaddle, and did.

Annie was crying. "My party is ruined. I, uh, uh, wanted to please everyone so much and, now it's ruined."

Carlton led her to the settee and held her hand. She folded into herself, sobbing. Her husband looked totally bewildered. He nodded to Myra, who quickly sat with her friend and shooed Carlton away.

He returned to the dining room where he found the two red headed women shooting eye-daggers at each other.

"Miss Dubonet. Clear this table and quickly put the tablecloth to soak. Bring fresh linens, plates, and silver to the sideboard. You will serve the meat course with thick slices of bread. We will eat sandwiches like the English. Do not forget the horseradish sauce." He turned to Marguerite. "Perhaps you could help Missus Myra with my wife. Tell them we will be eating soon."

Chapter Seventeen
July 1, 1901
It's All Relative

Uneasy peace settled as the adults returned to eat their, by now, cold roast beef sandwiches. Both red heads had their hair back into place, and neither looked at or got near each other. Lulah Marie retreated to the kitchen. The table conversation was all about Carlton's proposition.

"I know for a fact the rich people of Havana want flour for their bread like the Americans. I also know for a fact farms there can't grow wheat." Carlton beamed. "These two men are going to get my flour into the bakeries of Cuba."

CB raised his hand. "Slow down a minute. We said we would check into it." He looked at Myra, who touched her engagement ring. He nodded. That beautiful yellow diamond was payment for man smuggling on the *Sallie Lou*. She smiled.

He's back in business, she thought.

Marguerite saw the exchange and smiled, too.

CB continued. "We will talk after I see about the roll-off in Havana. You need a receiving agent. You can't just leave it settin' on the wharf."

"That's right, man," Jack said. "We can probably get it there. Can you move it where it belongs? We're puttin' a lot on the line, you know."

"You two get it on the dock, I'll get it off." Carlton nodded to his wife. "I'm good at my word, aren't I, my dear?"

"That you are." Annie beamed. "Carl and my father were partners. After Father went to fight the Indians and got himself killed, bless his heart, my wonderful husband protected Father's interest in the business. Father left me a legacy that remains." She leaned forward. "Now I am taken care of by both the men who loved me."

She blew one kiss to the foot of the table, and another toward heaven. No one noticed the kitchen door sway.

Carlton raised his water glass. "Let us toast to possible good fortunes, safe seas, and a continued friendship among like-minded fellows. Cheers."

"Cheers," was the unison reply.

"Now, I want to see what sweets wait in the kitchen." Carlton rang the silver bell. No answer. He rang it again. "Where is that girl?"

Annie stood. "Husband, stay where you are, I'll check. You know your temperament." It was she who carried the pies to the table, wearing a grim expression. "We have gooseberry and we have fig."

Carlton was slowly turning purple. He banged his fist on the table. "Where in God's name is that idiot?"

"I don't know. I don't know." Annie's trembling voice was almost inaudible. "Her apron's on the floor, and the children said she didn't go out the back way. She just disappeared."

"I've had enough of her madness. She didn't disappear. She's somewhere in the house. There are servant steps, you know." Carlton looked around the table. "Let's eat pie."

"That sounds good to me. Come dear friend, sit down." Myra smiled at her hostess. "May I cut? Let's taste both." She served the table small slices of each flavor. The polite conversation skirted the topic of the missing woman and settled on the newly planted fig orchards of LaPorte.

"These are not from our yard trees, but I have great hopes for next year," offered Annie. "All our neighbors have the saplings planted." She shook her head. "I just don't know about our weather. Let's hope they have strong roots." Everyone nodded in agreement.

As soon as the pie comparison was finished, CB stood. "Please excuse me, but I'd better gather the children. Jack?" He nodded to his partner. "Come help me wrangle them. I'm sure Flossie Mae needs to be brought to her mama."

Jack nodded and left the room with CB. Soon the back screen door slammed. The women all helped with the clearing of the dessert plates. They could hear soft talking on the stoop.

"What in the world is going on with Marguerite and that woman? Even a blind man can see there's something."

Jack nodded. "She never told me about the witch's hair, only about her being some kind of kin." He scratched his head. "They sure resemble."

"Well, this has got to stop. We've got a deal to make. Those two can't go ruinin' it." CB looked hard at Jack. "We need this flour business. Gold runners are slowing down, and property taxes are due soon. Damn it, man, I don't have the cash. Even with the rent you two pay, there's still not enough between us to cover the due."

"You should have told me sooner," scolded Jack.

"I haven't even told Myra. She's so busy with the children. I can't bother her with money problems." CB frowned. "We gotta get back in the movin' business or we will be movin' to the poorhouse."

"You gather the children," said Jack. "I'll talk to my wife about this princess problem right now." He grinned. "If you hear cats squallin' in French, keep the children outside. They might pick up a few choice words that don't need learnin'."

"Aye aye." CB saluted and headed to the alley, calling "Annie, Annie over, can Daddy CB come over?" He heard them down the way. The baby was still sleeping, so he joined the game, allowing time for whatever might happen in the house.

Jack found his wife helping in the kitchen. Lulah Marie's apron was back on the pantry peg, no princess in sight. Carlton's cigar smoke wafted from his study. The ladies looked up.

"CB misplace the children?" Myra asked.

Jack shook his head. "He's playing Annie Over with them since there was no hungry baby crying." He looked at Marguerite. "I need to talk to you. Please excuse yourself and meet me in the parlor."

Marguerite looked at the women, set down the tea towel she was using on the crystal, and followed her husband.

"*Oui?*" They sat on the loveseat by the steps. "*Qu'Estce que c'est?*"

"What is the connection between you and that woman? You have cursed her since the day you met her." Jack lowered his voice even softer than it was. "Today takes the cake. I want you to go find her and get her back in this house. It's time to settle this. Our business may depend on it. Do you understand?"

Shrieks echoed down the stairs. "Mother, mother, how could you do this to me? You know I was your favorite. Ohhhh."

Crash. Thunk.

Carlton and Annie met at the same moment by the newel post.

"Arabel," they said in unison, and quickly climbed the steps. At the top, Carlton called, "Jack, I need your help. Bring your wife."

Uninvited, Myra joined the Smiths at the top landing. Arabel Gaithers was on the floor of her room. Annie was sitting fanning her sister, who seemed to be rousing from her faint. Princess Lulah Marie Dubonet was sitting at the boudoir breakfast table, staring into a small glass ball. She looked up at the new occupants.

"I'm sorry, but you did not make an appointment. Perhaps we can see each other another time." Her eyes returned to the glass.

"What? My sister-in-law is on the floor, you ruined my wife's party, and you, you idiot, tell me I have no appointment." Carlton sent the crystal ball flying, shattering it on the opposite wall.

Lulah Marie looked up. "Why did you do that? I wasn't hurting anybody." Her shoulders straightened. "You have destroyed my property. Please pay for it."

For the first time in his life, Carlton Wilson struck a woman. The round-house slap knocked Lulah Marie to the floor. Stepping on her hair, pinning her down, he reached over and pulled the chenille off Arabel's bed. The seer was quickly wrapped in the spread. "Jack, do you have enough strength to carry this sack of sh...uh, garbage down stairs." Carlton turned his attention to Marguerite. "I hope you will help me with this little problem. It appears you two know each other."

"Yes she will." Jack answered for his wife. He hoisted the wild haired mummy over his shoulder and smiled at Carlton. "'Bout as heavy as a bag of flour, but I like to use kegs. They roll."

"You can roll this thing down the steps if you want, I don't care." He turned to his wife. "When Arabel is able, I want her to join us. She's a part of this disaster, too."

Myra scurried down to the kitchen and out the door. "CB, CB, where are you?" she called.

"In the alley with the children. Is it time to go?"

"There's trouble here. I'm taking the children home. You need to stay."

"Coming. Flossie's waking anyway." CB hollered down the alley. "Come on, y'all. Mama says it's time to go. Theo, bring the carriage." He hurried to the stoop. "What?"

"Red heads with hot heads. Carlton may need a referee with muscles." Myra kissed her husband. "I'll take the young'uns around the side of the house. Please be sure to tell Annie thank you for all of us." She directed her voice to the alley. "Don't make me get a switch. Now move it."

The crew was soon down the street, Theo proudly leading, pushing his crying sister in her buggy.

CB found the parlor rearranged. The love seat was across from the settee, each on opposite walls. Marguerite and Jack sat together, he was gripping her hand. The red headed cocoon sat opposite. Carlton stood behind her, holding her captive, a hand firmly entwined in some of her twists.

Annie put her arm through CB's as though expecting to be escorted down an aisle.

"CB," she said. "My sister Arabel is needed down here. May I show you her room so that she can be helped with the steps? She's a tad unsteady on her feet just now."

"Of course, Missus Annie, is she sick?" Annie was leading them to the stairs as he spoke.

"Somehow she fainted." Annie tilted her head to CB. "I think she's just trying to not face the music about Lulah Marie. My sister might be in a real pickle. We'll soon see." She chuckled. "Carl's too old, or he'd drag her down himself."

CB was used to moving cargo, and quickly strong-armed the reluctant Arabel Gaithers to the parlor, where she was offered a seat by her dear wrapped princess. Annie sat in her husband's Eastlake, CB standing beside her. Everyone looked at Lulah Marie and Carlton, waiting.

"Ah hem," Carlton cleared his throat. "My wife and I are owed an explanation as to why her dinner turned into a donnybrook." He tightened his grip on his prisoner's hair.

"First. Arabel, you did not come to your sister's party. You entice the help from her duties, and then you scream and faint." Carlton shifted his weight behind of the settee, tugging on the twists. "You are my wife's sister and our guest. Because of that, you owe us an answer."

127

"I'll pay you. I'll pay you for everything." Arabel glared at Annie. "But it's not like you need it. Mother just told me about your wealth and how you two hid it from Emily and me."

"You owe an *apology* to your sister, not money." Carl was seething.

Annie's eyes went wide. "What are you talking about? Mother is dead. I never hid anything from you two, no matter how things were between us."

"Mother talks to me every day. Doesn't she, Princess?"

The mummy nodded.

"Mother loves me the most. She tells me each time she appears in my room." Arabel was close to shouting. "Mother told me how your 'fiancé' gave you money long before he married you. At least Emily and I were decent enough to wait for holy matrimony before being supported by a man." Arabel jumped up and took two steps toward Annie. "I can only guess what that makes you."

CB was in front of his hostess before her sister's second footfall. "Missus Arabel, you will not insult my friend." He made a long stride, meeting her face to face. "Sit down." He remembered his wife's parting words. "Don't make me get a switch."

Arabel sat.

"Woman, how dare you insult my wife." Carlton was yanking on Lulah Marie's twists with every word. "My wife was a maiden until our wedding night. You have no right to say otherwise."

Annie raised her hand to shush the room. "This is about me. Let me speak." She took a deep breath. "Arabel, you and Emily supported Mother and me properly. For that I thank you. Carlton invested Father's half of their mill business. He presented Father's legacy to Mother, and Mother decided that I would need it after she was gone. She knew that there was a great possibility that you two would not continue maintaining me. Mother returned the money to Carlton to invest. She did not tell you two because she felt it was our business, not yours." Annie pointed to her sister. "Yes, the money grew. Yes, my husband is a wonderful business man, and because of that, you two sleep under our roof." Arabel stood. "Sit down. We are not finished." She swung her arm to Lulah Marie. "You have caused much trouble here. How in God's name did you get this information?"

"Spirit told me."

"Liar," spat Carlton. "You must have been listening at the door." He pulled her head backward, looking hard at Lulah Marie. "Miss Dubonet, how do you know Mrs. Jack Smith? Mrs. Jack Smith, how do you know this woman here?"

Both sat silently. Carlton nodded to Jack. "Your wife seems very distressed in the presence of our maid, and I use that term loosely. Please ask your wife to help us with this problem."

Jack squeezed Marguerite's hand even tighter. Still no sound.

Carlton gave the twists a particularly hard yank. "Ouch, ouch," wailed Lulah Marie.

Carlton practically lifted Lulah Marie straight up. "Talk, witch, or I will pull you bald."

"All right, all right, let go. I'll talk." Carl relaxed his hand. Lulah Marie shook her head. Her arms were tight in the chenille, and she couldn't rub her tender scalp.

"My name is Princess Lulah Marie Dubonet, and I am of a long line—"

"You are from a long line of thieves and frauds." Marguerite spat the words. "You are nothing but a dirty gypsy."

"That may be so, but, my precious hotsy-totsy big house pretender, I carry his name. Why don't you?" Lulah Marie curled her lip into a false smile. "Have you forgotten your Maman? She was the whore our father left to marry my mother. That makes you a *connard*."

Marguerite was across the room before you could say 'bastard.' Grabbing the twists out of Carlton's hand, she slammed the wrapped, screaming Lulah Marie to the floor. Sitting astride the woman like riding a horse and holding the red reins in one hand, Marguerite punched Lulah Marie's face with the other, full strength. No one stopped her. She did it again and again. Lulah Marie screamed foul curses at her attacker. Marguerite stayed put.

Finally the Princess quieted and closed her eyes, Jack stood beside his wife.

"Are you finished?" he asked.

"No." Marguerite looked at Missus Annie. "May I use your kitchen shears? I might be illegitimate, but she's going to lose her hair. I don't want anyone to ever say we favor again."

Lulah Marie's eye popped open. "Nooooo, you can't do that. My hair is beautiful."

"That disgusting rat's nest is not beautiful," said Carlton. "I like this idea. I'll fetch the scissors."

Marguerite cut short every one of those red twists. She handed them up to Carlton, but he refused to touch them. In the end, Jack carried the long strands to the dustbin. "I've hauled much dirtier bags, but, Missus Annie, my hands need washing. Please show me the head, er, bathroom."

"*Mon cher*, may I follow you? I need to use the basin." Marguerite flexed her fingers. My hands are *tres sale*, too." Jack helped his wife off her mount and they followed Annie down the hall.

CB sat up the dazed woman. "All right if I loosen her? She might need to stretch."

Carlton nodded. "I wrapped her, you unroll her. Help her stand and get her into the kitchen. There should be some of the lemonade ice left for her bruises. I'll meet you there after I talk to my women." He stood by his wife. "I am so sorry that our house guests have been so disrespectful to you, my love. Earlier Miss Dubonet stated that she would be leaving, and I certainly don't want to hinder her." He looked at Arabel. "How much money have you given that woman?"

Mrs. Gaithers pouted. "I paid her fair for her services."

"Madam, that was not my question." Carlton stepped square in front of her. "I noticed your ruby brooch is missing. Did you give it to her? You wore it every day until that charlatan arrived. Does she have it?"

Arabel looked at her ring-covered hands. She picked at her fingernails. "I pawned it one day when you two were out. I needed silver dollars to pay her." She took a quick breath. "I gave her one every time our mother came to visit."

Annie looked at Arabel but stayed seated in her husband's chair. "Oh, Sister, poor dear Sister, I am so sorry. I am the one who started this by bringing her home."

Arabel glared. "Don't call me poor. In case you have forgotten, I still have my jewelry. Now, if you will excuse me, thanks to your husband, I have broken glass in my room to clean."

The silent assembly watched her leave.

Carlton nodded and joined CB in the kitchen. Lulah Marie was holding a towel against her cheek. "You will leave my house tomorrow. I am going to search your room. You will give back all that you have taken from my sister-in-law. If the silver is on your person, I will have the women strip you. Then you will be gone." Carlton tilted his head to CB. Wordlessly they each took an arm. "Search or strip? Where is the silver?"

"My room, I'll show you. Then will you give me my crown? I earned it. I served dinner."

"Hardly," grumped Carlton. "Now move." The men stepped behind her, blocking her escape.

The room search revealed silver dollars, cheap trinkets, and a train ticket to Austin, partially punched.

"Austin?' Carlton was curious. "Who's waiting for you? Why Austin?"

"They sent me there to have more princess lessons. I don't need them, so I got off the train. Ended up here."

"Well, madam, this is your lucky day. You get to go back to school. Pack your bag." He handed her two dollars and the ticket. "You will get that pile of rags as you step on the train."

The next morning Carlton kept his word. Princess Lulah Marie Dubonet, her shorn head covered with a babushka, stood with Carlton and Annie. As the train approached, Lulah Marie looked up at her host. "I still don't know why you did this to me. I am royalty."

"You are a royal idiot," Carlton growled.

Screech. The train stopped in front of them. Annie did not say a word. Carlton handed her the yards of fabric that once controlled her twists. She shoved it under her arm, picked up her grip, and waited until the porter offered her a gloved hand.

Head held high, she mounted the steps and sat in the ladies' coach, her valise on the seat beside her. She removed the scarf, quickly wound on her turban, and waited for someone to serve tea.

Annie and Carlton watched the train disappear. Lulah Marie had been too busy with her head wrap to notice that the Wilsons did not wave.

Chapter Eighteen
October, 1901
Isaac Who?

Harry took his role of taskmaster seriously. Junior was put to work in the store for all the hours on the OPEN sign. Since the boy was kept busy, the uncle did not notice that Junior was talking and smiling less and less. All Harry noticed was that the new store was kept clean, the displays were looking tip-top, and people were getting their orders delivered on time. The front door chime seemed to be ringing more and more. Dickenson's Grocery and Dry Goods II (the II stood for the fact that this store was the replacement for Dickenson's Grocery, Dry Goods, and Masonic Temple) was a very busy establishment.

Ting a ling. The front and back doors both had bells to announce customers. Ada looked up from behind the notions case. She gasped.

"Oh, my dear God in heaven, Ike. Is it really you?"

The man smiled. "Yes, Missus Ada, it is."

Ada was around the side of the counter and took hold of the man in the doorway, dragging him to the center of the store. There she kissed both cheeks of Ike Jameson, widower of her dear lost friend, Julia. He smiled and planted a big ol' smooch on her forehead. That's when she noticed his hat. It was a beanie just like Rabbi Joe wore. She crinkled her left eyebrow at him. "Jewish?"

"Yes, ma'am. Born and raised."

"Hmmmm, so that's how you know Joe's wife. People said it was from way back when." Ada had heard the gossip. "I couldn't figure all that out since we sat on the same pew at church."

"Long story needs to be told another time. Sure is good to see you." He kissed her forehead again.

"Is Ikey with you? You know so many children died or got sent away after the storm." Ada led him back to the checker barrel and they both sat. "Is he here?"

"Yes, but he lives with Joe and Esther. I'm rooming by the docks while the counting house is being rebuilt." Ike shrugged. "Even if the wood is new, the wharves are no place for a child, especially a growing boy. You know what was, still is." Ike made a curvy woman-shaped gesture with both hands.

"Oh, excuse my manners. Ike, would you like a cup of good hot coffee? I do." Ada stood.

"Yes, of course. And, would you please call me Isaac? That is my 'born and raised' name." Ike, er Isaac smiled up at her.

"Did Julia know?" Ada blurted.

"She knew on our wedding night." Isaac emphasized the word *night.*

"Well, I'll be." *Hmmmm, that girl sure could keep her secrets.* "You sit tight. I'm going to get Harry. We have something to tell you."

Next thing Isaac knew he was being bear-hugged by Harry Dickenson. It seemed that each time someone from BH -before hurricane- came in the store, Harry would get emotional. Ada always said he had the biggest heart, even if he didn't always show it. The hurricane took so many of his Masonic Brothers and other town friends. Finding that some still lived "helped fill his heart back up," she would say. Harry pulled another chair to the barrel and used the game board as a tabletop for their coffee.

"Missus Ada said you have something to tell me." Isaac's tone was cautious. "Is it more bad news?"

Harry's grin contradicted that thought. "Your brother-in-law is the proud papa of a baby girl."

"What? Who? How?" Isaac had heard Julia's brother had survived, but that was all he knew.

"Your brother-in-law, CB Ledbetter, married our Myra right after the storm. They have a house in LaPorte."

Isaac collapsed, his arms rested on the checker board, and fell totally apart. All of the horror of the hurricane, the grief of losing his wife, and the building of his new, true life had been handled with rigid stoicism. This news pushed him over the edge of false strength he'd maintained for the sake of his son. Ada rescued his coffee and they sat quietly waiting for his sobs to pass.

"Oh, thank God. Oh praise Jesus." Isaac didn't care if he was a renewed Jew. "You mean to tell me there is a little bit of Julia in LaPorte? I never thought there would be any family left. Oh, Jesus, oh Jesus. Thank you for telling me."

Ada smiled at his language. "Would you like to know her name?"

"Yes, yes."

"Your niece's name is Flossie Mae Ledbetter." Ada figured that would be the icing on Isaac's cake. She wasn't wrong.

He started blubbering all over again. "Julia's name, her real name, oh Jesus, oh God, oh, Missus Ada. I can't believe it."

Ada took his hand. "Our Julia lives on. You will have to go to LaPorte sometime. Myra, CB, all the children except for Junior—he's with us—live there. Even Miss Annie lives there, but she isn't Miss Annie anymore. She's Missus Annie, married to Carlton Wilson." Ada took a breath. "Annie's sisters are widowed, and Carlton is taking care of them. You can imagine how that is."

"You remember how bad those biddies treated her?" Harry made a sour puss.

"Now, Harry," Ada scolded.

"Well, they did. Those tables are turned. According to anyone with eyeballs, the sisters are so out of joint, they can't walk straight."

"Enough, husband."

"That's all right, Missus Ada" soothed Isaac. "Julia, God rest her soul, would mention now and again about Miss Annie and how she was kept at home to tend their mother. I don't think she ever mentioned Mr. Wilson, though."

"Yep, that was some secret," said Harry nodding to Isaac. "But yours," Harry leaned over and tapped Isaac's yarmulke, "well, that beats 'em all."

Ting a ling

Junior came through the front door, carrying his empty delivery box. He liked making deliveries. Sometimes he got a ten cent tip. He always walked fast to the customer's house and slow back to the store. *Those cans'll wait their stackin'.* He heard talking in the back corner.

"Junior, so good to see you," called a voice from the checker barrel.

His eyes popped. "Mr. Jameson? Ikey's daddy?" Junior strode to the barrel.

"Yes sir, it is." Isaac stood, beaming. "Just wait 'til I tell Ikey you're here."

The boy broke away from Isaac's embrace. "Where is he? Does he still have all those marbles he won from me? You know he used to pick all my plums." Junior was smiling, remembering when they would play Picking Plums on Ikey's front porch. Ikey was really good at getting the best marbles from anyone he played.

"I'm not even sure if he has any. Everything washed away." A flash of sadness showed on Isaac's face.

"We sell marbles," offered Ada. "We got a new batch just the other day. Why don't you send him around to pick out a dozen as a gift from us?"

"Um, Auntie, my marbles are gone, too. How about me?" Junior smiled hopefully at his adults. "Please?"

"Well now, son," began Harry, "Did you earn a dime with your delivery today?"

Junior's face fell. *Here we go again.*

"Harry, not now." Ada's sharpness held a warning.

"All right, boy, you can get a dozen, too." Harry had heeded her tone. "You're going to have to wait until Ikey comes in and then you can trade off turns with your draws. That should make your games even." Harry winked at Isaac. "Got to keep these boys on the up 'n' up, you know."

"I'll be stopping at Joe's house tomorrow. You can just about bet Ikey will be by the store very soon." Isaac headed to the door. "Um, Missus Ada, do you sell kosher?"

"Just pickles. I need to know more about Jewish things." Ada touched his arm. "By the way, is Ikey called little Isaac, now?"

"No. Ikey is still Methodist. Julia wasn't Jewish. It always follows the mother." Again the shadow passed his eyes. He blinked. "You are so lucky to have everyone." The shadow was replaced with a smile. "You have little Miss Flossie Mae Ledbetter, and now, so do I. "

Harry grabbed Isaac's hand and shook it hard. "Well, sir, that makes us sorta kin. If I can figure it out right, I'll let you know. For now, welcome to the family, Nephew."

Isaac's grin said it all. "Thank you, Uncle. Thank you, Aunt." He extended his hand to Junior. "Hello there, uh…uh…Cousin."

Junior giggled as he shook hands. "You tell my…uh…second cousin, Ikey, that his second cousin, Junior's, hopin' to see him soon. Tell him we got plums to pick."

Isaac opened the front screen door. The bell ting-a-linged.

"Oh, I forgot to tell you. Joe wants you to know lodge time has been changed to six from six thirty this month. Something's come up. He said he'll tell why at the meeting." Isaac nodded to his friends. "Good-bye, family."

Harry stood there, scratching his thinning white hair. "Well, what' d'ya know, Jewish. Don't that beat all."

Chapter Nineteen
October, 1901
Rotten Plums

Ikey Jameson showed up the very next day. He sure was glad to know that someone from his old life was still around. Losing his beloved mother, house, and all his things were bad enough, but now he was living with strangers who said they were related to his father in the deepest sense. They said their blood ran longer and stronger than time itself. Ikey had no idea his father was a Jew until Ike Senior prayed aloud in Hebrew during the middle of the hell that was the hurricane. Now Young Ikey was staying in a household who said funny words and wore funny hats, and his dad was living someplace else. When he was told that Junior Gallaway was living with his aunt and uncle, Ikey knew that he and Junior had more than history between them. They had no-good dads. Why else would his father leave him with the rabbi and Junior's stepfather leave him with his uncle? Dirty rats, both of 'em.

Aunt Ada cooked them whatever they wanted to eat, and the boys were allowed to choose the best marbles in the case. Uncle Harry gave Junior his full dinner hour to play. Both chose ham and cheese sandwiches with leftover breakfast rice mixed with sugar and cream for dessert.

Ada smiled at Ikey. "Missing good old food?" was all she said as she handed the boys their plates.

"Yes'm."

"Let me know if you want more."

"Yes'm." Ikey blew Ada a little kiss as a thank you. "You know I will."

After several sandwiches and two bowls of creamy rice washed down with big glasses of milk, Junior led them back into the storage room to play. This is where he slept.

Stock wasn't too high to cover the windows, and they were out from under foot and away from the grown-ups.

"I'd take you out back, but Uncle Harry's rot dump is there and rats are everywhere. Ya can't sit on the ground 'cause the things might bite." Junior drew the taw on the floor with chalk. "Plums?"

"Yep. Bets?"

"No bets." Junior remembered Ikey collecting his due with his fists. He'd promised himself to never wager at marbles with that boy again. "Just plums."

The game lasted 'til Uncle Harry hollered Junior back to work. The boys collected their marbles, and Ikey scuffed the taw with his shoe. The shooting line was almost erased.

"Don't worry about it, man. I'm soon to oil the floor. Gotta do it every month."

"They sure do work you here, don't they?" Ikey stood looking hard at Junior.

"Yeah. They think they can teach me manners, or how to love my mother's husband, or somethin'." Junior's voice started to growl. "Or maybe they just want a slave to boss around. All I know is I'm learnin' nothin'."

Junior was almost to the storage room door when he heard Ikey say something real low.

"Huh?"

Ikey came up beside him. "Man, you work too hard. You need to get out." Ikey was whispering. "Wanna do something tonight?"

"What?" Junior knew he would never be allowed out after dark, but he didn't let on. "Whacha got in mind?"

"Naw, never mind, forget I said anything."

Ikey stepped out into the store. He approached Ada. "Thank you so much for your dinner. I haven't had good regular food in a long time." He did a hat doffing, roll down bow like he saw someone do in a show once. "Thank Mister Dickenson, too, if you don't mind."

"Please call me Aunt Ada and my husband Uncle Harry. You're welcome. Would you like to come again? I'm sure we could work it out with Joe and your father."

"Oh, may I? Thank you so much." Ikey formally shook Junior's hand, winking as he did. As he stepped out of the store, he called over his shoulder, "Sugar bowl."

Junior had no idea what that meant. The thought of going out at night stayed with him all day and into the next.

What the heck can you do after dark?

Ikey showed up Thursday, just in time for dinner. Ada was pleased that Junior had a friend to spend the hour with. The child was always wearing a grumpy face when they sat to table. Maybe Ikey would make a difference. She could only hope.

The boys ate every bite and then some. Soon they were in the back room again. The taw was still there, so they started the lineup.

"Hey, Ikey, what did you mean by sugar bowl?" Junior was sorting out all his reds. "That didn't make any sense."

"Yes it does." Ikey leaned back on his heels. "It's like this. You're livin' in a salt cellar. It's all you know. I'm livin' in a sugar bowl." He rolled his blues in his hand. "Sugar bowl life is sweet, a whole lot sweeter than this salt mess you're in."

"You're right about that. This store work is no fun." Junior set his reds on the taw. "What do you mean that you have the sweet life? You're living with a rabbi, for God's sake. That can't be fun."

"It'll do. The fun happens at night," Ikey lined his blues, "and what they don't know, won't hurt them. You shoot first."

The Checkerboard

Chapter Twenty
October, 1901
Sugar Bowling

Aunt Ada and Uncle Harry lived in the apartment over the store. With one bedroom, parlor, kitchen, dining room, and a real bathroom, this arrangement was perfect for the Dickensons. When Junior moved in, they set up a bed in the back storeroom for the boy. The plumbing from the apartment allowed a toilet downstairs. Once supper and evening activities were done, Junior said 'Good-night' to the adults and settled into his first floor nest. More often than not, he was asleep within minutes.

Junior figured the sneaking would be easy. All he had to do was walk out the back door. The plan was to meet Ikey down two blocks from the store. Junior had no idea what sugar awaited him, but he wasn't about to pass it up.

"Good-night, all," he called up the steps.

"Same to you," Ada called back.

Junior went into his room, grabbed his sack of marbles, and headed to the door. Ikey said sugar costs.

"Yikes, I forgot about the bell." The chime was at the top of the door, and bolted to the frame. One movement would ring it. "What the heck am I going to do?" he grumbled under his breath.

Walking back to his room, muttering every swear word he could think of, Junior noticed the window. Still not piled up with boxes, he knew exactly what to do.

Windows don't ting-a-ling. Hah!

Slick as snot on a mirror, the window went up, and the boy slipped out.

Ikey was waiting down the road. "You ready?"

"Yes, sir. I snuck out a window. They'll never know."

142

"Good. Have I got some sugar for you." Ikey gave Junior a wink and took off, long strides, in front of him.

"Hey, wait, where we goin'?" Junior ran to catch up.

"You'll see, come on." Ikey was almost trottin'. "You ever kiss a girl?"

"Um, no, just my baby sisters." Junior stopped dead still. "Are we gonna do some kissin' tonight?"

"Yep. Keep movin'."

"Jumpin' Jehoshaphat, who?" Junior was beginning to understand what 'sugar' meant.

"My sister, and she ain't no baby." Ikey turned, walking backward so Junior could get the full effect of his words.

"Sister. When did you get a sister?"

"Well, she's not my real sister." Ikey stopped walking. "You know I live with Rabbi Joe and his wife. Missus Esther has a girl from way back that's two year's older 'n me."

"And?" Junior couldn't figure what his friend was getting at.

"And Sarah has titties." Ikey knew that would explain everything.

"So?" Junior still didn't understand.

"For God's sake, man, titties mean she's ripe."

"Ooooh." Junior's voice was a whisper. "Do you...um...you know?"

"Jesus, no, hell, no, I ain't gonna be a daddy this early. She's fresh, though. She really likes kissin' and pettin'." Ikey grinned. "She says, 'Keep your britches on, and we'll have a good time.' Can't make a baby with your pants on, ya know."

They were almost to the house of Rabbi Joe.

"Where do you get the sugar?" asked Junior. "I bet her folks don't allow this kind of stuff."

"Oh God, no, they'd kill us both." Ikey pointed to the oleander hedge that surrounded the house. "We hide in the bushes."

"Oh. Is she waiting for us?" Junior peered through the darkness at the shrub line.

"She's waiting for me. You stay here 'til I come get you. I kinda forgot to tell her I was bringing a friend." With a 'shhh' gesture, Ikey disappeared.

Junior thought he heard some giggling, but he wasn't quite sure.

Do girls giggle when they kiss? Mama and CB giggle a lot, but never when they kiss.

That brought back some of his anger, but the thought of smoochin' a girl wiped it away fast. In its place were those big boy feelings he'd been getting recently.

Ikey better hurry up. Kissin' don't take all day. I wanna get me some sugar.

"Psst, psst, come on."

Junior startled. It was like Ikey could read his mind. Junior ran around the bushes and smack-dab into Sarah. Ikey was right. She had tits. She held him in a big hug.

Sarah smiled at Junior. "Ikey says you want a kiss. Zat so?"

Junior nodded. His words were gone.

"Ikey says you never kissed a girl. Zat so?"

"Yes," he croaked.

"You want my sugar? Ikey says to give you sugar."

"Yes." Junior couldn't have said 'no' if he tried. Sarah kissed him full on the mouth. Then she did it again, pushing her chest hard against him. His big boy feelings 'bout exploded.

The third kiss, this time sticking her tongue between his lips, pert near knocked him out. Junior wiggled out of her hug and stepped back, doubling up trying to hide his excitement. She stood there, hands on hips.

"You like my sugar?" She shook her shoulders, making her titties swing. "See if Ikey will bring you back. I think you're cute." Sarah looked at the house. "Better get in before they miss me."

Smiling, she blew kisses at both boys and walked away.

"Oh Jesus Christ, that was something." Junior was still bent over.

"Yep. By the way, you'll get used to the boner. Then you won't be lookin' at the ground so much." Ikey slapped the front of his trousers, laughing. "Get down, boy."

Junior slowly stood straight. He did not follow suit with a slap. He reached in his pocket and offered Ikey his pouch. "Pick your plum."

Chapter Twenty-One
October, 1901
Gate Liftin', Beer Sippin', Butt Whippin'

Ikey became a daily dinner hour visitor to the store. Ada appreciated his "yes ma'ams" and his food compliments. "He's such a good boy," she told Harry. Before Ikey would return to school, the boys would go into the back room to play. Ada was happy Junior wasn't so lonesome anymore.

All Junior could think about was kissin'. As the boys played marbles, they whispered about the next time.

"Last night, when we were done, she asked me to bring you around again." Ikey was eyeing the line. "She told me she likes you."

"Oh, jeez, that's nice." Junior smiled, remembering Sarah's little tongue.

"Ya gotta bring your shooters this time." Ikey knuckled down and fired. "My bag's full of plums."

"Yes sir." Junior was already digging in his pouch.

"Ya know what else is fun?" Ikey picked off two more.

"What?" Junior couldn't imagine anything better than kissin'.

"Beer." Ikey licked his lips with an exaggerated slurp. " Damn, I like drinkin' beer. You got any money?"

"Um, yes." Junior had never had anything except watery communion wine. "Sometimes I get tips for deliveries."

"I know someone who can get it for me at the bucket shop." Ikey took his last shot. "I need a nickel for the beer and a nickel for the man. You got a dime?"

Junior dug his back pocket, handing over the coin. Ikey flipped and caught it. "Gotta go. You be ready tonight." He bagged his marbles, dropping the dime in last. He walked out of the storeroom. Ada was standing at the counter.

"Oh, Missus Dickenson, your dinners are so good. Thank you for such a great meal." Ikey smiled and touched his cap bill. "You're the best cook in town."

"Thank you, young man." *Such good manners.* "Remember to call me Aunt Ada, and you come back soon."

"Yes, Aunt Ada."

Ikey walked down the street. "Heh, he'll never know I'm the beer gittin' man. Just made myself a nickel," he thought aloud. "Tonight's gonna be some kind of carryings-on."

He began singing and didn't stop until he reached the school steps.

"Ha, ha, ha, you and me.
"Little brown jug, don't I love thee.
"Ha, ha, ha, you and me,
"Little brown jug, don't I love thee."

That night Junior met Ikey by the oleander and got his sugar from Sarah. This time she kept her lips closed, making sisterly pecks at him. Junior tried to hug her, but she just kept poking her head at him, keeping her body out of reach.

"What's the matter? Ikey said you liked me." Junior's voice was full of confusion.

"I do, just waiting." She looked at Ikey. "You got it?"

"Yes, ma'am, be back soon." Ikey went behind the hedge.

"What's he getting?" Junior was more than puzzled.

"I thought you knew, since you paid for it." Sarah made a drinking motion with her hand.

"Oooh."

Ikey walked around the bushes with a tin pail. It was about half full of foamy brown liquid. Junior had never seen beer before. He stared. "Why does it have soap bubbles in it? I thought people drank it, not washed with it."

Ikey laughed.

"You sure do make the funniest jokes," giggled Sarah.

"Uh, yeah." The twilight hid his embarrassment. "You got something to dip it with?"

The three children sat around the bucket, sharing one teacup filched from the kitchen. The necessity of passing the cup caused each one to drink their portion straight down.

Junior'd never felt anything like this before. After his second round, he found himself lying on the ground. Sarah scooted over and next thing he knew, she had his head in her lap and was kissing him all over his face. She had four lips.

He almost made it home before the beer came up. The mess missed his shoes by the shortest of margins. His return through the window was accomplished headfirst. He slept in a rumple, curled up below the sill.

The next day they did it again. The kissin' was fine, the beer was wet. It took three teacups to make Junior dizzy this time. All of a sudden, Sarah was gone and Ikey was standing over him. He had a crooked smile. Junior squinted up.

"Wha chu want, looking at me like that?"

Ikey held out a helping hand. "Get up, man. Have you ever been gate liftin'?"

"Nuuh." Junior tried to grab one of the many Ikeys he saw.

"We're going liftin'." Ikey hoisted his unsteady friend to his feet.

Junior swayed. Dizzy up was worse than dizzy
down. Ikey put his arm around his shoulders and started
guiding him along the street softly singing. Junior joined in.

"Ha, ha, ha, you and me,
"Little brown jug, don't I love thee.
"Ha, ha, ha, you and me,
"Little brown jug, don't I love thee."

After a block or so, Junior got the hiccups. That led
to a fit of giggles. The boys stopped in front of a newly
built house with fancy iron fencing and a swinging gate.
        "Shhh. I know, hic...where we are...hic." Junior
pointed at the house. "That's Constable...hic...Turner's
house. He's one of Uncle Harry's Masons."
        "Ohh, Rabbi Joe's a Mason, too." Ikey was
whispering. "This is perfect. He knows both men who
aren't the boss of us." A low, deep laugh escaped. "Ya
wanna lift him?"
        "Oh, yeah." Junior knew what liftin' was, though
not done it.
        The boys left the gate three houses down. They
never saw the parlor curtains move.
        The third night Junior called his "Good night" up
the stairs as usual and walked in his room. Shutting the
door behind him, he went to the mirror. Running his fingers
through his straight black hair, he admired his reflection.
"Lookin' good, lover boy," he told himself.
        Junior slid his window open and was half way out
headfirst when his world came to an end.
        Squeak. Slam. Smash. The windowpane crashed
down. He was half in, half out, pinned like a badger in a
trap.
        "Boy." He heard his Aunt Ada behind him. "Boy."
He felt the first blow.
        "Owww. Owww. Get me out."

149

Aunt Ada's broomstick found his bottom again.

"Owww. Stop. Please stop. Owww."

"You." Swack "Will." Swack "Not." Swish, swack. "Ever, ever do that again."

"No, Auntie, no," the boy screamed. "I won't ever drink beer again. I promise."

Down crashed the handle. "Drink beer? You've been drinking beer?" The blows got harder. "All I know about is you moving Constable Turner's gate." Swack. Crack. The broomstick broke in half. With the broom end, she continued with, "You. Will. Not. Be. A. Hooligan." Brandishing her broken weapon, Ada stomped out of the storeroom, leaving the crying boy still caught in his trap.

"Son." The voice was not Aunt Ada's. Junior raised his head. "Son. You have broken your Auntie's broom and my trust." Uncle Harry was standing out in the yard. He squatted so that he was looking straight into Junior's eyes. "When I open this window, you will pack your valise. You can no longer stay under our roof."

Junior stared. Uncle Harry's eyes did not blink. "But, but it wasn't my...."

"Shut your mouth." Uncle Harry pulled open the window and shoved the boy back in. "Shut your mouth and get your stuff. Now."

Constable Turner stood waiting by the cashier counter. With a nod to Harry, he handcuffed Junior and took his things. Once at the jailhouse, the officer silently removed the cuffs and pushed Junior into a small dark room at the back of the jail. He threw his valise in after the boy. There was only a transom over the door and not one window. Unlike a cell, this room had no cot or blanket. A rusty pail stood in the corner.

"Boy." The constable had no nonsense in his voice. "That there bucket's your necessary. Don't piss the floor. That's where you sleep." The door slammed behind him.

Junior heard the key turn. The room was dark, darker than the thoughts of hell. The boy stepped back and felt the wall. Finding his grip, he slid down beside it and pulled it into his arms. He cried holding and rocking his belongings like a baby.

"Mama, oh Mama," he crooned. No one answered.

Chapter Twenty-Two
October, 1901
Judgment Day

Telegrams flew between Galveston Island and LaPorte. A plan was made. Every adult agreed, including Constable Turner. Junior was to remain in the closet, his only air and light coming from the open transom, eating bread and drinking water for however long it took the *Sallie Lou* to return. Then there would be court time with a judge, a very special judge.

Beatrice Turner let him out of his hellhole the third day.

"Child."

The light from the opened door startled Junior. He squinted. There was a round, white-headed lady standing there. It looked like she'd forgotten her skirt. As his eyes adjusted, he realized she was wearing men's overalls.

"Uh, Ma'am?" He stood. "Ma'am?"

"Yes, child, I am Mrs. Turner, Mrs. Constable Turner." She took a few steps in. "Smells like you might be needin' to empty your slops. Get your bucket and follow me."

Mrs. Turner led Junior past the cells and out back to the privy. "Dump your mess, do your business if you want, and rinse your bucket at the pump. I'll wait here." She stood, never taking her eyes off the boy. "Oh, dear Jesus, he is so young," she murmured to herself. "Bless his heart." She fixed her face to a scowl and called out, "There's soap in that-there can by the pump. Wash up. You need it."

Junior did all that he was told.

"Come on, boy, the judge is here." Mrs. Turner's voice sounded rough. "He's not gonna want to wait."

Junior stood still. "Judge? What, what judge? I... uh... I..." his voice trailed.

"Yes, a judge. You broke the law. Gate lifting is a crime." *Well, in this situation it is.* "Step on it, time's a wastin'. Y'all gotta pay for what ya did." Mrs. Turner took the child's arm and firmly led him back through the jail. Walking past the cells, they turned left out the front and entered the next door down.

It was a courtroom, brand new built. There was a man in a black preacher's robe, sitting behind a big desk. He was holding a wooden hammer. Short walls with chairs behind came out from each side of the desk, but no one was using them. Junior stared. The sunlight from one window barely lit the desk. No lamps or electric lights glowed.

"Come here." The judge sounded loud in the empty room. "Come here and state your name."

Head down, scared steps took Junior to the desk.

"Look at me, boy, and state your name."

"Everett Gallaway, Junior." His head jerked up. The judge's eyes looked funny. "That's my daddy's name. Everybody calls me Junior."

"I will call you Everett." The judge did not smile. "Everett, sit in that box over there." He pointed with his hammer. "Now."

Junior walked behind the barrier. The chair was too big for him. Once seated, legs dangling, he looked straight ahead. In the gloom of the back row of benches, he saw his family enter, all of them, including his stepfather, CB Ledbetter. Constable Turner was behind them.

"Mama." Junior started crying. His mother sat silent, tears dripping on her sleeping baby.

Down came the hammer.

BANG.

"Quiet, prisoner." The judge shifted himself behind his desk. "Who brings charges against this man?"

"But, but, I'm a boy." Junior's voice echoed in the room.

"Quiet, prisoner. Do you have a hearing problem?"

"No. It's just that I'm a boy."

BANG.

"I repeat, who brings charges against this man?" The judge looked at Junior, daring him to open his mouth.

Constable Turner stood. "I do. Your honor, may I approach?"

"Yes."

Robearde Turner, dressed in his Sunday uniform, walked straight to the other side and stood behind the short wall. "Judge, I brought my own Bible for the swearing. Is that acceptable?"

"Of course, hand it to me."

Constable Turner's worn Masonic Bible was passed to the judge. He turned to the boy. "Stand."

Junior obeyed.

"Raise your right hand and put your left on the Bible."

Junior obeyed.

"Do you swear to tell the truth to this court, so help you God?"

Junior nodded.

"Speak up, man." The judge did not sound happy.

Junior pouted his lower lip. "Yes. Sir."

"Sit." The judge turned to the constable. "What are your charges?"

"Criminal mischief and drunkenness, your honor. This young man was obviously inebriated when he lifted my new wrought iron gate. It was found several houses down the next day."

The judge scratched his bearded chin. "How do you know he was drunk?"

"Mrs. Turner and I watched the whole event from our open parlor window. He was weaving and singing 'Little Brown Jug'."

"I know that tune." The judge nodded to the constable. "That's a drinking song, all right." He turned to Junior. "Can you deny these charges?"

"Um, no sir, but…"

"But what?" the judge snapped.

"But I wasn't by myself. If Constable Turner saw me, he saw Ikey." Junior's pout was getting stronger. "Why isn't he sitting up here, too?"

The judge carefully stood and leaned toward Junior. "I don't care if the entire island of Galveston was with you. You are the one being charged. You are the one who was turned over to the law. You are the one who is sitting in the hot seat. And you, young man, are the only one I am talking to." The judge sat with a hard thump and a huff. He swiveled to the other side. "Thank you, officer. You may step down."

The court room fresh cut floorboards squeaked as Robearde Turner joined the rest in the back of the room.

"Stand, young man. I have decided your punishment."

Junior stood, his hands tight around the rail atop the wall in front of him. His shaking knees were hidden, but his defiant tears were not.

"I, Judge Calhoun, sentence you, Everett Gallaway, Junior, to one complete voyage as deck boy on the merchant vessel, the *Sallie Lou*. You will be directly commanded by Chief Mate, Sure Foot Ledbetter. You will leave this room and go directly to the ship."

BANG.

"Court is closed." The judge stood and, using a cane, shuffled slowly down the middle aisle. Everyone except Junior saw him wink at CB.

Chapter Twenty-Three
October 23, 1901
Shipped out

Junior's arms and legs were frozen. *Whaaaat? Did he say I had to go to sea with CB? No, no, no.*

CB walked to the front of the court. Junior had never seen him in full uniform. "Young man, my name is Sure Foot Ledbetter."

"Huh?" Junior was beyond confused. "You're CB. You married my mama."

"I repeat, my name is Sure Foot Ledbetter. I am Chief Mate of the *Sallie Lou*. Judge Calhoun has handed me your custody. You are sentenced for one voyage as deck hand under my command. You will call me Chief Ledbetter. Do you understand?"

"Uh, yes."

"Yes, what?"

"Yes, sir." Junior felt his arms and legs start to tingle, a signal that he would start shaking again if he didn't soon move. "Uh, Mister Chief Ledbetter—"

"Call me Chief."

"Chief, may I go see my mama?"

"We board soon. I'll tell you when time's up." Sure Foot took the boy by the shoulder and walked him to the back benches.

"Mrs. Ledbetter, your son needs to say some things to you." Sure Foot stood by the door.

"Thank you, Mr. Ledbetter." Myra's eyes sparkled with tears and mischief. She handed Flossie Mae to Aunt Ada and held out her arms to her eldest, pulling him to her lap. Myra noticed that Junior's feet almost touched the floor in their embrace.

"Son," Myra cooed. "My big boy."

"Mama," Junior sniffled.

"This is the second time a child of mine's seen the inside of a jail."

"Mama." Junior snuffed up his runny nose. "Mama, it wasn't my fault. Ikey——"

"You got caught. Enough said." Myra pulled his head to her bosom and stroked his thick black hair. "You look just like your daddy, God rest his soul. You will not shame his name." She smoothed the hair from his forehead and kissed him. "You may not know it yet, but your Daddy CB, Chief Mate Sure Foot Ledbetter, loves you like all get out."

"Mama," Junior's words were muffled. "Mama, he is not my daddy."

"I know, sweetheart, but he is my husband, and that ain't changin'." Myra gently pushed her son from their embrace, turning his head to look eye to eye. "I'm going to tell you two truths. You will never get your daddy back. You will never be the oldest male in our household again."

Junior poked out his lower lip. "But...but... Mama, I hate him. He changed everything."

"Yes." Myra smiled. "He changed everything. He made us whole."

"Deck Hand Gallaway." Junior startled. Chief Sure Foot Ledbetter was holding the boy's valise. "Stand and kiss your family, time to board."

Myra and Ada crushed him between them and almost bumped heads as they tried to cover him with goodbye kisses. Junior hugged his baby sister and reluctantly shook his uncle's hand.

"Wait by the door; I need to kiss my family, too. Here, take your things." CB pulled off his uniform cap, swooped up his wife, and gave her a 'you are mine' kiss that said it all. He petted Flossie Mae and smiled at Aunt Ada and Uncle Harry.

Uncle Harry grabbed his hand and pumped it hard. "Fair seas, my nephew, fair seas to all."

CB touched his brow in a salute. "Aye aye, sir. I will keep him safe."

Cap back in place, Chief Ledbetter escorted his ward away from the courthouse and down to the docks. Not one word was exchanged the entire time.

Junior was shown his hammock and the head by a sailor with three earrings. The boy left his things and went straight to the necessary. He'd been in a two-seater at school, but nothing as big as this. The long row of porcelain toilets with buckets beside them was all new to him. Peeing was easy, it went in the hole. He figured the buckets with water to wash things down if you left a mess. *I wonder where it goes. Guess I'll find out soon enough.*

His hammock was strung between two posts down in the hold. "You don't get to sleep with the crew. You're a punk kid and don't belong." The earrings swung as the sailor walked away.

Four bells rang. Junior saw all the men walking toward the same place, and he got in the line. Each carried a plate, cup, and utensils. "Jeezy Pete, I'm hungry," Junior said aloud. He felt a hand on his shoulder and startled. The hand squeezed.

"Don't turn around," whispered a voice behind him. "Just listen. Your stepdaddy is Chief Ledbetter. I am First Mate Smith. You are Everett." The hand squeezed a little tighter. Junior nodded. "The men won't like it if they find out we know you. They'll turn on you quicker 'en you can say 'Bob's your uncle'. Understand?" Another nod. The hand and Jack Smith left the line.

Cookie was putting out ladles of beef stew, red beans and rice, and huge slabs of corn bread. The sights and smells of that fine food made him so hungry. Junior's stomach reminded him that he had not seen anything but bread and water for what seemed like a month o' Sundays. He had no plate. He didn't know how to eat stew without a bowl, but he was gonna try if he could.

"Who are you?" The cook looked hard at the boy. "Why are you in chow line? And without your mess kit? You one of them stowaways?"

"No." Junior's voice barely sounded. "I'm—"

"Gentlemen." The voice spoke from the galley door.

Junior's head jerked at the sound. He knew that voice. All hands looked up. The Captain never came to galley.

"This new boy is Everett Gallaway. Cookie, give him a kit and feed him good. He's gonna need it." Captain Calhoun paused. "Men, I trust you will show him the ropes, but he will answer to Sure Foot only. Don't think you got yourself a personal slave." The mess hall was dead silent. "This boy was ordered to be here by a judge. I say it's a heap better than lock up. What you all say?"

"Aye aye, Cap," the men called in unison.

Captain walked up to Cookie, took two pieces of cornbread on a plate, and turned to Junior and whispered, "Yes, it's me." He nodded to the stunned boy and left.

Cookie filled Junior's plate with sailor-sized portions. Junior ate everything, tasting nothing. Belly full, he went straight to his hammock where he cried himself to sleep. His dreams were filled with visions of traps. The rats caught all had straight black hair.

Chapter Twenty-Four
October, 1901
One Step at a Time

Junior woke up just before he hit the floor. Face down. He caught himself with his elbows right at the hurting part. When he stopped seeing stars, he rolled over. Two strangers in regular clothes stood above him. One of the men was really fat, and they were holding Junior's hammock high.

"Hey, kid, how'd you get this? Nobody else got one."

Mr. Fat Man was hangin' on to the hammock, swaying. His rope-holding buddy seemed to be dancing with him.

"Huh?" Junior tried to stand. He felt like he'd been drinkin' beer.

"Houthu get a hammock? You payth ethtra?" Rope Holding Buddy had missing teeth. His tongue kept popping out when he talked. They dropped the hammock.

Back on his feet, the boy started doing the same dance as the other men. "Are we moving?"

"Been." Fat Man offered his hand. "Howdee, my name's Ollie. My friend here's called Jake."

Junior tried to shake but missed the hand offered. "Name's Ju…uh, Everett. You two sailors?"

"Thit, no, we're prothpectors." Jake scratched his stubbled chin. The three seemed to be getting the same sway rhythm going. "I didn't know those two thowed kids, too."

"Yeh, them sommybeaches must be hard up to stowaway a kid. How much did you give 'em?" Ollie seemed to be standing still, with his backside against a pillar and legs wide apart. Junior started to answer.

"I'm a—"

"Gallaway, who you talking to? Chief wants you topside."

Junior jerked around. A uniformed sailor stood at the door. Junior looked over his shoulder. No sign of Ollie and Jake. "Nobody, I was talking to nobody."

"Well, come on, kid, we ain't got all day. You can talk to nobody on your own time." The sailor stood still. "I'm 'sposed to escort you. Just what in hell did you do that you gotta be escorted?"

Junior tried to walk and barely made it three steps when he fell sideways, landing flat on the deck. "Ouch. I didn't do anything, Ikey did."

"Get up, landlubber, can't walk on your butt." The escort continued to wait.

Junior pulled himself up another pillar. Holding tight to the post, he tried to stay standing.

"Bend your knees, lubber. Let's go." The sailor walked toward the boy. "Watch me." It seemed as though the man was walking on dry land. "You'll get your sea legs soon." He held out his arm and Junior grabbed tight. The escort rearranged them so the man supported the boy. They made it out into the gloomy morning without any further spills.

Chief Mate Ledbetter stood on the deck. "Thank you, sailor."

"Aye aye." The sailor disengaged Junior's arm. "Sir?"

"Yes?"

"He's a lubber."

"I see."

Junior wobbled straight to the rail, hung his head over the edge, and lost what was left of last night's chow.

Sure Foot stood beside him, but not too close. "You done?"

"No. I. Am. Not." Dry heaves broke the sentence. Raising his head, he looked at the man his mother called 'husband.' "Help me. I. Am. Dying." Vomit hit the deck, splashing his own shoes but luckily, missing Sure Foot all together.

"See that full water bucket over there?" Sure Foot pointed beside a coil of rope. "Get it and rinse my clean deck. We're going to see Cookie."

"Can't eat." Junior stumbled behind the Chief, pukin' in the empty wash pail as he walked.

"Come on, Cookie'll fix you up. Can't have you too weak to work." Sure Foot walked ahead to the galley.

Jack met them half down the passageway, saw the bucket, and raised his eyebrows. " I'll get him to Cookie. Can't have the men wonderin' why you are carin' for a puker."

With a grateful smile, Sure Foot headed off to Captain's quarters. *Probably some pukin' there, too.*

Cookie installed Junior in a makeshift bed atop two bags of beans in the galley pantry and exchanged his pail. Junior couldn't lift his head, let alone the bucket. He kept the boy in the galley all day, giving him alternative doses of peppermint tea and ginger syrup, all the time working at the stove. His mess hands ignored Junior. Cookie had dosed lubbers before. Junior spent the night on the beans, covered with an old apron. He never knew Sure Foot and Jack pulled chairs to the pantry door, sleeping close by 'just in case.'

Cookie always arrived before his mess hands, way before sunrise. Just like the captain, Cookie had known the two sleeping officers since they were nine years old. It made no sense to him that they would guard this boy.

"Sure Foot. Jack. Wake up." Cookie clanged his biggest stew pot lid right in front of them. "Why are you in my galley?"

"The boy," answered Jack, sittin' up and stretchin'.

"You two better tell me what's going on. Captain has never taken on a kid crook before. Who the hell is this boy?" Cookie's ladle found its mark once again on the lid.

Sure Foot grabbed for the spoon. "Stop banging. Don't wake him."

"Who is this kid?" Cookie did not relinquish his drumstick. "You two need to tell me now."

"He's Myra's boy, my stepson."

"And my step-nephew," added Jack, looking around. "You got coffee ready?"

"Hell, no, been too busy waking y'all up. Give me a minute to get the fire hot. Talk to me while I work."

Sure Foot and Jack pulled the chairs close to Cookie as he worked. Quietly, so that no one else could hear, Sure Foot told everything, including the anger at home, sneaking out, beer drinking and gate lifting. "There was a mock court run by Captain Calhoun and punishment assigned." Sure Foot sighed. "The boy hates me for loving his mama. Myra and I thought Junior and I might be forced to work things out. We figured he couldn't run away in the middle of the Gulf of Mexico."

"We can't let the men know." Jack spoke wistfully. "Remember how they did me? Some of the men saw my skin and that's all. Ya never know what they would do to him if they thought he wasn't a hoodlum working off his crime. Don't want to wish that stuff on another soul."

"You're right about that. They sure done ya bad until they stopped seein' your color." Cookie ladled boiling water into the china pot, added the filled tea ball, and set it on a tray. "Jack, you stay here. Sure Foot, go serve your captain, if you can wake the sot. Tell him I know and will help."

Sure Foot smiled for the first time in a long time. "Thank you, man. All I want is to turn my son around." He covered the teapot with its quilted cozy, picked up the captain's morning tray, and left.

"Jack, see if you can get the boy up and moving. I'll dose him before he hits the deck." Cookie filled a small pan with water and added some mint. "This tea should help. You get him to the head, and if he doesn't puke, I'll do another spoonful of ginger syrup." He turned from his stove. "Sure Foot needs all the help he can with this new family. I don't know if I could take on all those young'uns."

Jack nodded. "Yep, and a new one, t'boot." Another stretch. "I'll go stir that sleeping bag of bones. Wish us luck on the head walk."

Junior was still curled up on the bean sacks. Jack stood for a second, just watching the child breathe. "Dear Jesus, watch over this boy and keep him safe," he prayed. "Please help him shed the lubber and give him his legs. Amen."

"Amen."

"Good morning, boy. I didn't realize I was talking out loud to the Lord." Jack smiled. "You want to add anything before your amen?"

"God bless Mama, Aunt Ada, and the children. Amen."

Jack raised one eyebrow. "No blessin' Daddy CB or Uncle Harry?"

"No."

"Well, rise and shine. Today you're gonna learn to walk without pukin'. You up to it?"

"Can't stay here. You know, it's just like where Constable Turner locked me up. Closets and me don't get along." Junior struggled to stand. He fell straight into Jack's belly and pitched backward.

Jack caught him by the arms and, holding his elbows from behind, turned him around. "Look straight ahead, not down, not sideways. Bend your knees. Don't worry, I'll hold you. See the door on the other side of the galley? Look at it. Ready?"

164

The trip to the head and back was uneventful. Jack finally released Junior when he sat him in one of the chairs by the pantry door. "Cookie, he's earned his dose. I have to get goin'. Duty calls."

"See you at mess," Cookie told Jack. "Don't know if he'll be eating anything, but you stop by. Maybe some soda biscuits or tack will stay down."

Jack made a quick tip of the hat salute and left. Cookie kept his back to Junior, cutting thick slices of bacon. "So, you're Missus Myra's boy, Junior."

"Uh...uh... my name is Everett Gallaway."

"Yes. Everett Gallaway, Junior." Cookie emphasized *Junior*. "Your dad told me."

"Humph," the boy pouted. "Not mine. That man is not my dad. My father, Everett Gallaway, died of cholera when I was little. Don't need no damn substitute."

Cookie spun around, knife in hand. "Listen, to me, Junior Gallaway. You are in my galley and you will not disrespect any officer on this ship." Cookie took one step toward Junior. "You better clean up your language and—" He stabbed the air with his bacon knife. "You better clean up your heart." He turned and buried the weapon deep in the slab waiting on the cutting table. "Now, git over here so I can dose you."

By evenlight the boy had his legs and his stomach back. Cookie spent the day giving him peppermint tea, ginger syrup, and stories of Sure Foot and Jack's childhood on the *Sallie Lou*.

"You're tellin' me that CB's daddy sold him to the captain?"

"Yessiree, he did. But CB, er Sure Foot, outdid him that day by getting the man drunk and picking his pockets of the money and bond contract Captain gave him. From what I know, Sure Foot would have paid Cap to get him away from that man." Cookie looked over to Junior. "He ever use a belt on you?"

"Oh, Go—uh, goodness, no. He's never even used a switch on me." Junior couldn't hide the shock in his voice. "Did his daddy do that?"

"Him, his sister, and his momma. You are blessed to have the likes of Sure Foot in your house." Cookie wiped his hands on his apron. "His daddy was no daddy. Sure Foot Ledbetter is." He picked up a tin of lard. "You up to walking to your berth? I got cornbread to make for tomorrow."

He reached for the bell rope by the pantry. CLANG. A sailor appeared at the galley door. "Kid was so sick, I doubt he remembers where he supposed to sleep. Show him his hammock. I cured him. Tomorrow he's gonna start doin' his work."

The sailor nodded. "Come on, lubber. Follow me."

Junior snuggled into his hammock. Right before he drifted off, he thought he heard singing. The voices were familiar.

"Just a closer walk with thee,
"Grant it, Jesus, is my plea,
"Daily walking close to thee
"Let it be, dear Lord, let it be."

Junior softly added the counterpoint, "Just a closer walk, just a closer walk." He was privately harmonizing with CB and Mr. Jack. That night the boy dreamt of home, and no one was wearing a belt.

Chapter Twenty-Five
November, 1901
Ollie and Jake

The young prisoner was set to deck work as soon as he proved his sea legs. It kept him busy. He took orders from Jack and only saw CB when he passed through mess, carrying the captain's tray. Junior's black hair was a benefit, as his skin went from inside work white to outdoor work brown, not burnt red. The men taught him how to wrap his head in a kerchief to keep the long hair and sweat away from his eyes.

One midmorning, Junior realized he'd forgotten his head rag and went back to his bunk crate. The man who dumped him that first night was asleep in the hammock.

Turnabout's fair play.

Junior gave the hammock a hearty push. Jake did a fine rock-a-baby, but did not fall out.

"Thit, man," grumbled Jake. "Can't you thee I'm thleeping. Go away."

Junior swung the bed harder. No luck.

"Thop it, just thop it. You're makin' me thea thick."

Junior grabbed the ropes and yanked backward. The hammock stopped moving, but Jake didn't. This time Jake hit the deck, his head bouncing on the wood.

"Jethus, kid, why'd you do that? You don't thleep in the day. Whath wrong with tharin?" Jake rolled over and sat up. "Ollie and me don't have any plathe ta thleep 'thep the floor. You ain't here in the day, tho we take turnth nappin'." Jake yawned and rubbed his head. "I think thath only fair. After all, your bunk ain't hung with the reth of the men, tho you muth not be a real thailor."

"And you two are not real passengers, so there," Junior shot back. "Real passengers have real places to sleep."

"You got us." Ollie sidled from behind a stack of barrels. "We are official stowaways. What are you?" He held out his hand to his buddy. "Come on, Jake, I'll hoist you."

Junior shoved back his hair and tied on his kerchief. "I'm a criminal, and it's not my fault."

"And..." Ollie replied.

"And the other kid got away with it."

"And..."

"And I gotta do my time on this boat."

"And..." Ollie sounded really curious.

"And that's all. Stay out of my bed." Junior headed to the door. "Whatever an official stowaway is, well, it ain't as bad as a time-servin' criminal, so you just better leave my stuff alone."

"But, kid," Ollie started, but Junior was long gone. He turned to Jake. "Flip ya for the rest of the day." He pulled out his lucky nickel. "Heads."

Jake finished his nap behind the barrels, and Ollie was soon snoring in the hammock.

That night, Junior went hunting for the men. He found them sitting close by on a pile of rags, eating the same mess Junior just finished. The boy lit his lantern and sat cross-legged with them, watching.

Ollie looked up from his plate. "Thanks for the light." He gestured to the food. "Want some?"

Junior shook his head and stared. "How did you two get Cookie's chow?"

"We're thowawayths, but we don't tharve. We paid for thith trip." Jake crumbled his cornbread in his beans and rice so'd he could get all the broth.

Ollie smiled. "I guess we better tell you about us now that we know you are a convicted criminal. Don't want no trouble." He reached behind him and brought out two bowls of peach cobbler. "Sure you don't want some? Good stuff, ya know."

Junior leaned back in the rags. "Had some in mess. How'd you get it?" he asked.

The two men looked at each other and gave a slight nod.

"Black Jack. Him and Sure Foot sneaked us on, and Black Jack feeds us." Ollie was talking with his mouth full. "Yum, these peaches are good."

"What? How? Huh?" Junior's words were gone.

"Yeh, them two got us on board in those barrels over there. We're headin' to the gold."

"Where?" Junior still couldn't talk in sentences. Mr. Jack, CB, stowaways in barrels—none of it made any sense.

"Nome, Alathka," offered Jake.

"Uh, um, I hate to tell you this," Junior said slowly. "In school, we learned that Alaska is north and west from Texas. I think we're headed south and east."

"Yep, you're right." Ollie started laughing. "I never thought about it before. We're going bass-ackwards. Come on, Jake we better start swimmin' the other way."

"Uh, you'll never make it back to Texas. You'll drown or get eaten by a shark or whale or something." Junior's concerned tone stopped Ollie's merriment.

"It's all right, kid, we know what we're doing. We're heading to Panama to catch a train across the land strip. Another boat will take us north to Nome." Ollie's face got serious. "We been told what happens to people when they cross those mountains heading toward California. They say the mountains make you eat your dead."

"No, can't be." Junior felt his chow unsettle.

"Yep, we heard it for a fact. A whole group of them named Donner ate each other." Ollie scraped the last of the dessert on his spoon and into his mouth. "Peach cobbler sure beats eyeballs."

Junior ran for the head where he lost his own dessert. When he returned to his spot on the rags, the two gold seekers were playing cards.

"You know how to play faro?" Ollie was dealing.

"No. Never saw it before."

"Well, kid, don't learn. Ya see Jake over there?"

"Yes." Junior watched the men pick up their cards. There was a stack of facedowns between them.

"He got cheated out of his entire stack of traveling money." Ollie laid down two cards and took two from the top of the middle pile. "Them faro dealers are all dirty." He pointed at Jake. "That's how come I punched him."

"Thit, I didn't know." Jake looked at Ollie. "Thand pat."

"That's why we're here now. I gave Sure Foot and Black Jack my traveling money to get us both to Panama." Ollie punched Jake's arm. "Ain't gonna leave my prospectin' buddy behind. We're a team."

"Yeth thir, we're a team." Jake smiled. "Thorry I loth the money."

"Sorry I knocked your teeth out. You'll pay me back when we're both rich."

Junior stood. "I gotta get some sleep. Don't burn the lantern too long." He crawled into the hammock. "Uh, you two?"

"Yeth?"

"What did you do before you became prospectors?"

"Ollie wath an undertaker. I wath a preather 'til I loth my teeth." Jake laughed. "Can't preath without teeth."

Sleep was slow for Junior. This time the dreams were of cannibal snakes, one with no eyes, and one with no teeth.

Chapter Twenty-Six
November, 1901
Tantrums and Truth

Junior found Black Jack at breakfast mess.

"Liar, liar, pants on fire, damn it, Mister Jack."

He slammed his kit on the closest table and ran head first into Jack's chest.

"Liar, liar, liar," the boy yelled.

Junior locked his arms around the man and butted him like a Billy goat. The hall went dead silent. The men watched the skinny, but strong grandson of a slave calmly raise the boy by his elbows and drop him to the floor. Then he scooped up the stunned prisoner, threw him over his shoulder, and nodded to his audience.

"Men, I'll take care of this little problem. Y'all enjoy your grits. Hope Chief doesn't shackle him."

Jack hauled the boy to his own quarters, not CB's. He dumped Junior on the cot and sat beside him, keeping him pinned down with the pressure of one hand.

"What the hell is the matter with you? You gone crazy?" Jack pushed with each word. "You must be plum dumb out of your head."

The boy stared bug-eyed at the man. "Ahh. Gluk. Cah bre." Jack lifted his hand. "Uh...uh...uh." Air went where it belonged. He lay there until the gasping stopped, and then started bawling. "I thought you were good, I thought you were good." The boy rolled on his side, away from Jack, and continued his sobbing chant. He finally fell silent except for a hiccup or two.

Jack waited. "Child, I don't know what's gotten into you. All I know is that kind of behavior won't help." Silence. "You can't lay there all day. Roll over and talk to me."

"No."

"I'm not leavin', so you better start talkin'."

"No."

"Child, 'nuf's enough." Jack stood. With one quick flip, he had Junior rolled and sitting, legs dangling, on the side of the bed. Jack pulled up a chair and sat square in front of him. "Now talk."

Junior took a deep breath and swiped his drippin' nose with the back of his hand. "Him I understand, but you?"

"Me what?"

"You're a worser criminal than I am." Junior spat the words. "You and that worthless pile of shit, CB, are—"

CRACK.

Jack's slap struck the boy's cheek, full force. "You shut your mouth. Now. I will not let you say another word against your stepfather and my friend." He swung his hand back. "You can think or say that filth about me, but you may not curse the one man on this earth who loves you no matter what." Jack lowered his hand, leaned forward, and stared. "Who are you? You can't be Missus Myra's boy. She didn't birth anything the likes of what I been lookin' at."

Junior rubbed his cheek and stared back. "I know about the barrels. I know you two get money from men with no tickets. I met Jake and Ollie."

"Who?" Jack sounded truly puzzled.

"Your stowaways. They told me everything."

"Oh, so that's their names. Never knew." Jack nodded. "It's true. We are just like you, real bad criminals."

"I'm not a real bad criminal." Junior's lower lip started trembling again. "I'm just a boy who got caught."

"Then I guess CB and I aren't real bad criminals, either." Jack stood. "Come on. Let's you and me find the chief. I'm gonna let him handle this." He rubbed his palm. "I'm gettin' tired of hearing your voice, and I'm damned tired of knockin' you around." Jack stepped toward the hallway. "Don't make me pick you up again. Get a'movin'."

Jack swung open his door just as CB was reaching for the latch. Jack gestured with his thumb at his bunk and stepped aside. "He's had a rough day. Hope his face don't bruise too deep. I'm going topside."

CB waited until he knew the door was closed. "I heard all about that temper tantrum you pulled in mess. The men are sayin' 'that punk kid should be put in irons' or at least we drown you." CB scratched his blond head. "I know you have a burr up your butt about me. Why you mad at Jack?"

"'Cause," pouted Junior.

"Not an answer." CB waited.

"'Cause you 'n' Mister Jack sneak men on ship for money. I know you use barrels. I know you feed them. I know you are both dirty criminals." Junior's voice was rising. "My daddy never did anything bad except get sick and die. I'm gonna tell my mama on you." He was screaming. "She'd of never married you if she knew. My mama's gonna divorce you when she finds out you're low down."

"Son." CB put both hands on Junior's knees and leaned into his face, whispering. "You do that. When she is done telling you where that fine house in LaPorte came from and all the other nice things our family has, I think you will sing another tune."

Junior glared back.

CB stood. "Your behavior is out of line. Your extra duties will help you learn why you're here. Go to your workstation. You missed breakfast. Hope you have better manners at dinner." CB waited by the door.

"Oh, by the way, when you tell your mama about me, you'd better call her those same names. After all, your mama and my sister were our man movin' helpers before the hurricane." CB's mouth set straight. "I guess that makes us all dirty criminals." He gestured with his chin toward the passageway. "Son, I love you. Don't make me beat you. Now get to work."

Chapter Twenty-Seven
November, 1901
Cuban Complications

CB and Jack usually didn't spend much time ashore in Cuba, but now they needed to make sure the Havana roll-off would be safe for Carlton's smuggled flour. This commodity was so valuable that extra precautions were needed in case of theft. The sailors knew a declaration of keg content to the deck master would triple the price, due to fees and tariffs. The two officers wore seamen clothes to avoid drawing attention. That didn't work.

"Hey sailor, ho sailor, lookin' for a high time?" The dock whores recognized new meat. Three of them surrounded CB and Jack, speaking English. "Come with us. We can take care of you and your piece of chocolate, too."

"Excuse us, ladies" said CB. "We're busy lookin' for something other than your fine company. Y'all know where the independent rollers stay? We're lookin' for a man to give a little work."

"You'll find the good rollers already workin'. Them at the taverns ain't worth wastin' air talking to 'em." The whore held out empty hands. "They'll rob ya quicker than ya can get your skirt down."

One of the 'ladies' was cozying up the Jack. The rest started moving on since their sister in sin was makin' her claim. She eyed him from toes to nose and back again.

"You sure are one tall piece of candy. You must got a lot of good sweet chocolate to share."

Jack blushed. "I am a married man. My business is hers and hers only." He looked at CB. "Come on, let's get moving."

CB tipped his cap. "Thanks for the warning," he called to the departing woman. "We're looking for

175

someone to trust, paid well, of course." He looked around. "Sure you don't know anyone?"

Jack's admirer spoke up. "My brother works. You say you pay good?"

CB was reaching in his pocket for a five dollar piece. "Yep, where can we find him?" He played with the coin, flipping it between his fingers. He looked at his hand. "Bring him here, and this is yours." One more flash of gold, and the money was gone, safe in his pocket. The whore nodded.

"What's your brother called?" asked Jack. "We can't be talking to a no-name."

"You can't be talkin' to Tomas, anyway. He has *poco* English." The whore smiled. "I'm not a no-name. Call me Terese. Pay more, and I'll translate."

Jack jerked his head. "Come on man, we don't need her or her brother. Time's a wastin'." The two started walking. Five steps later they heard, "I'll get him. You wait."

They did. She got her gold.

Tomas had more than a little English and was quick to understand what was expected of him.

"*Si*, I get barrels to wagon, no questions. Wagon man pay me." He eyed his sister. "She pretty, no? She make you happy. You want her?"

"We don't do that," said CB firmly. He looked at Terese. "When we come back, you get Tomas for us? We'll make sure there's a little something in it for you."

"Naw, I find him for free. He brings me plenty of business. I do the same for him." Terese kissed her brother's cheek. "*Adios*." She disappeared into the crowd of sailors on the wharf.

CB and Jack watched their new employee saunter off. CB chewed the inside of his cheek. "I don't guess we'd better tell Carlton he's paying a whore monger to move his flour."

"Nope, don't guess we'd better." Jack shook his head. "Can you imagine living in a world where it's all right to shop out your sister?"

"Not me." CB looked up to the heavens. "My, ahem, daddy sold me. God knows what would have happened to Flossie if she hadn't gotten away. I am so glad she became Julia." He blew a kiss to the sky.

The two mates were deep in thought as they climbed the plank. They didn't notice Junior swabbing deck, heading the other way. Captain was in his chair, but something seemed off. They hadn't looked at him lately. His hair was almost as colorless as his face. His shirt couldn't button over his belly. He was slumped into himself, snoring.

Jack looked at Sure Foot. "He's either bad drunk or sick. We better check."

"Yeah, I don't think he's been noticable skunked in a long time. Something's wrong." CB and Jack squatted on each side of the captain's chair. "Sir," Sure Foot yelled. "Sir."

Captain Calhoun lifted his lids. Both sailors recoiled. His eyes were deep yellow.

"Dear God, is he a demon?" Jack crossed his fingers. "We gotta get Cookie, he knows everything." Sure Foot looked around and saw a conspicuously turned back. "We might need some help. I'll get the boy. You stay here."

"Hurry."

Sure Foot walked up behind Junior and touched his arm. "Son." The boy continued swabbing. "Son, I need for you to get Cookie."

Junior stopped.

"Why? You gotta feed Jake and Ollie, or didn't they pay you enough?"

Sure Foot felt his muscles tightened, but kept his voice even. "I need you to get Cookie and tell him he is needed topside. I need this done now." His calm voice started to strain. "Captain is sick and needs help. Get Cookie and bring him here. That's an order."

Junior hung the mop, sneered an "Aye aye," and headed to the galley. It seemed forever before he returned, Cookie in tow. Captain was deep asleep. Junior stood to the side and watched.

"Why you call me? You two know how to take care of this."

"Raise his head, look at his eyes. Jack thinks he has a demon." Sure Foot didn't know what else to tell him.

"I am not squattin' down. I do that all day long workin' the stove." Cookie stood straight. "You two lift his chin." Cookies pried open his right eye.

"Oh Jesus, he done did it." Cookie stepped back. He looked at Junior. "Make yourself useful and help these men carry him to quarters."

Sure Foot looked at Cookie. "What is it?"

"Look at him. His skin, hair, eyes, they're all yellow." Cookie wiped his forehead with his apron. "Goddamit, boys, he's done drank his liver to death." He took a deep breath. "And he shit himself. You boys are on your own movin' this one. I'll meet you below with hot water." Cookie headed straight to the galley.

Chapter Twenty-Eight
November, 1901
Our Fathers Whom Art in Heaven

There was no hiding the captain now. All topside stopped their loading and watched. One sailor started wagers on how long it would take to move him. Sure Foot and Jack were seriously stumped. It was going take more 'en two men and a boy to get the comatose captain down to his quarters.

"He's drippin' down his leg," said Jack. "I ain't hoistin' him on my back."

"Me neither, but we gotta get him below quick." Sure Foot stood staring at his captain.

Junior was studying the situation, and remembering. "Mama said that when my daddy got the cholera, she pulled him out of the necessary and into the garden barrow. That's how she got him to the back stoop." Junior circled the captain in his chair. "This is kinda like the same thing. We could push him onto the lift and lower him to cabin deck."

"I think you've got something there." Jack was off, quick to return with a cargo trolley.

"Son, hold the handles steady." Sure Foot and Jack, at arms and legs, slung Captain Calhoun like he was a sack of allspice berries. One of the watching sailors rang for the lift. The barrow full of Captain, Sure Foot, Jack, and Junior rode the slow descent down. Cookie was waiting as they rolled into the Captain's quarters.

"Mama said my daddy was like that, all dirty." Junior looked at Cookie. "Does Captain Calhoun have cholera? Mama said she had to burn everything he touched." He took a step backward. "We went to go live

with Aunt Ada and Uncle Harry 'cause we could catch it."
Junior took two more steps and hit the cabin doorframe.

"This is not cholera." Cookie shook his head. "This
is drink." He looked at Sure Foot. "I think you better
handle this with your boy while Jack and I clean him.
We're gonna need some sort of towel to use as a diaper.
Liver shits don't stop."

Sure Foot gestured with his head. "Come on, son.
Those two have work to do." He walked to the door. "Son,
I have something to tell you." Wordlessly, Junior let his
stepfather lead him to the Chief Mate's cabin. Junior sat on
the bunk and waited. Sure Foot pulled his desk chair close
and began.

"Captain William J. Calhoun saved me when I was
nine years old. That's when Cletus Ledbetter, the man I
used to call Daddy, sold me as a bonded boy." Sure Foot
smiled. "I got my contract and money back before we
sailed. Cookie told me he told you."

Junior nodded. "He did. He also told me about the
belt. I'm sorry about that."

Sure Foot grimaced. "Me, too."

"Thank you for never whipping me."

"I promise that will not happen to anyone in our
family." Sure Foot looked at his hands. "He even hung up
our hound and lashed it to death. Made us watch."

"Jesus…uh…jeez." Junior corrected his cussing.

"Anyway, Captain Calhoun and Cletus both loved
drink. Cletus is dead, someday I'll tell you about it, and my
captain is soon there." Sure Foot put his face in his hands.
"Son, the man who loved me like a real daddy has drunk
himself to the edge of death." Sure Foot started crying.
"I'm losing mine just like you lost yours." He gulped air. "I
love that man. Oh, dear God, I love that man." Sure Foot
did not hold his tears.

Junior sat. Finally, Sure Foot mopped his face and
looked at Junior. "Boy, we need help taking care of

Captain, but if this is too much like your daddy's cholera, just let me know."

"CB." The words came as a whisper. "I was too little to help with my daddy. I am not too little to help with yours. Let's go see what we can do." He stood and saluted. "Come on, Chief, we have work to do." CB followed his boy, still wiping his tears.

Sure Foot couldn't sit vigil. He had a ship to sail. Junior and Jack traded shifts, watching and cleaning their captain. Three days past Cuba, Captain William J. Calhoun opened his eyes. "Boys. Where's my boys?"

Jack jerked his head toward the door. "Run Junior, get your papa. He's with tiller man. Hurry. Tell him Cap is talking."

Junior had him back quicker than two winks. Jack and Sure Foot knelt side by side at their captain's bed. A yellow hand inched from beneath the sheet. Both sailors held it, one woven with the other.

Captain's voice was barely audible. "Look at that. My two boys make a checkerboard. One is black, the other white." A tiny smile showed on his lips. "They said a mixed ship would never sail. Oh, my sons, I'm so proud we proved them wrong." He was breathing shallow gulps. "I want to hear you sing one more time. Would you do that?"

Sure Foot started crying again. He laid his head on that checkerboard of fingers, his blond hair covering the hands. Jack withdrew his and pulled out his harmonica. He began playing 'Softly, Tenderly, Jesus Is Calling.' It was the first song the two ever sang to their captain after Jack learned to play. Sure Foot slowly raised his head. Junior joined and three voices serenaded their captain with the chorus.

"Come home, come home,
"You who are weary come home;
"Earnestly, tenderly, Jesus is calling,

181

"Calling, O sinner, come home!"

Captain weakly gestured toward his desk. "Look in the carved box on my bottom shelf...uh... later." His voice was surprisingly strong. "I love you, boys. I love you." His hand fell, his eyes closed, and he softly, tenderly went home.

CB covered the body with a tear-stained sheet. "I don't know what to do next."

Jack turned to the shelf. "He said to look in the carved box. Maybe he's got private papers or something he wants us to read." He lifted it to the captain's desk. "Should I open?"

CB nodded.

The lid squeaked with the sound of a long closed hinge. There were stacks of envelopes and folded papers. The top sheet was addressed to 'CB Ledbetter & Jack Smith'. It was silently handed to CB. "You're listed first, you read."

CB opened the letter and began:

Dear Boys,

I am dead, but you know that. It's been coming for a long while, but this past year told me it was sooner than later. You boys took very good care of me. Thank you. Now there's one more thing to do. Bury me at sea.

My life was the *Sallie Lou*. I have no relatives. You men are my family. Look for an envelope in the box from the Galveston Port Registrar. I order you, CB Ledbetter and Jack Smith, to have a good life.

William J. Calhoun

Jack took what was next in the box. It was a large business sleeve with their names on the front. He unwrapped the string tie and removed an envelope addressed to Captain William J. Calhoun.

"I'm thinkin' we're supposed to see what's inside."

Jack carefully opened the flap and pulled out a document. He unfolded and silently read it. Without a sound, he crumpled to the floor. CB read the paper and joined his friend.

Junior watched CB Ledbetter and Jack Smith sit in stunned silence, staring at each other. He didn't know what to do, so he sat on the floor with them. Taking the vellum from his stepfather, Junior read aloud the transfer of certificate of enrollment for the merchant vessel *Sallie Lou* and all its contents upon the death of William J. Calhoun to CB Ledbetter and Jack Smith, share and share alike. It was signed and sealed June 10, 1898.

"Jesus." This time Junior did not correct his language. He looked up. "You didn't know?"

"No." CB croaked. "Oh dear God, we didn't know." He looked over Junior's shoulder. "It's dated way before the 'cane. He gave us the *Sallie* years ago, and we didn't know it." He took the paper and put it on the desk.

Jack's eyes got wide. "Wonder how many grandsons of slaves own their own ship?" He chuckled. "Sure wish my daddy could see me now. He wanted me to stay and pick cotton. Heh, heh, heh, I'm gonna ship cotton."

"I can pay the taxes now. No more tavern checker games. No more man movin'." CB sniffled and stood, offering a hand to his long legged friend. "Come on, partner, time to get to business." He nodded to the bunk. "We need to take care of our captain."

Junior looked up from the floor. "I know an undertaker and a preacher. You want me to go get them?"

"How you gonna do that?" asked CB. "We're in the middle of the ocean, not in Galveston."

"Wait right here. You'll see." Junior was out the door before another word was said.

CB reread the document, having not trusted his eyes the first time. No words had changed. The *Sallie Lou* was theirs.

Jack started singing, paraphrasing a well-known plantation song.

"Swing low, sweet *Sallie Lou*
"Comin' for to carry us home,
"Swing low, our *Sallie Lou*,
"We're sailin' on the ship we own."

CB joined with the bass counter of 'Swing low, *Sallie Lou*, Swing Low, *Sallie Lou*.' They were almost ready to high step jig around the room when "Ahem" came loud and clear from the cabin door. The celebrants froze. Cookie stood with his hands on his hips.

"I see you looked in the box."

"How did you know?" asked a puzzled CB.

"Look closer at the registration. I was the witness." Cookie smiled. "He loved the *Sallie Lou* like nothing else except the girl he named it for."

Jack interrupted. "He had a girl? That's news to us." Jack unconsciously touched his chest. "Were they ever married?"

"No," said Cookie. "She was his only sweetheart, but he loved sailing more than anything. She needed a man who would always be at home. Cap told me last he knew she lived on a ranch in Austin." He walked to the bunk. Gently he lifted the sheet and silently said good-bye to his friend. CB and Jack joined him. "You boys know he loved you like sons."

"Yes, sir," replied Jack. "We knew long ago."

CB's tears started again. "He was better than my real daddy."

"I know," said Cookie. "A real daddy would've never sold his son to a stranger and walked away."

"Yeah," added Jack. "A real daddy wouldn't have used his belt on his son's best friend, 'bout killin' him."

Jack and CB looked at each other. Only their wives knew that Cletus B. Ledbetter had been sealed in a shipping keg, bound with his own strap. Two days later the bung was pulled and that foul load was rolled overboard to sink to the bottom.

CB wiped his face on his sleeve. "I am proud of how we were brought up. Captain William J. Calhoun was a good man."

Tap. Tap.

Junior and the stowaways were at the door. "May we come in? I fetched the undertaker and the preacher."

Ollie and Jake were standing in the hall shadows.

"Come in, son, and bring your men with you." CB extended his hand. "Gentlemen, I know we met under different circumstances. Sorry, I don't remember your names." CB nodded to the boy. "Junior said he brought an undertaker and a preacher."

Ollie nodded. "Name's Ollie. Been an undertaker all my grown years until now." He nodded to his friend. "Jake's the preacher, but he don't talk so good. I knocked out his front teeth."

"Yeth thir." Jake shrugged. "I gueth my preathin' dayth are over." He looked at the bunk. "Thunior thed the captain ith dead. He thed you could uth our help."

"We sure do." CB stepped away from the bunk. "Mister Ollie, do you know how to do a burial at sea? Captain Calhoun left written wishes." CB glanced at the wooden box.

"Never done it before, but I was taught by my uncle, and he did one." Ollie looked at the captain's face. "Drink?"

CB nodded. "As long as I've known him."

"In a way that's good. He'll last a bit longer." Ollie looked around. "I'll do it. We need a washbasin, soap, and towel. Does he have a dress uniform? Captains shouldn't be sent out in their birthday suits." He nodded to Jake. "You remember any burying words? We'll need some."

CB and Jack were talking softly in the corner of the cabin. Jack nodded.

"Gentlemen," said Jack. "I remember the night we met. Two for the price of one, thanks to a card cheat." He gestured to CB. "My partner and I have agreed that it is only right that we return your passage fee as payment for caring for our captain. You will get to Panama with money in your pockets."

"Thank you, thir. We thur do apprethiate it, don't we, Ollie?"

"We sure do." He looked back to the corpse. "I'm going to need a hammock, something heavy like bricks, and a sail's needle and thread. You got that?"

"I see y'all got everything under control." Cookie headed to the door. "Come on, Junior. I'll show you where the new hammocks are."

"Uh, could we use the one I sleep in? It's pretty old and, anyway, Jake and Ollie's been hot beddin' it, too." Junior wrinkled his nose. "Those two don't wash, and—" He lowered his voice—"I think they have bugs. Could they have their own for the rest of the voyage?"

"We'll see. Come along, boy, gotta get the sewing supplies," was all that Cookie said.

CB went topside and rang the bell, not in the time giving pattern, but a continuous clanging. Sailors left their stations and gathered on deck.

"Men," Sure Foot's voice choked. "Men, our captain is dead." He lowered his bare head. "Our father, who art in heaven...." The crew pulled off their caps and finished the Lord's Prayer. Their leader raised his head. "He asked to be buried at sea. I'll tell you when at mess."

He turned and left the silent deck, heading to the tiller. He had a boat to sail.

Chapter Twenty-Nine
November, 1901
Eternal Father, Strong To Save

Ollie went straight to doing what he knew. Jake helped with the washing and the dressing. Jack stood by the door, not leaving the two stowaways alone in Captain Calhoun's quarters. He knew there was no trusting those strangers in this place.

"Trim his beard, don't shave it," instructed Ollie. He looked at Jack. "That all right with you?"

Jack nodded, smiling. "He'd want the fishes to recognize him."

Ollie took scissors to the raggedy ends of the beard wisps. "How long this boat been sailin' with him?"

"It was a year in when I signed on in '88. Captain Calhoun bought her new. His daddy had a boat before him." Jack looked around the messy cabin. "She looks older, doesn't she?"

"Yep." Ollie was working at getting the beard even. "I thought she'd been running since the war." Snip. 'There, that looks good."

"Captain did the best he could, considering…" Jack gestured at the yellow face. "CB and I don't blame him for nothing."

"He thur was lucky to have you two thailors in hith crew. I thought colored didn't thail with white." Jake handed Ollie a wet cloth to wipe the trimmed whiskers away. "Why did he hire you?"

"I really don't know. I was a strong kid, so was Sure Foot. I guess he was willing to take a chance. We grew up together. Until we both got married, we called the *Sallie Lou* home."

"Did the captain do it?" Jake passed the towel to Ollie.

"What? Marry us? No. Both of us had a God sanctified wedding." Jack chuckled. "You should have seen that Catholic Priest when CB, that's Sure Foot to you, insisted I be witness. The man 'bout had apoplexy when CB said I was his brother."

"Did the mackerel thnapper let you thine the paperth?"

"Yes sir, he did," replied Jack. "A lot of unusual things happened those few weeks after the hurricane."

"That's the truth." Ollie reached for the comb in Captain's shave kit. "This man's been sick a long time. Look how his hair's breaking. No wonder this ship shows bad."

"We tried." Jack was rummaging in the dresser. "You putting shirt and under drawers on him?"

"Yes. Get a clean set, socks and shoes, too." Ollie stepped back and admired his work. "I think he was a good looking man when he was young. We'll make him a welcome guest at Davy Jones' banquet table."

Jack heard scraping in the hall. Junior was dragging a canvas hammock like a sorry tail behind him. He stopped at the door. "Cookie rolled it up for me to bring, but I dropped it. Pulling the bricks is easier than carrying. Got the needle and thread in my pocket." He looked up. "Mister Jack, do I have to stay here? I'm remembering my daddy and, uh, I got a couple of new beds to hang." He handed over the sewing supplies. "Cookie said those two can keep sharing one between them."

"No, boy, of course not. You go, and thank you for bringing the hammock." Jack gave him a quick hug. "We'll be having the funeral soon. Do you think you could stand through the service? I'm sure Chief would really appreciate it."

"Yes, sir." Junior disappeared the way he came.

"What's so special about that boy?" Ollie was finishing the under dressing. "He told us he was some kind of criminal. Never heard of ships being used as a boy jail."

"He thur don't theme like a bad kid." Jake was separating the dress uniform pieces, shaking off the dust and laying them on the desk. "You an' him frienths?"

Jack touched his finger to his lips. "Shhh, I'm his uncle. CB is my brother."

"Huh? You're colored."

"Remember?" Jack smiled, "we're 'getting CB married' brothers."

"Ooh." Ollie and Jake nodded. "Tho, heth The Bee's boy?"

"Stepson. Needed a lesson taught, and the family thought a voyage would fix him. Captain agreed." Jack added a silent *rest in peace*. "Sure hope it works. He was headin' to a bad way."

The men worked in silence, moving, rolling, and preparing the body. Ollie tried to button the uniform jacket, but had to cut the back. "Can't make it fit over his belly," he commented. The last step was crossing his arms in the final pose. "Time to sew him up," said Ollie. "Say your goodbyes,"

"Already have." Jack stepped to the bell pull and rang the chief mate signal. "CB will be here soon. Let's wait for him."

"Will do." Ollie looked around the cabin. "We're going to need a plank to tip him. You got anything close by? Me 'n' Jake can't go wandering around looking."

"We'll find something when CB gets here." *I'm not leaving Cap to go find some board.* "We'll get him laid out," he said aloud.

"Yes?" Sure Foot was at the door.

Ollie gestured to the bed. "Gotta sew him up. You want some time."

Sure Foot approached the man he loved, the man he thanked for making him all he was today. Jack stepped up beside him, and slowly they raised their hands in salute. Standing at attention, CB's voice faltered and then grew strong. The two sang.

"Rock of Ages,
"Cleft for me,
"Let me hide myself in thee;
"Let the water and the blood,
"From thy wounded side which flowed,
"Be of sin the double cure;
"Save from wrath and make me pure."

"CB, I'll be back with a plank." Jack walked to the door. "Want me to tell Cookie? He can let the men know it's soon time."

"Tell him to feed 'em fast. I'll ring 'all hands' when we're ready to go." Sure Foot wiped a tear. "Thank you, you two, for this fine job. Uh, Jake, you sure you can say the funeral words? I'd understand if you didn't."

"Oh, no thir, I can thay the preather parth juth fine."

"Then you will." Sure Foot stepped back as the two stowaways wrestled Captain William J. Calhoun into the hammock. Ollie put bricks around the body and began sewing the canvas closed.

Jack soon returned with a sturdy board. All four lifted the shroud and laid the captain flat.

"I'll ring the men." CB began a continuous pull on the Captain's bell rope. He rang a full five minutes.

Each man took a corner of the plank and carried the body to the lift. A sailor was waiting. Soon all were topside. The entire crew stood at parade. Junior was with them. A low murmur rose at the sight of the strangers. The pallbearers placed the board on the rail, feet first. Jake stood by the head and nodded. Cookie spoke.

190

"Men, these two *passengers*, Undertaker Ollie and Reverend Jake, have been of great help. We are lucky to have such talented *passengers* on this voyage." The emphasized *passengers* said it all. Cookie came forward and took Jake's place at the pall.

Jake turned to the crew. The man facing the sailors stood preacher tall, preacher proud. His voice boomed. "The lord ith my thepherd, I thall not want." All joined in to finished the psalm. Jake stepped back to the board. "We commit thith man unto the thea."

He began lifting his end and the men understood. Captain William J. Calhoun slid into the ocean he loved, sinking swiftly out of sight. All stood at salute.

CB and Jack went straight to Captain's quarters. Jack stripped the bunk of the death sheets while CB tidied the desk. He secured the letter of transfer in its envelope and put the box back on the shelf. A soft knock and a response of 'enter' brought a sailor with a tray of mess for each.

"Uh, Chief, sorry about the captain," the sailor said. He looked at the food and winked. "Cookie orders you two better eat."

"Thank you, sailor, tell him we will." CB looked at the laden tray. "Did he send any coffee for those cups?"

"Yes, sir, left it in the hall. Couldn't carry a tray, a coffee pot, and knock all at the same time, you know." He set the tray on the cleared desk. "Be right back."

"Thank you. Let the men know we will be here most of the night in case I'm needed."

The sailor saluted and left. Jack pulled up the side chair and poured them cups of that strong coffee they'd used to sober their captain. "Looks like Cookie knows what we need to do."

CB sat at the desk, took a bite of black-eyed peas and a swig of the brew. He looked at his friend. "Man, we're in a shit pot of trouble."

Chapter Thirty
Late November & Early December, 1901
Change of Command

Jack set down his fork. "Shit pot of trouble? How's that? We own this boat. You can pay the house due, and I can be a cap…" His voice trailed. "Oh, yeah, I forgot. Two can't captain the same ship, and I'm colored."

"That's what I'm talkin' about, my friend. *We* are in a real bad pickle. You can't captain a white ship. There'd be instant mutiny." CB bit into his biscuit. "Heck, there may be mutiny when the men find out who owns this boat. Some still remember their daddy's Rebel stories. I can hear 'em now. 'No goddam nigger's gonna give me my pay.' Some of 'em sleep under blankets done up like Confederate battle flags." CB mixed his rice with Cookie's good gravy. "You'd think their kin was on the winnin' side."

"Yeah, and I thought my kin was." The sparkle in Jack's eyes was gone. "Just because my skin is brown… shut up, Jack Smith, nothin' you can do about it." He put his head in his hands. "Nothin' you can do about it," he repeated.

"We gotta take care of this." CB poured himself some more jamoke. "The paper has both our names on it. It says 'share and share alike,' and we will." He poked at Jack's arm. "Hey, what 'cha think of this? I tell the men that the paper says I own it and keep my mouth shut about you."

"Cookie knows."

"Cookie ever treat you bad? Call you names? Short your tray?" CB laughed. "Damn it, man, he even stopped calling chocolate cake 'brownies' so the men wouldn't get after you. Calls them 'tasty delight bars'."

"Well, that's dumb." Jack raised his head. "I never knew why he used such a fancy name. He did that for me?"

"Yep. If you think about it, Cookie's taken care of us as long as the captain has." CB grinned. "Remember when he used his best boning knife to dig that bullet out of your butt?"

Jack's sparkle returned. "Yep, you deserved that broken nose for shooting me. Hmmm, never thought about it before. Cookie is like another dad to us."

"Uh huh, guess we needed two. He'll keep this quiet." CB scraped his last bite of stew. "Come on, man, eat up. We got work to do. I can't captain a ship if I don't even know what's in her quarters."

Jack started his chow. "Excuse me, Captain Ledbetter, who's your best man?"

"You are, Chief Smith. Always was, always will be."

"Men'll gripe at that one."

"Tell them to take it up with the captain." CB looked at the high shelf. "Want to have a toast? Cap taught me about brandy."

"Might as well." Jack wrinkled his nose. "Does it taste like whiskey? I hate whiskey."

CB poured a splash of the liquor into their coffee. "Worse." They clunked their mugs and drank.

By morning, CB was set up in the captain's quarters and Jack's gear was in the chief's. CB kept Cap's reminder chain hanging on its hook. *No need to take it down. I can use it to remember him.*

Neither man slept. First light, they headed to the galley. Cookie thought the plan would work. CB Ledbetter was now Captain of the *Sallie Lou*, Jack Smith was Chief Mate, and the dual ownership would remain secret. After a quick plate of left over biscuits and red gravy, Jack fell asleep in his chair, and Cookie let him. Without a word, he grabbed his butcher knife, an empty coffee pot, and followed CB into the hall.

The new captain stretched his full five foot four inches as tall as he could. He quietly cleared his throat. "Gentlemen." The din of mess covered his voice. CB looked over to Cookie and nodded.

Bang. Klang. Cookie whacked the galvanized pot with the side of his knife. All heads turned.

"Gentlemen, this is your Captain speaking." A slow rumble of voices rolled through the room. 'Klang' went the coffee pot. Silence prevailed. "Our late William J. Calhoun deeded the *Sallie Lou* to me. Cookie witnessed the transaction."

Cookie raised his knife. "Captain had me sign the papers with him in 1898. This young man did not know about it until last night." He stepped closer to the tables, brandishing his knife. "Mr. Calhoun had no heirs, no family. CB owns this ship straight up and legal." He waved the weapon over the tables. "Any questions?"

Dead silence.

"Gentlemen, I have appointed Second Mate Smith to Chief. He knows everything I know about the charts. We learned from the best." CB felt his throat start to close. "Men, I promise to honor our dead captain. I,…ahem,…ahem, thank you for your,…ahem,…help during this time." CB teared. "I will miss him."

He turned and walked back to the galley. Cookie lowered his knife and followed. The noise of hungry talking men filled the hall. Cookie heard 'nigger' and 'ass-kisser' but kept those words to himself, only hoping CB didn't hear. CB did.

The two tiller men soon learned that CB was right. Chief Smith knew his charts. The long route to Panama was easy sailing. The straight voyage south past the Cayman Islands and east of Honduras and Nicaragua would be good practice for Jack. He knew the return north with all those port stops, would be his sailing come-to-Jesus. And, by God, he wanted to prove he could lead the choir.

CB was working Captain's Log. He found that Mr. Calhoun kept two, one for the harbormaster and one for the truth of the matter. CB learned his captain was running rum that first year when he was nine and Cap gave him the key to the side locker. That's where the supply of brandy was. It was also filled with cases and cases of undeclared hooch. The boy grew up moving liquor boxes. Captain always said CB's legs were short enough to stand in his closet. The second log was proof of that endeavor. William Calhoun had moved many hundreds of thousands of dollars' worth of contraband since 1887.

"Where the hell is it?"

"What?" Jack was standing at the cabin entry.

"Didn't realize I was thinking out loud." CB gestured with his head. "Come in and shut the door. You gotta see this."

The two poured over the pages. There were fifteen years of records. Jack spoke. "Remember when we were moving a lot of men, and we were taking jewelry?"

"Yeah." That special cloud of grief for his sister flashed over CB's eyes. "And…"

"We couldn't spend what we didn't earn. Captain Calhoun probably couldn't either." Jack stood and started pacing around the desk. "That money must be here somewhere." He stopped and stared at CB. "I bet his cash is on this ship. Jesus, man, there might be a ton of gold stashed away in these boards." He walked to the wall by the bunk and started rapping his knuckles up and down, listening. "He might have it hidden in this room. That money is ours."

"Shhh," CB cautioned. "Somebody will hear you knockin' and wonder what in the world's happening in this cabin. We don't want nobody knowin' about nothin'." CB shut the ledger. "I'm going to hide this book."

"Is there a load of liquor in the locker right now? I'm thinkin' Captain didn't plan to die. You got the key?" Jack held out his hand.

"Dang, man, you're too tall to fit. I'll go look." CB stood. "Me goin' in and out of that closet when he was alive was one thing. Everybody knew I was fetching his brandy. Now there is no cause for me to go in there." He opened the door, looking both ways. "You stand watch, can't draw attention."

Jack did not see a soul. He also didn't see the shadow.

CB was back quick. "Jeez, man, it's packed full. What in the world are we gonna do with it? The tradin' was one thing he never taught me." He pocketed the key. "You ever hear him talk about the tradin'?"

"No." Jack looked at the desk calendar. "We got three days 'til Panama. That'll give us time to think."

"You reckon Cookie knows?"

Jack nodded. "Probably. Better I talk to him instead of you. Men are used to not seeing their captain."

"By the way," CB cricked an eyebrow, "why are you down here? Hiding from someone?"

"Oh dang, I forgot. Come to tell you to get topside. Weather's up. Flags are telling our future."

CB closed the other ledger and put them behind their favorite book, *The Tales of King Arthur*, setting the book title straight up, keeping the shelves neat. Jack nodded acknowledgement of the hiding place, and the two climbed up into a brewing squall.

Sailors were already making sure nothing was loose. They needed no orders. Jack stopped being Chief and started being Mate. CB watched his men do what they did best, work together. Then he realized something. Junior was not with them.

"Where's that boy?" he hollered to one of the sailors. The man shrugged and kept moving. "Anybody see the boy?"

"With Cookie," came a reply, yelled over the wind. "Been pukin'."

"Thank you, sailor, glad he's not overboard. Didn't want to go fishin' in this water." CB left the deck and headed for the galley. Junior was back in the pantry with a bucket.

"Storm gettin' you?" CB sat on a sack of beans next to the boy.

"Uh huh." Junior looked up from his puke pail. "Thought I was over this."

CB smoothed the boy's stringy hair back and took out his own kerchief. "Raise you head, son. Let me get your hair out of the way." Junior let CB wrap his head, which went right back into the scuttle. "I'm sure Cookie will get you dosed up. See you on deck when you are able. We need all hands."

CB left him to his misery, knowing the boy wouldn't be leaving the galley any time soon.

Chapter Thirty-One
December, 1901
Ship Rats

It was a regular blow and was gone in a few hours. Cookie covered the boy and let him sleep on the beans. The crew changed watch, and the tired sailors enjoyed their hard-earned rest. CB and Jack headed to their cabins. CB found his door ajar.

"Gotta be more careful," he said to himself. "Left too fast, I guess." He shut the hatch behind him.

Stripping down to his shirt and drawers, he turned to his bunk. Right in the middle was a dent. It looked like someone had stepped on his blanket. He froze and cursed under his breath. Quickly he looked all around. The room seemed in order, so CB began to relax.

Maybe Jack leaned on it while we were talking.

He pulled loose the bedding and hit the sack. CB's sleep was quick and easy after being awake for the last twenty-four hours.

It was Jack who woke him. "Hey, man." Jack pulled his arm. "Rise, shine, give God the glory, glory," he sang.

CB opened his eyes and smiled. "Children of the Lord," he responded. "What time is it?"

"Not sure, but the sun is high, and we are dry. Up and at 'em." Jack went back to the song. "Rise and shine and *clap* give God the glory, glory, children of the Lord."

CB was sitting on his bunk side when he remembered last night. "Uh, yesterday did you get on my bunk while we were talkin'?"

"Huh?" Jack was on the verse about 'come on children, don't be weary' and it was at camp meeting volume, hands wavin' in praise. "Say what?"

"I asked you if you had been on my bunk yesterday."

"Why would I do that? Got me a real bed of my own." Jack stopped his revival. "What's going on?"

"Not sure. When we went up to the storm, did you see me shut my cabin?"

"Nope,"

CB stretched. "Found the door open and a crevice in the covers." Standing, he scratched a spot on his arm. "Looks like I done got bit by something."

"Not surprised." Jack looked at his buddy's straight blond hair. "Want me to check you? That's one good thing about being colored. We don't get lice, we're too curly."

"Naw, not crawlin'." CB started dressing in fresh clothes. "Did I give you the key for your cabin?" He pulled his middy over his head.

"No, where is it?" Jack started rummaging on the desk. He reopened William Calhoun's box. CB heard the lid squeak.

"How did that get there?" CB's arms began to prickle.

"Was sittin' on the desk. Thought you might have put the cabin key in it." Jack kept rootling through the papers.

"Stop," CB was unnaturally loud. "Stop."

Jack raised his hands. "What's going on? I didn't do anything."

"Not you, the box." CB stepped up to the desk. "I know I put that thing back on the shelf." He looked around as though to find something more out of place. "Open door. Messed up bunk. Box on desk. Oh jeezie, Jack, someone was here. Somebody's been in the box."

"Damn it, man," said Jack. "That can't be. All hands were working the deck last night. I checked. Everyone was accounted for."

199

"I don't care if it was the ghost of Davy Jones, someone was in this cabin." CB started digging in his pocket. "Here's your key. Now I gotta find the one for me. I think we got rats."

Jack was wandering the outer edges of the cabin, quietly tapping on the walls. "You hunt your key. I'm checkin' the walls."

CB was getting irritated. "Let that go for now. We got work to do." He looked at his partner. "I gotta find that key. Come on, put your eye on it."

"Aye aye, Cap." Jack did a salute and a high kick with a heel click. He landed and felt his foot slide out from under him. CRASH. That tree tall man fell like timber, landing on his rump. "Oomph. Ouch. What did I step on?"

CB looked at Jack's feet and picked up the cabin key. "Thanks, man, you found it. Must have dropped it heading out to the storm." He scratched his itchy spot and held out his hand to Jack, "Ya need a lift?"

CB made sure the cabin was locked and the two went to galley. Cookie had coffee waiting. "Boy's done bein' sick and gone to work," was all he said about Junior. "You two want grits this morning? There's some good sausage and the netter got a few shrimp for the mix."

"I was wondering if the storm would stir things up." Jack was licking his lips.

"Well, do you?" Cookie was beating the dickens out of the grits, getting them full of air and flavor.

"Sure, sounds mighty fine." CB sat at the galley table. "Cookie, I think there might be a problem." He took a long slug of his brew.

Cookie kept whippin'. "What kind of problem? Sickness? A woman? Nah, that couldn't be it. What else is there?"

"Someone was in my cabin last night."

Cookie stopped. "You didn't lock up?"

"Must not 'of. Came in after the storm to see the door open." CB refilled his mug. "Found what looked like a footprint on my bunk and, this is the bad part, Captain's wooden box had been moved."

"Did you check the liquor closet?"

"Had that key in my pocket. Jack found the cabin key on the floor this mornin' when he fell." CB gestured with his thumb. "You'd think he was eleven, the way he was high steppin' around the room."

"You hurt?" Cookie was back to stirring.

"Nope, landed on my sitter." Jack walked to the stove, looking over Cookie into the pot. "'Bout done? Smells good."

"Soon, now back off. I'm talking to my captain."

CB blushed. "Jeez, I could never be your captain."

"Hell, boy, you're the crew's captain, and I'm part of this crew. Ya better get used to it." He ladled out two bowls of the creamy white stuff. "Little or lots?"

"Lots."

He topped CB's bowl with his shrimp gravy. "What about you, Chief, little or lots?"

Jack nodded at CB's bowl. "Same."

Cookie served his own and sat at the table with his mug. He called 'Chow' to the mess hands waiting in the hall. They carried the breakfast pots to the hungry men. Cookie knew storm fighting had taken it out of them.

"Make sure they eat their oranges," he hollered out the door.

"Aye aye, sir."

Cookie filled his mouth with breakfast and took a big slurp of coffee. "Damn, that goes down good."

"It sure does." CB took another bite. "Shrimp's great. Where did you get that spicy sausage?"

"Picked up a barrel in Havana. You like?"

"Yep. Uh, Cookie, what are we going to do about the cabin?"

Cookie was chewing. "Casing's tough," he observed to no one in particular. "Lock the damn door from now on," he grunted after he swallowed. "Ain't nothing else you can do." He wiped his mouth with his apron. "Now you two finish up and get out of my galley. This sausage's so spicy, I guarantee you won't want to be sittin' next to me in about ten minutes." He burped. "See. It's startin' to talk already."

CB and Jack stayed long enough to scrape their bowls clean. They could hear Cookie's loud digestive dilemma announcement as they walked through the noisy hall. CB elbowed Jack. "Phew, that was close. You go on. I'm going to talk to the men."

Jack nodded and walked out of the mess.

Once again, CB pulled himself tall. "Gentlemen." This time they stopped what they were doing. "Gentlemen, thank you for your hard work yesterday. You all showed your stuff. Huzzah." They all returned the cheer. "Enjoy your breakfast."

CB went straight to his cabin, half expecting the door to be open again. It wasn't. He sat at his desk and worked his charts. Nothing bothered him for the rest of the day except for that danged bite on his arm. By afternoon, even the itch was gone.

Chapter Thirty-Two
December, 1901
One Day Out

One day out to Panama, CB asked Jack to fetch Junior. Things had been smooth enough between them, and CB thought the boy might be wanting to write to his mama. CB wrote letters every night. Some were posted from Havana before the captain died, and each day afterward he sat at the desk, sharing his new life as a captain with his wife. The postal boat from Panama sailed north faster than the *Sallie Lou* because of her stops at Belize and Frontera to trade.

"Yes, sir?" Junior stood at the cabin door. "Am I in trouble?"

"Come in, son. No, you are not." CB gestured to the side chair by the desk. "I'm proud of your work."

The boy's face lit. "Been tryin'."

"I know." CB smiled back. "I was wondering if you would like to write to your mother? Landing's tomorrow and we can send it then. I have a fat packet of letters for her, and you could add yours. That would be a nice surprise."

"I'm not good with spelling."

"Me neither." CB looked serious. "My daddy brought me to the *Sallie* when I was nine. I couldn't read. Jack taught me."

"Really? I didn't know colored—"

"Me neither. He taught me how to read music notes, too."

"That's really somethin'." Junior scratched his head. "Wonder if he taught Missus Marguerite how?"

"Jack told me her mama already knew. Bet Marguerite does, too." CB stood behind the boy. "You let me look at your hair? Saw ya scratchin'."

"Sure. Ollie and Jake are itchin' all the time." Junior was used to his mama checking him. The white nits showed easy on his black hair. "At least I don't have to share the hammock anymore." He felt CB run his fingers along his nape. "That's how mama does it."

"She taught me. Said she wouldn't marry a man supporting an extra family living on his head."

Junior laughed. "Do you see any cousins?"

"Let me get the comb. Looks like you're having a reunion." CB slowly, meticulously got all the critters and nits he could see. "You know what's next."

"Yes sir." He pulled his head rag from his pocket.

"Not that one, probably full of eggs." CB opened his top drawer. "We'll use one of mine. It's clean." He grabbed the oilcan and soaked the handkerchief with kerosene, wringing it out in the basin. "Here ya go, wrap up. Should be done working by morning."

Junior made sure nothin' straggled, 'cause he knew the treatment worked best if the hair got sweatin' hot. "I promise to stay away from matches," he joked.

"So, you want to tell your mama about life on board?"

"Sure, but my belly's talkin'. Must be dinner soon." Junior stood.

BONG.

CB shook his head. "Your belly must have a watch in it."

"Can I come tonight to write? If I don't, it'll be too late."

"Sounds good." CB walked him to the door. "See you after duties."

204

CB picked up Junior's head rag and dropped it in the basin, wetting it with kerosene. "Die, boys, die." He left it soaking.

The day before docking was always busy. The sugar cane from Cuba, designated Panama, needed to be separated from the barrels to be rolled off in Central America. Port day also meant four hour shore leave, and Captain Calhoun always issued partial pay to his men for 'lady visits,' as he called them. CB knew that was something he needed to continue. Problem was, he didn't know how to open the pay safe. The *Sallie Lou* was too small to employ a Purser, and Cap had always handled the money. CB closed his door and moved the shelved books that hid the small safe. He was stumped. It had a combination lock.

"What the heck are the numbers?" He was staring at the knob when he heard a sound in the hall. He put the books back in place just before he answered the knock.

"Come in."

A hand entered.

"Sir, Chief needs you topside. Seems two men decided to go at it over which whore they wanted to visit. Chief says you get to decide."

"You'd think they'd both visit her." CB flipped the door lock and followed the sailor to the deck.

The Romeo with the bloody nose was sitting astride his opponent, pounding away on his head. Most of the crew was standing around watching and passing off bets. Jack left the crowd and joined CB.

"Good God, it's Donneley and Zico," said CB. "No wonder they're fighting. They're so ugly, I'm surprised any whore'll have them."

Jack was shaking laughing, keeping it inside. "Well, Captain, what are you going to do?"

"Put ten on Donneley." CB joined the silent shaking. Laughing aloud was not fitting for peace keepers. "Go get the buckets."

"Aye aye, sir." Jack was soon back with large tins filled with sea water. "One, two, three." The fighters were doused. Jack stepped back. "They're all yours."

CB spent a lot of time learning from his captain. He knew exactly what to do. He was too short to break up a fight, so he grabbed the bleeding Donneley and pulled him sideways off the battered Zico. He nodded to the sailor standing closest who dragged the Irishman away, shoving him against the rail. CB put a foot on Zico, pinning him.

"You break his nose over a whore?"

"Yeah."

"Why?" CB moved his foot. Zico stood.

"His nose is too ugly for my woman."

CRUNCH

CB rubbed his knuckles. "And now so's yours." He turned to the men. "Whoever put down money on this sorry lot better get it back. The fight's a tie, and neither gets the girl." He flexed his fingers. "Mr. Donneley, Mr. Zico, tomorrow is your lucky day. You get to save your money because you both are confined to quarters." He walked to the ladder.

"Go see Cookie about those noses," he heard Jack say.

CB smiled. Cookie knew how to pack a nose. He'd done his.

Captain Ledbetter spent the rest of the day on reports and stewing about the combination. Was it random? Had it been set to special numbers that could be remembered when drunk? CB looked at the books on the shelf where the safe was hidden. All the books were upright, all except one.

CB smiled. "Thank you, my friend." With a few twirls,, the safe was open. All the crew's pay was stacked, ready for the men. CB put the cash on the desk and secured the safe behind the books. He opened the duty ledger. He separated the bills and coins into piles for distribution.

"I gotta concentrate," he muttered to himself. "Can't make any mistakes."

He did not hear the door swing open.

THUNK

CB's head hit the desk, sending the money flying. He saw stars and the moon. Then nothing.

Chapter Thirty-Three
December, 1901
Dreams and Nightmares

"Listen to me, child. You have got to stop tormenting your brothers." Nora Lee had Franky all het up again, bawlin' over somethin' or t'other. CB was beginning to realize that, just because a child is cute as a button, does not make that particular child an angel. Miss Nora Lee sure could devil the life out of her brothers.

Nora Lee swished her skirt and batted her eyes. "I didn't do nuffin'."

"Stop the silly talk. You are not the baby anymore." Franky bawled louder and tried to climb CB's leg. He hoisted the boy onto his shoulders. "Hush. She didn't hurt you."

Franky started whacking CB on the head "Nora Lee can't get me, Nora Lee can't get me." Franky drummed a cadence with every other word. The girl ran straight into CB, wrapping her arms around his belly, squeezing tight.

"Whoa howdy, child, you're 'bout to knock us over." CB staggered. Franky stopped banging on his head and put his arms under his chin. "Hey, boy, you're choking me. Let lose my throat."

"Thut up, ath hole."

CB's eyes flew open. "Whaha…."

The filthy, oil soaked kerchief was stuffed in his mouth. He was staring straight at Jake. For some reason he could still feel the children hanging on him. He looked down. Ropes, not arms, circled his chest and legs. The choke pressure increased.

"Ollie'th gonna thlit your throat if you don't thit thill." CB did not move a muscle. "Thath a good little Captain. We heard the thailors talkin' about gettin' thum of their pay tomorrow. That ain't gonna happen. I got what you wath countin'. Now you're going to give uth all the reth of the money." Jake stepped back. "Where ith it?"

"Gallk," CB gagged on the rag.

Ollie pressed his knife harder against CB's neck. "Answer, man. I've used this knife on many a corpse, can easily use it on you."

CB grunted louder. He could taste the kerosene.

"Don't kill him 'til he gith uth all the cash," Jake stage whispered to Ollie. He put his face at CB's. "You'll talk thoon. We'll wait."

Ollie looked around the cabin. "Hey, Buddy, can you pull me up a chair. My back's startin' to hurt, bending over like this."

"Thur." Jake slid over the desk's side chair. "You thit. I'm gonna thart thirching." He looked at CB. "Where'th that fanthy wood box you had on your desk. All we saw wath papers."

CB tried to gesture with his chin, but Ollie pushed the knife.

"We told you to hold still."

It was dawning on CB that he was hopelessly helpless.

Can't talk to tell 'em, can't move to show 'em. He closed his eyes, hoping to conjure a dream of the children. *Tell me, Miss Nora Lee, what we gonna do now? Any suggestions, Franky?*

He heard his room being ransacked.

Please don't tear the books. They are so precious.

He started to doze.

"Thit, Ollie, there ain't no money here. I even looked under hith mattress."

"Keep lookin'. Did you feel his pockets?"

"Thath the firth thing I done when I knocked him." Jake held out a few coppers. "Thath all I found." He tossed them on the desk. "He can keep thoth. We'll be gittin' all the good thuff."

Jake started dumping CB's clothing on the floor. CB slitted his eyes, watching the thief shake out his shirts and underdrawers, looking for the payroll.

Idiot.

Supper mess bell rang.

Six. They've been at it a while. Jeezie, my neck is tired.

CB moved his head. Ollie jerked. The blade sliced.

"Shit," cursed Ollie. "I cut him. He's bleeding like a stuck pig."

He turned the knife and cracked him with the hilt. Once again, CB saw stars, but not the moon. He let his head hit the table, squeezing his chin down and stayed still.

Chapter Thirty-Four
December, 1901
Son Shine

Supper chow was nothing to write home about. You could tell provisions were running low. Red beans, fat back, rice as much as you wanted, but no onions to bring the flavor. The hot water cornbread was made with bacon grease instead of lard. Coffee was thin, no sugar. No one complained.

"Gonna get me a hot bath." One sailor was listing his plans for the next afternoon.

"Who ya gonna git to scrub yer dirty hide? No one'll come close enough to ya, you stink so bad." His tablemates were throwing him the razz-ma-tazz.

"I don't care, 'slong as she don't care."

"Make sure she's got a crab comb." All the men laughed at that one.

Junior usually sat on the end bench and had gotten used to their words. The men, for the most part, figured out he was no bad criminal, just a kid needing a lesson. They treated him like true crew and did not watch their talk. The boy smiled.

I'm muscle strong and world traveled. Ikey's a milk sop, living a schoolboy's life. Bet nobody talks like this at his supper table.

"What 'chu smilin' at, boy? You gonna git a whore to comb your hair?" The man across from him had raised his voice for the benefit of the others.

"Uh, no sir, prisoners don't get paid." Junior showed his hands, palms up. "Got no money. Gonna stay put."

"Just as well," called a voice from down the table. "No whore wants from a boy what he ain't got."

The crowd roared at that one.

Junior shrugged and stood with his empty plate. "From what I hear, you men are gonna need more than a bath to please a woman. Y'all might want to spend your money on good food, instead. That steak dinner sounds mighty fine. Bring me some scraps when you get back."

Junior walked out to the sound of whistles, cat calls, and something about giving a dog the bone. He didn't mind. Tonight he was going to write a letter to his mama. He started composing it as he headed to CB's cabin.

"Hoy, Gallaway." Junior stopped.

That was Jack's voice. When he called him his last name, it meant there were others around. He turned.

"Yes, Chief?" Junior made the required salute.

"I need you to carry a message to the captain. I can't get away from my duties to deliver it myself." Jack reached in his middy and handed Junior an envelope. "Thank you. Captain will handle this with his other paperwork." Jack winked.

"Aye aye, will do." Junior winked back. "Good evening, sir." Junior took Jack's letter addressed to Marguerite, fitting it in his pocket. The boy continued toward the cabin. As he walked, he noticed that same smell he and his mama knew right before the hurricane, the smell of doom. Outside the closed door was CB's dinner tray, untouched.

"He never doesn't eat," Junior said to himself. Suddenly he smelled something else, his hammock mates. "What the…"

Junior's curse was interrupted by a loud thunk and a moan. The boy stood frozen, listening.

"Jethus, man, now what we gonna do? Heth bleedin'."

"Shit, Jake, now I got to kill him."

Junior's eyes darted all over his surroundings. He pocketed CB's dinner fork and knife off the tray.

"What else? What else?" Cap's reminder chain hung in its usual place. Junior grabbed it off the hook, dropped the open lock in his other pocket, and kicked open the cabin door.

"Get away from my dad," Junior's voice echoed in the room as he swung the chain.

It hit Ollie upside his head, the end whipping around his face. Junior jerked the reminder like a rope, the links dragging part of Ollie's face with it. The knife went flying. Junior swung again, this time catching Ollie's neck. The chain wrapped tight, a chokehold strangling the man's screams. Ollie went down.

Jake dove for the knife. Junior stepped on the blade.

"You little weathel, the captain really ith your dad." Jake grabbed the boy's ankle. "Thit, now we gotta kill you both."

Holding the chain tight, Junior fumbled in his pocket, pulling out the first thing he felt. With all his might, he buried CB's dinner fork in the hand that held him. Junior collared screaming Jake with the other end of the chain. He yanked the fork. Jake stupidly watched his blood oozing from three perfectly formed holes and started to cry. Junior shoved Jake over next to his partner and pushed him down.

CLICK.

The padlock held the travelers neck and neck. He then picked up Ollie's knife and threw it out the door.

Junior ran to the bell rope and rang and rang and rang. Leaving the alarm, he threw his body on CB.

"Daddy, Daddy, Daddy." The man did not move. Junior yanked the rag from CB's mouth. "Oh, Daddy, Daddy, breathe."

Chapter Thirty-Five
December, 1901
My Daddy Don't Drink

Jack couldn't believe what he saw. The stowaways were wrapped in chains, the cabin upside down in complete chaos, and CB was in Junior's arms, both of them crying. Junior was holding a bloody head rag to CB's neck. Coils of rope lay on the floor.

"What the...? Jack blocked the doorway. He picked up the thrown knife.

"Move, boy." Cookie was behind him, pushing. "Move." One step got him to CB. "Can you stand?"

Junior looked up. "Cuh, cuh Cookie, Mister Jack," he stammered. "They tied him up, they cut his neck. They tried to kill him." The boy was sobbing. "They tried to kill him."

"I did not. Ollie did. Heth the one who cut him. I tried to thop him."

Jack casually walked over to the chained men and kicked each one in the ribs. "Shut up, dogs," and kicked them again. Turning to his partner, he repeated Cookie's question. "Can you stand?"

CB looked at Jack and then down at Junior's arms holding him tight.

Jack understood. He knelt in front of the two. "Son, you need to turn him loose. We can't tend him 'til you do." He very carefully lifted Junior's hand from the bandage and took it tight in his own. "Let him try to stand. Cookie will staunch the blood."

Cookie walked CB to his bunk and laid him flat. The wound blood was already clotted on the rag. The ringing alarm had the hallway packed with sailors. Cookie shot off orders for warm water, soap, sulfa powder, and clean bandages. "They're all in the pantry, left side, behind the cornmeal, in a box marked with a red X." Two men ran up the steps. He continued. "I need four of the strongest men out there to take these two rats up deck. Make sure they are securely shackled in the sun."

The room was soon cleared, and the remaining sailors left the hall to watch the chaining.

Junior, still holding on to Jack, stood beside Cookie. "Is he gonna die? Can you take off the kerchief to see how bad he is?"

"Will do when the supplies are here." Cookie looked around. Miraculously the thieves must not have seen the brandy bottle on the top shelf. "Chief, would you reach me down that hooch? We may need it."

"My daddy don't drink."

"Yes, Junior, I know." Jack dropped the boy's hand. "We might need it to clean the cut."

Jack handed the decanter to Cookie. "You gonna pour it on him? That's gonna sting."

"Can I have a sip?" CB spoke very softly. "I think it might help the pain."

Cookie nodded. "Just a little."

Jack found a drinking glass and poured some. CB took the tiniest sip, and carefully shook his head 'no.' "Bleah. Rather hurt."

One of the messmates appeared at the door. "Here's your box and a kettle of warm water. I see Captain's tray in the hall. I'll take it away. Where's the silverware?"

"Uh, the knife's in my pocket." Junior handed it to the mate. "I stabbed Jake with the fork. Don't know where it ended up."

Cookie looked up from his patient. "Gig that frog good?"

"Yes sir, in the hand." Junior grinned. "I think it might've gone all the way through."

"Good job," Cookie smiled back. He looked at his messmate. "Take this glass of brandy and pour it on the prisoner's wound. Do nothing else."

"Aye aye." The mate saluted, brandy in hand.

Junior watched him leave. "That's gonna hurt."

"Yes, son, I know."

"Good."

Cookie took one of CB's wash towels and soaked it with warm water. He carefully placed it on the rag. "Gotta soften the blood so's we can lift that thing." He looked straight at CB. "Can you swallow deep?"

"Yes. Just hurts to talk."

"If you can swallow, you ain't gonna die."

CB smiled for the first time. "My son held the kerchief to the cut. He kept it closed."

Cookie smiled back. "Junior, come over here." The boy stood by the bed. "I want you to lift this rag. I want you to see."

"But, but it might hurt him."

"Son," CB looked at the boy. "Son, please, I need for you to take care of me."

"Yes sir." Junior handed Jack the wet towel. As carefully as lifting a newborn baby, he peeled back the bloody cloth.

"It's not bad." Junior passed off the rag. "It's not bad at all." He turned to Cookie. "Look. It's closed up." Junior started shaking. "My daddy ain't gonna die."

"No, thanks to you, I'm not." CB reached for the boy's hand. "You saved my life."

CB did not make a noise as Cookie powdered and plastered his neck, wrapping it 'round and 'round with bandage. The messmate brought trays for the patient and the son. Cookie took his supplies and left.

"Hey, Junior, you still got that letter I gave you?" Jack raised his eyebrows. "You know, that important message I gave you earlier."

"It should be in my pocket. Hope it's still there."
Junior checked. It was gone. "Maybe it fell out when I used
the fork. Let me look." He got down on his hands and
knees. "Here it is, on top of that pile of papers those crooks
dumped." He reached up and gave Jack the envelope. "Oh
jeez, I forgot." He got himself on his feet. "Tonight I'm
s'posed to write my mama." He looked at CB. "I'm
guessin' I better not tell her what happened today."

"Good idea, son. She can see the scar when we get
home." CB looked hard at Junior. "When we do, you want
to go to LaPorte, or to your aunt and uncle?"

"LaPorte, but just to see all the family." Junior
looked shyly at CB. "If it's all right, can I sign on the *Sallie
Lou* as a real hand? I want to be just like you."

"We'll see. We'll see." CB took a slow sip of his
coffee. "Let's get to America first." He chewed his biscuit
and lay down on his bed. "See if you can find a clean sheet
of paper and a pencil somewhere. You write, and I'll check
for the spelling."

Deer Mama,
    I miss you and everybody else. I have grown
strong arms. Daddy CB fixt the head lice. I am
lerning a lot of things. I am not a criminale
anymore. Love, Your Son, Junior
    P.S. There were bad guys on board, but now they're
caut.

"You think that's good enough?" Junior handed his
letter to CB.

"Scratch the part about bad guys. That'll make her
worry. I'll mark the spelling." CB was flat on his bunk, no
pillow. Cookie said he couldn't bend his neck until
morning. "Tell her about how you got over seasickness."

"Good idea."

Dear Mama,

I miss you and everybody else. I have strong arms. I don't puke anymore. Daddy CB fixed the head lice. Thank you for teaching him. I am learning a lot of things from him and Mister Jack. I am not a criminal anymore. Cookie makes good food, but not as good as you. Love, Your First Born Son, Junior

"I made it longer."

"I see." CB handed the letter back. "Anything more?"

"Nope, you can send it."

"I'm not allowed to move around too much until tomorrow. Would you get the mail packet?" CB gestured with his thumb. "Look behind my chamber closet. There's a space where I keep my letters to your mama. I don't think the rats found it."

"Nope, they didn't." Junior handed the thick packet to CB. "You sure do write a lot. Does Mister Jack write that much?"

"Sometimes he does, sometimes he's too tired. Let me put his envelope and your letter together. I'll get someone to post all this tomorrow." CB yawned. "Those two thumped me pretty darn hard. My head's really hurtin'."

"What can I do to help? Mama would put cool wet cloths on our head. I could…" CB was snoring. "I could sit beside you if you need me."

And Junior did.

Chapter Thirty-Six
December, 1901
Steak Dinner

Jack had the jitters. Today was his first docking and roll off since he became Chief.

"You nervous?" Cookie was keeping an early Jack in the galley for breakfast.

"Don't want him to hear all that dirt the men are talking," he muttered quietly over the pot of boiling water soon to be turned into grits.

"I can't make any mistakes today." Jack had heard Cookie's words. "You know, they'll be watching everything I do."

"I know."

"Not only our crew, but as soon as the dock men hear that the *Sallie* has a colored Chief, they're gonna be like flies on manure lookin' to fault me." Jack glanced around the galley. "Any yesterday cornbread? Don't think I can wait for the cooking."

"You can wait, and yes, there're a few cuts in the box. Get me a piece, too."

Jack buttered Cookie the bigger slab. "Here ya go." He sat at the table. "You check CB this morning? You know I was busy."

"Looked in last night, Junior was sound asleep in the chair beside him." Cookie smiled. "Just like when you two sat over there guarding the pantry. I reckon the boy's comin' around just fine."

"You think CB might be able to move today? Sure could use him helping with the docking…"

"And the roll off and loading," Cookie added. "You stir the pot, I'll go roust him."

Cookie found two snoring lumberjacks in the captain's quarters. Junior had crawled in the bunk sometime during the night and the two were flat on their backs, mouths wide open, taking down a forest.

"Well, I'll be damned if they don't look alike a'layin' there," Cookie observed.

"No we don't," CB whispered. "Shhh, let him sleep." Slowly, carefully, he worked his way up and over the sleeping boy. "I got yellow hair, he don't."

Cookie extended his hand. "Take it easy. Here, grab on, let me help."

"I'm fine." CB took the offer. "Just need to see if I got my legs."

Cookie and CB walked to the desk chair. "How's your cut?"

"Itchy."

"Good." Cookie unwrapped the outer bandage. The plaster was stained a light pink. "Looks like you're healing. No blood." He wound the gauze back around his neck. "Head?"

"Hurts, but not dizzy. Can I turn my neck?"

"If it don't pain ya any."

CB looked right, left, up, down. "Stings, but no real pain." He tilted his head toward the bunk. "He stayed."

"Checked on you last night. The boy was in your chair." Cookie scratched his stubble. "Hmm, gotta shave. I'm getting me a steak dinner as soon as we dock."

"Jeez, Cookie, I didn't ever know you stepped out." CB's astonishment was evident.

"Well, son, it's like this. You don't know everything about me, and you never will. And yes, I like steak dinners, but I never get dessert."

"Good morning." Junior propped himself on one elbow. "Daddy, are you all right?"

"Yes, son, Cookie checked me out." CB smiled. "Gotta call me Cap, don't forget."

Junior swung his legs down. "Aye aye, Captain." He looked at Cookie. "You sure he's good? Did he bleed? Last night he said he had a real bad headache. Did you check his noggin?"

Junior started rubbing CB's scalp. "He's got a goose egg right on top."

"That must be the first knock. They got me twice." CB started feeling his own head. "There it is, right in the back of the middle. That one feels like a crow's egg." He guided the boy's hand to the spot. "When they hit me the second time I pretended to be out so they'd leave me alone."

"Smart." Cookie was following Junior's fingers over the knots. "They could have got your temple." Cookie finished his exam. "You feel up to landing a boat? Jack sure could use a hand."

"Feed me first."

"Aye aye, Captain." Cookie jerked his chin at Junior. "You keep the boy until I see you walk into galley. Don't want to find you passed out on the deck."

"Will do. Be up soon." CB smiled. "Thanks, Cookie."

"Humph. Just don't go gittin' your throat slit again anytime soon."

"Do my best." CB watched him leave. "What a good man," he murmured. "Sure hope he doesn't eat dessert."

"What's wrong with sweets?" Junior's stomach started rumbling at the thought of something tasty. "I love Aunt Ada's gooseberry cobbler."

"Yep, that's my kind of dessert, yessirrebob." CB looked at himself. "I think I'd better change my clothes. No one wants to see a ship's Captain with a bloody shirt. There's going to be enough to-do on the docks when they find out Captain Calhoun is dead."

"Don't forget Jake and Ollie. You gonna throw them overboard?"

"Wish I could. Please hand me anything you think is wearable. They dumped all my clothes. Excuse me, haven't seen the head since yesterday." CB stepped into the chamber closet. His relief was evident. "Whew." He shut the door behind him. "I feel a whole lot better. You find anything presentable?"

"Yes, sir, got your clean uniform. Everything's laid out on the bunk."

Ten minutes and they were in the galley.

"You look a giant tad better than last night," said Jack with a quick hug. "Sure as shootin' didn't want to bury another Captain."

"What's this I hear about you needin' to dock this thing? You get us to Panama when I wasn't lookin'?" CB nodded to Junior. "You better get going to your mess. Roll off is hard work." Junior saluted and left. CB reached for a porcelain mug. "You got the coffee made?"

"When do I not?" Cookie poured a half cup. "See if you keep this down. Some people get the pukes after a head knock. You got two."

The three sat around the galley table, enjoying their first swallows and watching for any reaction from CB. Nothing.

"Top me off. I'm ready to help this greenhorn land."

Jack looked into his mug. "It ain't the green part they'll be watchin'."

"I know. You'll be fine. I'll stand with you." CB stirred some molasses into the bowl of grits Cookie set down. "Where's the rats? Did anyone kill them?"

"Chain spiked to the deck by the hold, gettin' hotter by the minute." Jack raised an eyebrow. "Got the men dousing them with sea water every hour or so just to keep them breathing. Salt'll ruin my deck, but I don't care. "

"Good. Don't want to give dead rats to the *policia*. Wouldn't look too good, me bein' the new captain and all." CB took another fork full of grits. "Thanks for feeding me, Cookie. You think my neck wrap will be all the proof we need to get them jailed?"

"Yep, we got lots of witnesses. I think every man on board saw your cut. You were just too busy trying to stay alive to notice." Cookie chuckled. "Found our half pay stuffed in their pockets."

"Oh, God, I forgot about that. Where is it?" CB stood up, swayed, and sat. "Whoa, not gonna do that again for a while."

"Don't worry. Jack got it all straightened out last night. Took the duty ledger and the money. Everything is ready for Captain Ledbetter to make pay." Cookie patted Jack on his back. "Ya done good. No man can say you didn't."

"We'll see after today." Chief Smith stood. "You ready, Cap?"

"Standin' slow, ready to go." CB wiggled his head. "Don't hear nuthin' rattlin'. I guess we got work to do." He stretched his full height. "Tell me, man, do I look like a captain?"

"No, too short. Do I look like a chief?"

"No, too tall."

"You boys look fine. Now go be what you are." Cookie shook each man's hand as a blessing. "Make us proud."

"Yes, sir," was the unison reply.

Chapter Thirty-Seven
December, 1901
The Checkered Flag

Jack was right about one thing, seems as though the entire Panama wharf was watching the *Sallie Lou*. News traveled fast when word of Captain's death got out. Jack was wrong about one thing. The wharf men weren't lookin' at him. CB stood on deck, his neck bandages on display. First hand down on the roll off told about the attack. Soon the *policia* were there. Jake and Ollie were hauled off to the *carcel*.

"Good riddance, rats." Cookie came up beside CB. "What they gonna do with 'em?"

"The *alguacil* said that President Roosevelt had lots of Americans all over the place, getting ready to cut a ditch. He's chain-ganging Ollie and Jake to one of the crew bosses. Those two get to dig their way to the Pacific." CB scratched his bandage. "Good grief, this thing itches."

"Have you showed it off enough?" Cookie squinted down at the dock. Jack was directing cargo traffic. "You know, not one word of 'nigger' has landed in my ears. He's doin' good, the wharf men are listening." Cookie crooked his mouth. "In a way, you being laid up is a blessing. It lets him take your place with the lists. He's proving he can read, write, and boss all at the same time. Be no question after this."

"Look who's working with them. Junior's makin' me proud."

Cookie nodded. "He's making himself proud."

"He asked me if he could sign on regular when we get home." CB shook his head. "I don't know what to think. He's awful young."

"He's older than you were."

"That's different."

"No it's not." Cookie chuckled. "You always said you were happy to get away from your old man.

"That's true."

"Junior wants to go away with his old man." Cookie scratched his belly. "You done deciding?"

"I guess. Gotta talk to Myra. She might skin me for taking her boy." CB noticed Cookie didn't have his apron. "You headin' out for steak?"

"Yep, I got me a chef friend who cooks 'bout as good as I do." Cookie patted his stomach. "You want me to bring you back dinner all wrapped up? Don't know about you, but I'm damn sick and tired of beans and rice."

"Bring back two, one for dinner and one for supper." CB grinned. "You make good chow, but you're right. Sure had enough of beans and rice these last few days."

"You want them to wrap up a couple pieces of cake to go with?"

"Sounds good, thanks." CB turned away from the rail. "I have to set up the pay station. You need yours now?"

"Naw, got plenty. Pay me when I get back." Cookie nodded. "Cakes' on me but ya owe me extra for two dinners." He headed down the plank.

"I owe you more than that," CB whispered. "I owe you my…"

"Cap." One of the sailors interrupted his thought.

"Yes?"

"First crew's ready for pay. You want us to make line?"

CB nodded. "Tell them to muster outside my door. I'll be there in five minutes."

"Aye aye, sir."

That night CB walked his ship, counting heads. All were safe. Most were passed out drunk in their hammocks.

A few were gathered in mess, bragging about their conquests. Cookie returned with two steak dinners for his captain and invited CB, Jack, and Junior to his galley for cake. He'd bought two.

Cookie raised his coffee mug to Jack. "Ya done good, boy." He cut the yellow one with the melted brown sugar drizzle. Jack smiled and took the offered first piece.

"Thank you, sir."

CB cleared his throat. "I want a slice of the one with the berries on top." He licked his lips. "Then I'll try the other."

Cookie handed him the knife. "Cut your own, Yer hand ain't broke." He redirected his attention to Jack. "Any trouble today?"

"Nothing new. Most all the men worked hard. That Zico complained that his nose hurt too much for him to do much, but I pointed at Donneley and commented on how hard he was working and that since he'd broken his nose, Donneley's must hurt a whole heap more." Jack chuckled. "The fools started jaw-jackin' about who was the stronger, and next thing ya know, they finished their loading." He took a third slice of berry cake.

"Mister Jack, I...uh...heard somebody talking about you." Junior was polishing off his second piece.

The men waited.

"Son, was it ugly?" CB's voice was cautious.

"I heard the dock master say it was the best checkerboard he's ever saw." Junior started swiping the back of his fork over the crumbs. "What did he mean?"

"A checkerboard ship is a mixed ship." CB stared smiled at Jack. "You know what that means?"

"I did us proud?"

"My friend, you sure did. I know dock masters." answered Cookie. "They gossip worse 'en any ol' washer woman about every ship they know. Good God, man, you've nothing to worry about at this wharf."

Jack grinned. "We ought'a raise the blue and white checkerboard signal flag. Ya know it's the letter N." He laughed. "That'll tell 'em who's chief."

CB caught Cookie's eye and nodded. "Sounds like a plan to me. I'll get it done tomorrow."

The flagman had never flown a signal flag as a banner, but he didn't question Captain's order. As the *Sallie Lou* pulled away from Panama, the blue-checkered flag flew proudly. They would be sailing north, stopping at Belize for mahogany and Frontera for allspice berries, capsicum peppers, and vanilla beans. Galveston was a short ten days away.

Chapter Thirty-Eight
December, 1901
Cleaning House

CB's neck was healing well. Cookie gave him gauze to wrap it as protection against his collar, but had taken off the plaster the third day. The biggest problem was keeping his hands away from the scar. It'd closed up crooked and itched like all get out. CB was glad to wear the bandage. The log work kept his head tilted and that helped, too. Today was easy sailing. He sat staring at Captain Calhoun's secret accounts. Something had been nagging his mind since the one time he'd looked at it. The numbers didn't make sense.

CB had been in and out of the side locker since he was a boy. Sometimes it was full of cases, sometimes not. Even though he had never been privy to Captain's rum business, he was very aware of his captain's drinking. CB knew that only a few crates of bottles moved with each voyage. The brandy boxes were in front, kept open, and new whiskey marked XXX was in the back. It was a puzzle.

Knock. "CB, it's me."

"I'm coming." CB unbolted his cabin door. "You need me up?"

"No, just takin' a breather." Jack sat in the side chair. "You working?"

"Looking at the other log. It doesn't go with what I know."

"Which is?" Jack turned the book so he could see it.

"I don't find how he can record all this money when I knew not much changed in that room." CB reached to scratch his neck and stopped. "He moved liquor, but these numbers read like he moved all the rum in Cuba. That doesn't add up."

"You start on the first page and work through?" Jack flipped to the front.

"Not yet. You want to put an eye to it?"

"Sure. I got a couple 'a minutes." Jack looked around. "You got a straight edge? I follow numbers best if I use a ruler."

CB handed him one from the desk's top middle drawer. The room stayed silent as Jack ran down the first page. Then he did it again, this time stopping five entries down. "When did Captain Calhoun buy the *Sallie?* I thought it was the year before I came on."

"I always thought it around that time. I remember Cletus looked for a new smellin' ship to sell me to. Why you ask?"

"It looks like our captain was a very rich man before the *Sallie.* This reads thousands of dollars before then. The numbers don't get smaller after 1887. It don't show anything about buying a boat." Jack looked at his friend. "Could this be an altogether sompin' or 'tother that has nothing to do with hooch movin'?"

"Maybe, but look further on in the book, he's listing liquor cases there." CB squitched his chin, trying to scratch. "Damn, I wish this cut would hurry up and go. Don't want to be fussin' with it at home."

Jack drew the straight edge down the second and third pages. "Hey man, look at this. He's got the same entry every six months. Says DAD to GNB and then $2103.07. Every six months. Where'd he get that kind of money?"

CB stood close behind Jack, leaning over him, staring at the book.

"Oh Jesus, I know what that means."

"You're squashing me." CB stepped back. "Here." Jack handed up the ledger. "You tell me. What does it mean?"

"DAD stands for dad. GNB stands for Galveston National Bank."

"And...?"

CB set down the book. "Cookie told me Captain Calhoun bought the *Sallie Lou* with the money his father left him. The man owned a fleet of ferries and was rich. Bet the $2103.07 is more of that inheritance." CB sank into his chair. "It looks like each one to the GNB has been withdrawn in cash."

"When's the last entry?" Jack rifled through the log. "September 4, 1900. That makes sense. Hurricane probably took the bank."

"Probably. No new nothin' in the last year."

"And no new rum money," CB stood, stretching. "I looked in the safe, regular pay cash is there."

Jack closed the book. "I been meanin' to ask, how'd you figure out the combination? You get a message from God or something?"

"Nope. Scheherazade."

"Huh?" Jack shook his head. "I don't get it."

"The day of half pay I was beyond stumped. I knew where the safe was, up behind *King Arthur* and this ledger, but had no idea the lock numbers." CB pointed to the bookshelf. "Take a gander. See anything?"

"Since you said Scheherazade, I'm lookin'. Jeez, it's upside down."

"Only book out of place." CB grinned. "One thousand one Arabian nights and..."

"Forty thieves." Jack finished the sentence. "The combination is 1-0-0-1-4-0."

"Tried that, no luck." CB moved *King Arthur*. "Watch. 4-0-1-0-0-1 Done." The pay safe swung open. "Captain William J. Calhoun was one smart man."

"Captain CB Ledbetter is one smart man, too." Jack slapped CB's back in congratulation. "So where the hell did he put the rest of the money?"

CB closed the safe, spun the dial, set the ledger in front of it, and put the King back in his place. "I just don't know."

"We'll figure it out sooner or later." Jack walked to the door. "Come on, man, let's go see how the boat's sailing."

Two days to Galveston and the men were getting jumpy. CB called a topside muster. It was time to clean house. He wanted to show the change in the *Sallie* in more ways than a checkered flag.

"Gentlemen."

"Aye aye, Captain." The sailors responded with a salute.

"Two days out. Huzzah."

"Huzzah."

"Today and tomorrow we are going to give this old girl a cleaning the likes of which she has not had in years."

Grumble. Groan.

"Now men, you don't want to be associated with a dirty woman."

Laughter.

"Well, I don't either." CB smiled. "I'm asking all hands to take their off duty time to bathe her, dry her, and to slap some rouge on her rump."

Junior leaned to the man next to him. "What does he mean?"

"Wax her brass."

"Oh."

"While we are here, I want to say something. This voyage has been real hard on all of us." CB touched the center of his chest. "We lost our captain, we had trouble with some robbers, and, well, all I got to say is, you men are the finest crew on all these seven seas. Thank you for your work. You should be right proud. Huzzah!"

"Uh, Captain." It was Zico.

"Yes, sailor?"

"I just want ta say that you're one decent sonofabitch, even if you did break my nose."

CB saluted. "Thank you, sailor. Dismissed." He headed to his cabin. *Needs a good sortin' and polishin'. Can't expect what I don't do myself.*

After charts and the like, CB sat himself in the center of what had come to resemble a pile of rubbish. He was humming the sailing song he used to swing Nora Lee.

Knock. "It's me."

"Jeez, Jack, we gotta get you a key. Wait a minute 'til I get up."

Jack looked around CB's cabin, snapped his suspenders, and puffed his chest. "Got mine done."

"Yeah, but you didn't have Jake and Ollie tearing up your room."

"Or tearin' up my hide. You need help?"

"Just company. Wanna sit?"

"Sure." Jack watched CB sort. "They really did a number on this room, didn't they?"

"Yep. Most of this pile is trash, anyway. Looks like the captain hadn't cleaned anything in years." CB looked wistful. "Never thought I'd be the one staying in here."

"Never thought I'd be half owner of the *Sallie Lou.*" Jack stretched out his legs and closed his eyes. "Ya know, we don't have to smuggle anything anymore. No men, no hooch, not Mr. Carl's flour. Yes sir, we can charge him regular."

"Should give him a discount, you know, as a friend."

"Could still move something. Kinda fun to..." Jack was sound asleep.

CB pondered that as he worked.

Should clean out the rum room, too much complication to run liquor.

He stood from his sorting, got the key and a lantern, and quietly left the cabin.

"Let's take a real look," he said out loud.

The cases had not been moved. All looked right, brandy in front, new whiskey in back. CB gave the room a good study. Those crates were fresh pine, yellow in color. The middle boxes were dull grey. He saw the dirt for the first time. Pulling a rag from his pocket, he wiped the dust off the closest middle crate. It was marked AB 40.

"Oh dear God in heaven," CB backed out the closet and slowly walked to his cabin. "Oh dear God in heaven," he repeated.

Jack opened his eyes. "Why you prayin"?

"Praisin' man, praisin'. Come on, got something to show you."

CB led Jack to the liquor closet. "You never been in here, have you?"

"Nope, too tall." Jack duck-walked into the room. "What you want to show me?"

"Look at the front rows and the back rows. See new crates?"

"Uh huh. So?"

"The middle rows are old, real old. Look at their color."

"And…" Jack had found a place to sit since he couldn't stand.

"Read the mark."

"AB 40. Hmmm." Jack eyes went wide. "AB 40. Well, I'll be damned. Open Sesame."

Chapter Thirty-Nine
December 23, 1901
Safe and Loving Harbors

CB, Jack, and Junior arrived at the house in LaPorte sitting on the buck of a wagon full of old boxes. Halfway down the street, the boy jumped out and ran.

"Mama, Mama." Up the steps, he crashed through the door like the homesick child he was. "Mama, I'm here."

Myra caught him halfway through the dining room. He grabbed her and hugged her off her feet.

"Darlin', put me down." She held him at arms' length. "Good Glory, you've grown."

"Told you I was strong. Did you get my letter?"

"Yes, son, thank you for writing." Myra looked around her empty house. "How did you get home?"

"Wagon." He started pulling her to the door. "Come see."

They got outside just as Jack was hitching the horse.

"Ma'am." He tipped his cap. "Where's my woman?"

Oomph.

Marguerite was in his arms, 'bout knocking him down. "Right here, *mon amour*, right here." They kissed like the newlyweds they were.

Jack broke away first. "See the wagon? Gotta get the load in the house." Marguerite pouted. Jack touched her beautiful lips. "Soon, my love."

Myra got her hungry kiss as well. CB looked around. "Young'uns in school?"

She nodded. "Last day. They get Christmas Eve and Christmas Day as holidays."

"Good. Don't need 'em underfoot just right now."

"You're not wantin' to, ahem, go upstairs, are you"? Myra stepped back from their embrace. "Can't it wait 'til—oh my lord Jesus—what happened to you?" She very gently touched his scar. "Darling, you didn't tell me you were hurt."

CB pulled her close and kissed her again. "Got my throat slit. The big news is that our son was the hero of the day." CB released the embrace. "My dear wife, Junior stopped the robbery, captured the thieves, and saved my life."

He gave a quick kiss and walked to the wagon.

"What, what?" she sputtered.

"Ask me later. We gotta get this cargo into the house." CB threw her another kiss and joined Jack and Junior.

The women sat on the front porch, watching their men carry crate after crate into the house, through the parlor and dining room to be stacked in the kitchen. It was cries of the baby waking from her nap that got them out of their chairs.

"Sit," Myra told Marguerite. "You keep an eye on what's going on. I'll be right back."

Soon Myra returned, a very blond Flossie Mae in her arms. She stood in the kitchen, waiting. CB put down the last crate and took his daughter.

"Will you look at yourself," he cooed. "Some old sailor man gave you yellow hair." He nuzzled her neck.

"Wonder who that might be?" Myra wrapped her arms around her husband and her baby. "Could that old sailor man be a Captain?"

"Aye aye, ma'am." CB went back to the nuzzlin'. "Little lady, your daddy's a Captain." Smooch. He planted a big one on that yellow hair and handed her back. "We better do something about these crates. God knows what'll happen if Nora Lee finds out what's inside."

"Um, Husband, just what is inside?" Myra sounded just like Aunt Ada.

"Yes, just what is inside?" repeated Marguerite. She stood arm in arm with her own husband.

"Ladies," said CB. "Jack and I have brought you a safe future. We present to you Christmas gifts beyond any you may have dreamed of." He nodded to Jack who handed him the crowbar from the wagon. "OPEN SESAME."

The nails in the crate screamed and then the wives did too. The box was filled with five dollar gold pieces. It looked like something out of a picture book. CB did a swooping bow toward the box.

"Captain William J. Calhoun not only gave us the *Sallie Lou*, but all contents. Each crate you see is filled with gold."

The women started crying. "We own all this?" asked Marguerite.

"Share and share alike," responded Jack. "We own half." He smiled. "Who could've imagined grandchildren of slaves and a whore house maid would have a house full of money and a sailing ship, too."

"Yeah," said CB. "And don't forget to tell her about the checkerboard flag."

And so he did.

The End

About the Author

Some people call Jacqueline T. Moore a snowbird because she spends so much time writing in South Carolina. Not so. She loves the Ohio winters with all the ice and snow. She says, "Traveling south in the summer makes me a sunflower… and a beach bum!" As a writer and educator, Jacqueline surrounds herself with words. She savors the sounds and sense of letters put together to create a lasting memory. Her debut novel, The Canary, is inspired by a most beautiful yellow diamond that rests on her finger and all the whispers about how it got there. Its sequel, The Checkerboard, continues the saga of Myra and her family. While The Canary caused her aunt to wag her finger, Jacqueline hasn't heard any family fussing about The Checkerboard. Shhh, perhaps secrets really aren't meant to be kept.

Please visit her at www.jacqueline-t-moore.com and on Facebook at Jacqueline T. Moore for conversations and updates on her next book.

Acknowledgements:

With deepest heartfelt love, I hug my daughter, Julie Anne Jacobs. She is my reader, listener, hand-holder, and most of all, my tow truck when I get stuck. Thank you, Beth Withrow, for your wonderful command of the comma. Thank you, Pat Rinehart, for your guidance through confusion. I appreciate your viewpoint. Thank you my son, Nathan James, for being such a wonderful supporter.

Social Media Links:

Website: http://www.jacqueline-t-moore.com/

Facebook: https://www.facebook.com/Jacqueline-T-Moore-476568419146045/

Twitter: https://twitter.com/JacquelinTMoore
@jacquelinTMoore

MISSUS ANNIE'S POUND CAKE

Adapted from a 1700's recipe

Pound Cake
1 pound sugar (about 2 cups)
1 pound butter
1 pound flour (about 4 cups)
1 pound eggs (10-12 depending on size)
¼ teaspoon salt
½ teaspoon mace (Annie used nutmeg when she didn't have mace)

Preheat oven 325 degrees. Butter and flour your pan. Annie used a tube pan because the cake had a nice crust all around and was easier to serve. Sift together flour, salt, and mace and set aside. Cream butter and sugar until well mixed. Slowly add dry ingredients, making sure everything is stirred in. Pour into the pan and bake 1 hour 15 minutes. Then check if center is done with a tester. Depending on your pan and your oven, you may need to bake 15 minutes or more until tester is clean.

HOT WATER CORNBREAD

Adapted from Smith family recipe

Hot Water Cornbread
1 tablespoon lard (Cookie used bacon grease)
¾ cup boiling water
1 cup corn meal
1 teaspoon salt

Mix all ingredients until you can tell it's right. Heat more bacon grease in large skillet until medium hot, not smoking. Gently drop a heaping spoonful of cornmeal mix in hot grease and flatten with back of spoon. Do a few more. Cook until they are brown on the bottom and then flip. Take out of grease when that side is brown. Drain and serve hot. Keep making more. Be sure to eat one yourself, because there won't be any left when you are done.

COOKIE'S GRITS
Adapted from an old family recipe
Grits

3 cups water
1 cup grits
1 teaspoon salt

Get your water boiling hard. Add salt. Keep the boil. Slowly stir grits into the water, keeping the water moving. When all the grits are in the boil, start whippin' the mix. Don't stop. Whip 'til your fork don't move. You're done. Mash in lots of butter.

ARABEL GAITHER'S PECAN PIE

Adapted from Amelia Hofferberth Flory's family recipe

Pecan Pie
1 cup dark syrup (Arabel used molasses)
½ cup sugar
1 tablespoon flour
1 teaspoon vanilla
2 eggs
¼ teaspoon salt
1 tablespoon melted butter
1 ½ cups pecan pieces

Mix and pour in an unbaked pie shell. Bake at 325 degrees for at least an hour until set.

Book Club Guidelines

The Checkerboard

In this book, two families, one colored and one white, live under the same roof in the fancy house in LaPorte, TX. This home was payment for man smuggling, signaled by a very special checker game played by CB and Jack before the hurricane. Discuss the other images of checkers presented in the story. For example: racial mixing; the checkerboard in the store; the signal flag.

The Checkerboard is two stories in one. Southern Texas in 1901 is not racially integrated. Marguerite must take the role of house help even though she and Myra are dear friends. Why would Missus Annie and Mister Carlton come to a reception for colored people? How do Marguerite and Jack feel about the party? Discuss racial tensions aboard the *Sallie Lou* and the world they live in. How does this change throughout this voyage?

We see life on land in LaPorte and Galveston Island and we see life at sea. How is the shared household beneficial or difficult for the women? What do you think would happen if CB and Jack had to leave the *Sallie Lou* after the captain dies? Would the household remain intact?

Junior Gallaway's anger toward his mother's husband causes him to get into trouble. He is sent away from home and eventually banished to sea. Do you think the adults in his life handled the problem correctly? What would you have done differently?

As The Checkerboard comes to an end, there are characters with unfinished business. Who are you curious about and what would you like to see happen in their lives?

64322209R00135

Made in the USA
Middletown, DE
16 February 2018